Josie smacked her head with her hand. "Sam! Caroline must have been killed by someone she knows! And the only person she knew before coming here was Layne. Oh, God, what am I going to do? I'll never finish this project on time short two workers!"

"Yeah . . . You're gonna have a real difficult time without Betty, I'll bet."

Sam and Josie looked up at Mike Rodney, framed in the unframed doorway.

"Betty?" Josie repeated her name. "What does Betty have to do with this?"

"I'm arresting her for murder. . . ."

Please turn to the back of the book for an interview with Valerie Wolzien.

By Valerie Wolzien
Published by Fawcett Books:

Josie Pigeon mysteries:
SHORE TO DIE
PERMIT FOR MURDER
DECK THE HALLS WITH MURDER

Susan Henshaw mysteries:
MURDER AT THE PTA LUNCHEON
THE FORTIETH BIRTHDAY BODY
WE WISH YOU A MERRY MURDER
ALL HALLOWS' EVIL
AN OLD FAITHFUL MURDER
A STAR-SPANGLED MURDER
A GOOD YEAR FOR A CORPSE
'TIS THE SEASON TO BE MURDERED
REMODELED TO DEATH
ELECTED FOR DEATH
WEDDINGS ARE MURDER

Books published by The Ballantine Publishing Group
are available at quantity discounts on bulk purchases
for premium, educational, fund-raising, and special
sales use. For details, please call 1-800-733-3000.

DECK THE HALLS WITH MURDER

Valerie Wolzien

FAWCETT GOLD MEDAL • NEW YORK

A Fawcett Gold Medal Book
Published by The Ballantine Publishing Group
Copyright © 1998 by Valerie Wolzien

http://www.randomhouse.com/BB/

Library of Congress Catalog Card Number: 98–93281

ISBN 0-449-15036-4

Manufactured in the United States of America

First Edition: November 1998

10 9 8 7 6 5 4 3 2 1

This one is dedicated to Lee Harris, Jonnie Jacobs, and Lora Roberts. Three fine writers, great travel companions, and good friends. Happy holidays, ladies!

ONE

"**S**O YOU'RE GOING to build a toy-land town all around the Christmas tree?"

"Yeah, just like the song says. Do you believe it?"

"I believe it, but I don't understand it. If you hate Christmas so much, why did you volunteer to do all this work?"

Josie Pigeon sat back on the heels of her workboots and brushed her unruly red hair from her forehead. She bit her lips. "It's not that I hate Christmas, it's just that I do it so badly."

"Josie, what is there to do about Christmas? You put up a tree, eat some cookies, and buy your son a present." Sam Richardson took a clean white handkerchief from his pocket and wiped a smear of dirt from Josie's cheek.

"Little do you know. My tree always looks dreadful—it's covered with faded felt ornaments and cheap junk I bought at the local five-and-ten years and years ago. The cookies will be as hard as rocks and probably taste like them too. And Tyler wants a new computer and I can't afford to buy him one. Does this sound to you like a cheerful time will be had by one and all?"

"I could . . ."

"No, you couldn't," she interrupted before he could make an offer. "Although I really do appreciate it. I just wouldn't feel comfortable taking money from you."

"I was going to offer to bake the cookies." There was a big smile on Sam's face and Josie couldn't help but respond in kind.

"You volunteered to do this because it was something you do well to celebrate the season. Smart," Sam said admiringly.

1

"That's not exactly true either. I mean, I can do it. I can build real houses, so constructing a town of miniature buildings is a cinch. But I volunteered to make this damn thing because I'm hoping it will be good advertising for Island Contracting. It's going to be displayed underneath the Christmas tree right at the end of the bridge when you get to the island. Everyone will see it. And there might be an article about it in the local newspaper. Besides, I don't have much else to do these days."

"I thought you had that big job starting next week—you even hired extra workers for it! You're not going to tell me it fell through."

"Flatter than any Christmas baking I'll do. And now I've got to figure something out. . . . Damn it!" She looked down at the white tower she had just smashed with one hard hammer blow.

"Tsk. Tsk. Such a way to talk—and over a church."

Josie Pigeon and Sam Richardson were in the office of Island Contracting. Fashioned from an old fishing shack that hung out over the bay on this barrier island, the room was compact and, at present, filled with brightly painted miniature buildings in various states of construction. Josie, a woman in her mid thirties, and Sam, almost two decades older, were very obviously a couple.

"This is just one of three churches. The Episcopal is the one giving me the most problems actually—I can't seem to keep the red shingles from sliding off the roof."

Sam looked around the room. "Hey, these are replicas of buildings on the island."

"As the person who's been putting them together ever since Halloween, I'm perfectly aware of that fact."

"How many are there?"

"Twenty-seven. They're supposed to be the most important buildings on the island."

"How did you choose them?"

"Well, some were obvious. The three churches, of course. The island school. The post office. The town hall and the police department. The fire department. The lighthouse. The old Coast Guard station. The new Coast Guard station. The life-guard's station. The movie theater. The two oldest homes on the island. The village grocery store. The Fish Wish bait shop. The drugstore—of course that's probably going to be closing now that that chain store has come to the mall. Sullivan's General Store—did you know that was the only store at this end of the island when I used to come here as a kid? A bakery . . ."

"The one you prefer, which is open only in the summer," Sam said.

"Yeah." She took a moment to crave their jelly doughnuts before continuing. "The pancake shop. The candy store. The bike rental shop. That new kite store—I couldn't resist because it's so colorful. And that fancy craft shop for the same reason—I'm going to hang lots of banners across the front the way they do in the summer. The Gingham Cat—I hate that frilly type of gift shop, but I couldn't leave them out completely. And, ah . . . the . . . well, your liquor store." Her winter pallor did nothing to hide her blushing cheeks.

"I'm proud to be included in such illustrious company. But aren't you forgetting a major segment of the island's economy?"

Josie looked around her. "What?"

"Realtors. There must be a dozen on the island. You've left them all out."

"That was intentional. I don't want to offend anyone who might give Island Contracting a recommendation."

"So they're all going to be asking why they were left out?"

Josie shrugged her shoulders. "I'll just point out that I didn't include Island Contracting's office either."

"Then why is this going to be such good publicity?"

"Because there's going to be a big sign saying Happy Holidays from the Island Chamber of Commerce and Island Contracting. That's why." She frowned.

"Problems?"

"I was worried that Christmas was going to be here before I finished these things, but unless that new job comes through, it looks like I'll have plenty of time."

"Josie, maybe it's all for the best. You had a busy summer. You must have saved enough to live on during the slow season. . . ."

"I did. But I thought we were going to be starting that new house out on the point next week, so I hired those women, and now that that project has fallen through . . ."

"You're going to have to let them go."

"I . . . I don't want to do that."

"What else can you do?"

"Well, if I get the job that I'm interviewing for this afternoon—and then maybe another small job or two . . ."

"Look, I can understand your loyalty to Betty Patrick. She's your friend and she's been working for Island Contracting for years. But those other women . . ." He saw the stubborn expression on her face and stopped speaking.

"I hired them when I thought I was going to get that job, Sam."

"But Josie, you can't afford to pay the salaries of people who aren't working. And these women are professionals, they know the reality of your business. They'll expect to be let go if things don't turn out as you expected."

"But Christmas is less than a month away, Sam. I can't fire them. It would ruin their holiday."

"Josie . . ." He decided not to waste his breath. He would always remember a professor he'd had his last semester of law school who had insisted that a lost battle wasn't worth fighting. He had kept that in mind throughout his career as a prosecuting attorney in New York City—and continued to find it relevant after he moved to the island and fell in love. He changed the topic. "So what is this job interview you're going on this afternoon?"

"I'm not sure. Some sort of remodeling gig. The only thing I know is that there's a kitchen, a bathroom, and at least one bedroom involved. And that it has to be started immediately. That's all there was on my answering machine."

"Immediately? This time of year? Isn't that a little unusual?"

"Listen, any work at all this time of year is unusual. That's why I'm hoping we get this job. I wish I knew whether the owner was a man or a woman. It was a man's voice on the machine—but sort of loud, like he was talking on a speakerphone or from his car." She bit her chapped upper lip. "I haven't asked Betty to go along with me, but maybe, if we're being interviewed by a man without his wife, I should give her a call. . . ."

"It's winter, Josie. Betty isn't going to be wearing a bikini. A heavy ski sweater is more likely."

"Betty looks as good in a bulky sweater as most women do in a bikini. And she's as worried about keeping her job as I am—she needs a new car."

"So that's why I saw her driving one of Island Contracting's trucks to church last Sunday."

"Yeah." She glanced down at her watch, difficult to read through its cracked crystal. "I should really get going, I guess. I'm meeting this man at the north end of the boardwalk."

"Not at the house to be remodeled?"

"Nope. It was the caller's suggestion. He said he goes there each morning for the air. I was just glad he didn't want to jog along the beach—it's a little chilly to get sprayed by the surf."

Sam reached over and kissed her on the nose. "How about dinner tonight?"

"Great! But why don't you come over to my apartment? Risa is making something special. She was buzzing around the kitchen cleaning squid when I passed her apartment."

"Fine. What time?" He didn't bother to ask if there would be enough for an extra guest. Risa, Josie's Italian landlady, was a fabulous chef whose idea of ample was more like most people's concept of gargantuan.

"Six."

"Good," he said, approaching the door. "This evening will be an excellent opportunity to try some of the new Rigailie rosé that just arrived last week. I'll give Risa a call, shall I?"

"Okay. See you later," Josie called out to Sam's departing back as she moved the Fish Wish bait shop off her worn navy peacoat. She put the coat on and left her office. Her truck was parked at the curb and she hopped into its cab, and headed out to the other end of the island. By the time she had traveled the almost seven miles to the end of the boardwalk, her beloved truck's ancient heater was finally beginning to breathe warm air across her chilled fingers.

But when she pulled into the parking lot, she realized she had some extra time. The boardwalk was empty. A brand-new van was parked close to the ramp. No other vehicles were in sight. She yanked her rough collar up around her neck and huddled down in her seat, wishing she had remembered to grab a scarf and gloves as she left home this morning.

The sun steaming through the windshield was making her sleepy. She had just drifted off when the sound of someone banging on sheet metal startled her into alertness.

"Hey! What are you doing?"

The voice came from outside the truck. And the noise seemed to be the result of someone, or something, slamming into its cherry red sides.

"What am I doing? What the hell are you doing?" Seeing no one out the window, she leaned against her door—which, with an ominous crash, made contact with something below her field of vision.

"What the hell?"

"Hey, hold on there! Don't I have enough problems without being decked by some dumb broad in a beat-up truck?"

"I'm not a dumb broad." Josie looked out the window and snapped her mouth shut. The man she was yelling at was in a wheelchair.

"You almost crush my chair and now you're afraid to yell at me because my body doesn't work? You've got very interesting standards, young lady."

"I . . . uh . . ." Josie took a deep breath and decided to start over. After all, she really had smashed the truck's door right into this man's wheelchair. "I'm sorry. I didn't see you . . ." she began.

"So let's all thank god I'm disabled and you're not. If you were blind, apparently you would feel you had the right to wipe out the rest of the human race."

"I didn't say that!" she yelled, her temper beginning to overcome her regret. "And, you know, I was trying to apologize . . ."

"Fine. Apology accepted. What other choice does a gimp

have?" And, miraculously it seemed to Josie, the wheelchair swung around and, gravel flying out behind it, took off across the parking lot. "Hey," he yelled out over his shoulder, "you're not the bird lady who owns that stupid contracting company, are you?"

Bird lady? Oh . . . "Yes, I'm Josie Pigeon, if that's what you mean," she yelled back.

"Oh, well, you might want to know that the man you just crashed into is the man you were meeting for that interview about the remodeling job!"

Josie watched the chair speed off into the distance. A bumper sticker on the back declared that he'd RATHER BE READING. She sighed. It certainly wasn't going to be a good Christmas after all.

TWO

"**S**O THAT'S WHEN I realized who he was. And that Island Contracting was not going to be getting that job." Josie, Sam, and Risa were eating at the bleached pine table in Risa's cheerful kitchen. Candles gleamed between tall wine goblets, hand-painted Italian ceramic plates, and colorful napkins. The dinner, a Tuscan peasant meal of squid with potatoes, was incredibly wonderful. The wine Sam had brought was, even to Josie's only recently schooled palate, excellent. But, for once, she was too upset to eat. "But he was horrible, just horrible!"

"You said you crashed the door of your truck into him. Maybe he was just upset. He must feel very vulnerable in that wheelchair," Sam said gently, accepting another helping with a nod at their hostess.

"Sam, you should see the side of my truck! There's actually a dent in it. I couldn't have done that by bumping into him once. I told you! There was banging. That's what woke me up—he smashed the side of my truck."

Risa gave herself another hearty helping and sat down. "What does this man look like?" she asked, picking up her fork.

"Ah . . . well, I told you he's in a wheelchair. . . . You know, it sounds stupid, but I didn't notice much else. I was upset and everything. And I know exactly how I sound. I did see more than a man in a wheelchair. He was sort of heavy and . . . and his hair was brown with maybe some gray at the sides, and he wore glasses."

"It sounds like Hugh Sylvester," Risa said, chewing thoughtfully. "He's a charming man. A professor. He studies something odd—intelligence theory, I think he calls it. He's just moving to the island. We have met on the boardwalk in the morning. I have been going for walks when the weather is fine. He wheels up and down the boardwalk sometimes when I'm there. He's a quadriplegic, but he has limited use of his arms and can work his wheelchair. I don't know him well, but he seems very nice." She shrugged. "You know how it is. We talk. As I said, he's charming."

"Risa, you think every man you meet is charming," Josie said.

"That may be because Risa is charming to every man she meets." Sam offered a solution.

"You think I should ignore what he did because he's in a wheelchair?"

"It must be a very frustrating way to live. I think perhaps you should make allowances," Sam answered gently.

Josie opened her mouth to reply, but Risa spoke first.

"This man . . . if he is Professor Sylvester . . . he would not agree with you, Sam. He told me that unwarranted kindness is just a form of prejudice. I didn't understand at first, but it is an interesting idea, I think."

"It is, actually," Sam agreed slowly. "What do you think, Josie?"

"I think he screwed up my chance of keeping my staff over the holidays. That's what I think." And she stuck her fork in a tender ring of squid, stuffed it in her mouth, and began to chew angrily.

"Who are these new women you care so much about?" Risa asked.

"Layne Finnegan and Caroline Albrecht are the carpenters. And Sandy Hart—she's a licensed electrician as well as a plumber. A real find. But it's not as though I know them well. I just promised them work and now they're not going to have it. It's . . . well, it's sort of a point of honor," Josie explained, wondering how long it had been since she'd thought of that term. Freshman English maybe?

"They could find other work."

"Sam, how many people do you know who decide to build

or remodel their homes between Thanksgiving and New Year's?"

"Not many, but what about repair work?"

"There weren't any big storms last fall. A hurricane or two can keep us in business over the winter, but there weren't any last year. No, I suppose I should just call everyone first thing in the morning and let them know they should start looking for other jobs."

"You know you cannot be responsible for the lives of everyone, *cara*," Risa said, filling Josie's wine glass.

"But it is nice of you to try," Sam added.

Josie frowned.

"Please don't let it upset your dinner," Risa said. "You must keep up your strength, you know."

"Josie?" Sam put a hand on her shoulder when she didn't answer. "What is it?"

"I think . . ." She put her hand up to her lips and listened. "Do you hear something moving around up there?" She pointed toward the ceiling.

"Did you bring home more cats?" Risa asked.

"No. . . . And that's not Urchin," she said, referring to the chocolate brown Burmese cat her son allowed her to take care of while he was away at boarding school. "Urchin barely weighs nine pounds. Those are footsteps. . . ." She got up from her seat and followed the sounds toward the front of Risa's first-floor apartment. Sam and Risa followed.

"We call the police, *cara*?" Risa reached out for the phone as they passed it by.

"No . . . it might be nothing. . . ." Josie stopped moving as the footsteps left her apartment and seemed to start down the stairs.

Suddenly there was a knock on Risa's door. She swooped to open it. "See, *cara*, it was nothing. Just a . . . just this gentleman."

A very tall young man with an almost impossibly short crew cut stood at the door. "I have something for a Ms. Josie Pigeon. I understand she lives upstairs. Maybe I could leave it here?"

"I'm Josie Pigeon." Josie stood up and smiled.

"Then this is for you." He handed her a large manila envelope and turned to leave.

"Hey, what is it?"

"A contract, I believe. Of course, you'll find out when you open it. Good evening." And this time he made it out the door before anyone could think of anything else to say.

Josie stared down at the envelope.

"You are going to open it, aren't you?" Sam asked. "After all, if there is a problem, there's a lawyer present."

Josie ripped the top off the envelope and pulled out what appeared, at first glance, to be Island Contracting's standard contract. She flipped through the pages. "I don't believe this. I really don't believe this."

"What did you say that paralyzed man's name is, Risa?"

"Hugh Sylvester."

Josie squinted. "Does this look like it says Hugh Sylvester to you?" she asked, passing the contract to the others.

"*Sí.*"

"Hey, you got the job! This calls for a celebration, doesn't it?" Sam asked, a wide grin on his face. "Do you still have the bottle of Tattingers I gave you waiting in your refrigerator?"

"Yes, but Sam, this doesn't make any sense. Why would Hugh Sylvester hire Island Contracting after what happened this afternoon?"

"Who knows? But you know what they say about gift horses. . . ."

"Then you think I should accept his offer?"

"Is it a fair offer?"

"I'd have to study it. Check out what sort of shape his house is in. It's over by the bay up at the north end of the island. Most of those homes were built in the sixties by a pretty reputable company. If it's been kept up, it should be an easy home to remodel."

She shuffled through the sheets of paper. "Did you say he was just moving to the island?" she asked Risa.

"*Sí.* He's staying on the mainland now I think."

"These are all modifications to make the house accessible for his wheelchair. . . ."

"That doesn't sound particularly difficult," Sam said.

"I don't suppose it is. I've never worked with these architects before, but everything looks fine. Of course, I really should spend some time with the blues before I accept his offer, but . . . it sure doesn't sound bad." She reached out for her wine glass, a smile on her face.

"*Cara,* then you think Tyler may get that computer he wants so much that will be so educational and good for him?"

"We'll see. There's a pretty good profit margin built in, but I'm going to earn every penny of that money if I have to work with that man."

"You will find him lovely. . . . Where are you going?"

Josie was getting up from the table. "I'd like to call Betty and see if she can meet me at the office early tomorrow. He asks for a reply in twenty-four hours. I'd like someone to go over the specs with me."

"Use my phone," Risa insisted as Sam reached across the table for the contract.

"Mind if I look?" he asked, knowing the answer.

"Feel free. I'll be back in a few minutes."

"And I will get dessert. Pears poached in red wine, lemon, and spices. *Bella.*"

"I could make espresso," Sam offered.

"No, you work with Josie. Help her get that computer for our little Tyler."

Josie, dialing Betty's number, smiled. Tyler wasn't all that little any more. In fact, at fifteen, he was towering over his mother's head. Away at an excellent boarding school in New England for most of the year, she was always astounded by how much he'd grown each time he was home or she went up for one of the two parents' weekends the school held yearly.

Betty, a young woman with a very full social calendar, wasn't home, so Josie left a message on her machine and returned to the table.

"I have been thinking about Christmas," Risa announced, placing a large ceramic bowl on the table, brimming with glistening ruby pears and slivers of lemon peel.

"And?" Sam muttered, his concentration still on the contract in front of him.

"Well, I will give my usual Christmas Eve seafood dinner for all my dear friends, of course . . ."

Josie's mouth began to water. How could she be hungry with all she'd just eaten! Was there no bottom to her stomach?

"And then I was thinking of making dinner on Christmas Day. . . . A real American Christmas with roast goose and plum pudding and all of what is called trimmings. Such a strange word, just like those ornaments we hang on the tree. Maybe you would both like to come?"

"Why don't you both come to dinner at my apartment?" The words were out of Josie's mouth before she had time to think.

"Josie, *cara,* you will be busy with this new remodeling project . . ."

"My mother will be here for the holidays and she loves nothing more than cooking for the family on Christmas Day. I was going to invite Basil and you both and Tyler and all the people I owe hospitality to on the island," Sam said.

"I can cook, you know," Josie announced.

The response to her statement could only be described as skeptical. "Well, yes, you do very nice boiled crab," Risa admitted.

"And your hamburgers and grilled cheese leave nothing to be desired," Sam joined in.

"And that nice meatloaf you made with dried soup . . ." Risa began.

"You've never had my Christmas dinner. I do a very nice goose. And . . . and plum pudding is a family specialty," Josie lied, wondering what exactly went into plum pudding. Surely plums were difficult to find in the middle of December? On the other hand, if she could build houses she could surely get a Christmas dinner on the table for her friends. "I was planning on inviting Betty and some of the crew as well," she added. You jump in with both feet and then end up over your head, she remembered her father saying. Well, Christmas was a time for family traditions, after all. She looked into the incredulous faces of her two friends. "It's what Tyler wants—a big family

Christmas at home," she finished, with the only argument she knew would sway Risa.

Sam, however, still looked doubtful. "Since when is your son so fond of your cooking?"

"He's never had my goose and plum pudding," Josie stated honestly.

"Well . . ."

"If it's what little Tyler wants, Sam."

"There's almost a month until Christmas," he said. "I suppose a lot can happen between now and the time to put the plum pudding on the table."

THREE

"I DON'T UNDERSTAND WHY you're so nervous about meeting this guy."

"That's because you've never met him."

"He couldn't possibly be that bad," Betty insisted with the assurance of a sexy young woman who rarely met a man who didn't automatically like her.

Josie took a deep breath. They were getting nowhere. Betty would see, listen, and then decide for herself—along with the rest of the crew. Hugh Sylvester had asked to meet everyone who was going to be working in his new home. Well, she corrected herself, actually he had insisted on it. She had picked up Betty earlier and they were meeting Layne, Caroline, and Sandy at the office. They would ride to the Sylvester house together.

"What about the project?" Betty asked. "Is it interesting? Profitable?"

"Looks like it's both. The architect is a picky bastard though, every single thing is blocked in and measured out to the last quarter inch."

"That shouldn't be a problem."

"No, it's just a little unusual."

"Do you think we'll be finished before Christmas?"

"I certainly hope so. Do you have plans for the holidays?" Josie added, remembering her decision last night. "I'm going to have a big dinner at my apartment and you're more than welcome to join us."

"No, I'm not doing anything," Betty answered. Josie was

surprised. She had expected Betty to be going off with some man, if not heading down to her family's Florida home.

"I'd love to come to your home. So what do you think of our new workers?" Betty asked, before Josie could question her further.

"Well, I hired them, so you can guess what I think. Have you met everyone?"

"Just Caroline and Layne. I was down at the office picking up my last paycheck and they were there dropping off some forms."

"The paperwork for workman's comp just gets worse and worse," Josie muttered. "So what did you think?"

"Of them?" Betty shrugged. "They seem nice enough. Have they known each other long?"

"I have no idea. Why?"

"Well, I know they're sharing a house on the island, and when they were at the office they were talking about jobs they'd worked on together. I got the impression that they were longtime buddies."

Josie was surprised. She had hired Caroline first and then, on her recommendation, had hired Layne, but she hadn't asked how they knew each other or for how long. And, as usual, she hadn't actually examined the applications of either woman too carefully.

"Where did you find them?" Betty persisted.

"Caroline answered the ad I put in the paper. She was spending a few days on the island on her way to Florida for the winter. She said that's how she usually works—Maine in the spring, summer, and fall, then down to Florida for December through April. She enjoyed the island though, so when she saw my ad she just came over and applied for the job. I hired her on the spot. She's had some rather unique work experiences."

"You're talking about those women's workshops she teaches in Maine in the summer."

"She told you about them?"

"Sure did. I thought it was fascinating. I mean, teaching women to build their own homes is a bit unusual, isn't it?"

"Women wanting to build their own homes is more than a

little unusual, I would think," Josie admitted. "That's what intrigued me, to be honest. I think Caroline will fit right in with Island Contracting's philosophy, don't you?"

"Sounds like it. Does Layne teach there too?"

"I don't know, but we can ask her on the way to our job—they're right on time!" Josie added, steering the company's ancient Jeep Wrangler over to the curb in front of Island Contracting's office.

Two women, probably both closer to forty than thirty, were standing on the tiny front porch of the building. They were bundled in navy down parkas with colorful scarves wrapped around their necks as protection from the chill winds that blew across the island at that time of the year. A third woman, younger than the others, and less warmly dressed, was perched on the stoop.

Betty opened the door on her side of the Jeep. "Hop in," she insisted.

"Hey, I thought you drove that neat old Chevy truck," Layne said, following Sandy and Caroline into the backseat.

"It isn't working. It's always had trouble starting on cold mornings, but I think this is something different," Josie said sadly. "There used to be this guy down at the Texaco station who kept it running for me. But he's semiretired and goes south for the winter now. I have no idea what's wrong with it and I don't know any other good mechanics—and I probably couldn't afford them if I did."

"Caroline can look at it for you," Layne suggested. "She's a whiz at cars."

"I'd be happy to," Caroline added, yanking her scarf away from her neck and pulling her long blond ponytail out of her jacket. "I like working on old cars—they have interesting engines—built to last and not computer-driven."

"That would be great. But you may not have much time. This is sort of a rush job. The owner wants to be in the house before Christmas."

"So why can't he live there while we work?" Layne asked. "Lots of people live in their homes while they're being remodeled."

"Well, right now I'm not even sure he can get in his own house—he's in a wheelchair."

"No temporary ramping?" Caroline asked.

"I don't know. I've never seen the house," Josie admitted. "This guy—Mr. Sylvester—is in one of those big power wheelchairs. I don't know if he could use a temporary ramp."

"Sure he could. In fact, it's easy to make short ramps. You just buy these metal ends and attach wood planks. They're sold at most hardware stores—to move wheelbarrows and the like around. Hell, half the contracting companies in the country have a pair in the back of their storage room."

"Of course, we have some ourselves somewhere. I never thought of using them for this purpose, though. It sounds as though you know something about this," Josie added hopefully.

"A little. My father had a stroke and was confined to a wheelchair for the last few months of his life."

"Actually, I've done some work with handicapped access. Worked on a nursing home up in Maine," Layne added.

"Good. Because I don't know a damn thing about it. I've studied the plans, but that's it. And . . ." Josie stopped, not sure how much to tell the other women of her impression of their employer.

"And?" Layne repeated her last word.

"And I know the owner wants to be in his home by Christmas," she ended weakly.

"In three weeks? He wants us to remodel his kitchen, build him a new bathroom, and make the entire home accessible in three weeks?" Caroline asked.

"Three and a half weeks really, and if it's one of the homes I think it is, I think we can do it. Look around, talk to the guy. We can go over the plans together back at the office. I really think we can do this," Josie repeated.

"You've got the orders for all the supplies and hardware ready to go, don't you?" Betty asked.

"Yup. I worked on it last night. And he's picked pretty standard stuff. So maybe it's all in stock. If that's true, the toilet, the sinks, and the hardware could be in by the end of this week.

Island Hardware has a guy off-island who's a whiz with Corian; the countertops could be finished as early as next week. In fact, the way things look right now, the supplies will be waiting for us and not the other way around."

"Well, it sure sounds like you're organized," Layne said, sounding doubtful.

Josie, peeking in the rearview mirror, noticed Caroline elbowing her in the ribs. "I am organized," she insisted. "But I'm not a fool. I know things always go wrong. All we can do is try to get everything finished on time—and if we're late, we're late."

"But he's in a wheelchair . . ." Caroline protested. "I mean, shouldn't we try extra hard for him to get what he wants?"

"Wait until you meet him," was Josie's only reply. "That's the house." She pointed to a gray-shingled one-story home at the end of the block closest to the back bay.

"Well, at least we won't be installing an elevator," Layne said, leaning over to peer out the windshield.

"Look, there's already a ramp in place," Sandy said as they arrived at the front of the home.

"So I guess Mr. Sylvester is waiting inside," Betty said.

They parked the Jeep and walked up to the house, heavy workboots clumping loudly on the metal ramp.

"Come on in," a man's voice answered Josie's knock. She opened the door and the women entered the house.

The house had been built in the late sixties in a modification of the then popular simple A-frame. A great room with a tall sloping ceiling was fronted with a glass wall, with sliding doors opening onto a deck that looked out toward the bay. The middle of the space was the eating area; behind that, divided by a long countertop, was the kitchen. A hallway to the right of the kitchen led to the bedrooms, usually three in a house this size. The one full bathroom was augmented by an enclosed outdoor shower near the back door.

These homes were usually bought and sold furnished. The furniture here was sparse, whether for the sake of style or ease of movement by the wheelchair, Josie didn't know.

The women pulled off parkas and scarves and arranged

themselves on the one long couch. Their winter clothing provided a contrast to the bright tropical cotton print of its upholstery. Josie, perched on an arm, spoke first.

"Do you want me to introduce everyone?" she asked.

"If you want," he answered, apparently disinterested. "I didn't mean to give anyone the impression that I was calling you all here for a tea party. I just wanted to get a few things straight before you start work on my house."

Josie, not sure how to respond, smiled weakly.

"In the first place, everything has to be exact."

"We are very good at following the architect's plans . . ." Josie began.

"To within an inch of the plan?" he interrupted.

"I'm sure we can manage tha . . ."

"That's exactly what I don't want you to manage. I don't want things built to within an inch of the directions. I want them exactly like the directions! If a countertop is an inch too low, it is worthless to me—my chair won't fit underneath!"

"Well, then we'll make them exact. . . ."

"Are you aware of the new bathroom equipment American Standard is making?" Caroline interrupted. "They're almost completely adaptable. The sink not only can move up and down, but around the wall to a certain extent. That way, if you replace your chair with another model, the room's furnishings will adapt. And there are handrails . . ."

"That's very nice for the paraplegics—but for me it doesn't make a whole lot of difference. My hands don't work."

"You must have people who help you get around," Layne stated.

"Yeah, but most of them can walk without holding on to the walls. Now walking and talking is a different story. Some of them can't do that to save their souls."

"Now, now, what are you saying about me, Professor Sylvester?" A middle-aged woman, who weighed about twice what any reasonable doctor would have thought she should have, appeared from one of the back rooms, her arms piled high with folded linens. She looked at the young women and smiled. "I'll have some coffee ready for you ladies just as soon as I put these things away."

"This is not a social call, Nellie. . . ."

"Never hurts to be polite, and sometimes it helps," the woman replied and, ignoring the scowl on her employer's face, she spun around on her heels and left the room.

"Was that your mother?" Betty asked.

"That is Nellie, and she's one of my goddamn aides—that is, she was. I'm going to fire her fat ass the second I get a chance to find a replacement."

"I heard that, Professor Sylvester. I heard that!" To Josie's surprise, there was a loud, unmistakable chuckle after Nellie's words. "I'll get that coffee out in a jiffy."

"So you considered the American Standard bathroom fixtures and rejected them," Sandy picked up the conversation where it had been left.

"Well, I don't think my architect showed them to me." For the first time Hugh Sylvester seemed less than sure of himself. "But Ms. Pigeon may not be able to order special fixtures . . ."

"In fact, I was going to place the order this afternoon," Josie interrupted, anxious for him to realize how busy she had been in the two days since signing the contract. "And I'm sure our supplier can get anything you want. We can get them in and, if you find them unsatisfactory, they can be returned. One of the advantages of being a contractor is that we make returns without charge. Do you want me to get the spec sheets on the fixtures Caroline is talking about? They can be faxed to me and I can bring them over . . ."

"Well, I guess you get credit for being prompt, courteous, and helpful," was Hugh Sylvester's surprising response. "On the other hand, I'm not sure I would have hired Island Contracting if I had known about all the people who have been murdered on your building sites."

FOUR

"**H**E MUST HAVE hired you for a reason, *cara*."

"Yeah, because he was looking for someone to yell at after he fires Nellie—she's his helper—he calls her an aide." Josie threw the book she was reading onto the floor and picked up another one from the large pile in the middle of her coffee table. She opened it to the index while Risa was speaking.

"*Cara*, no one picks their contractor for such a foolish reason."

"Wanna bet?" Josie muttered, running her finger down the printed columns and then, apparently finding what she was searching for, flipping through the book until she had located the page. She read for a moment, bit her lip, slammed the book closed, and then it joined the others on the floor.

"*Cara*..."

Josie picked up another book and opened it to the index.

"*Cara*..."

She searched for the reference she wanted. Found the page, read it, and tossed it aside before Risa asked her question.

"*Cara*, what in the world are you looking for?"

"A recipe for plum pudding. The recipe for the best plum pudding in the world. These all seem to be alike." Josie looked up at Risa, her eyes open wide. "They all contain suet—that's fat, isn't it? Can you actually buy it in a store or do you have to buy a bunch of steaks and hack off the outsides?"

Risa shivered at the thought. "Maybe you want me to make this plum pudding. . . . I know a butcher."

"I'll make the plum pudding. You just give me the name

22

of that butcher." She frowned and read through the cook-book for a few moments. "There! This is it. The definitive recipe for plum pudding. You soak everything in brandy for six weeks . . ."

"You're going to serve this for Valentine's Day?"

"No, but it couldn't possibly make any difference if I soak this junk for six weeks, six days, or six hours. . . . Do you have any idea what's in this pudding?"

"In my country, we go to the local bakery and buy a panettone to celebrate the baby Jesus' birth."

"When I was growing up, my mother bought plum pudding in a little can at the A & P. It was imported from England. That impressed me, but I can't say I particularly liked the stuff."

"Your mother . . ."

"Didn't bake. Period," Josie said, as always refusing to think of her family more than absolutely necessary. Sometimes a thought or two intruded . . . "But my grandmother made the best Christmas cookies in the world and mailed them to us in huge tins." She was silent for a moment.

"So who knows? Maybe you turn out to be a great baker like your grandmother," Risa said softly.

"Not a chance. All I want to do is produce one absolutely perfect meal, then I'll go back to depending on takeout and the microwave."

"*Cara* . . ."

"Of course, maybe I should start looking for recipes for roast goose . . ."

"Goose?" Risa's voice rose to a pitch just one degree less than a shriek. "Maybe you should stick to a turkey. One of those nice frozen ones that has the little plastic button that pops up when it is done. And some stuffing from a package. So convenient. So good."

"Goose," Josie insisted. "And chestnut stuffing . . ."

"But little Tyler . . . he does not like chestnuts."

"Little Tyler is old enough to be learning to . . ." Josie's phone rang. She leapt up and scrounged underneath a pile of Christmas catalogues to answer it. "Hello? Oh, hello! Sure. Sure. Yes. Yes. I'll be right there." She hung up and looked around for her coat as she explained to Risa. "That was Betty. She was up at the Sylvester house accepting deliveries and she thinks there's a problem. I've got to get right over there."

"But . . . but it's late. And it's Sunday. I thought you weren't going to work this weekend. You were going to plan for Christmas. That's what you told me. You said you would be at work Monday morning, bright and early."

"Well," Josie said, pulling her old green parka from where it had fallen on the floor behind her couch, "I guess this is just one work week that is going to begin on Sunday night, good and late. See you!" Much to her surprise, the keys to her truck were in her pocket.

"*Sí*. Do not work too hard." Risa picked up a cookbook and was apparently engrossed in one of the recipes before the door had closed behind Josie.

The barrier island on which Island Contracting was located was just seven miles long and it took only a few minutes for Josie to get to the Sylvester home. She found Betty sitting cross-legged on the deck that ran across the front of the house. In the summer, it was undoubtedly a lovely spot to perch on. But now it was covered with the remains of last week's snowstorm and a tarpaulin protecting piles of building supplies; Betty looked singularly uncomfortable.

"What are you doing there on the floor?"

"Trying to find the contents of my toolbox. The damn handle fell off again. I thought I'd fixed it." Betty shook her head, obviously angry with herself. "I just hope I didn't lose anything between the boards of the porch."

"I have a flashlight in the truck. Maybe if I crawl down underneath and beam it up toward you it would help," Josie offered.

"Nah. I can look better tomorrow. I think I have everything anyway. God, I'd hate to spend the money for a new tool chest just before Christmas."

Josie hated to think that she might too—especially as she herself was planning to buy Betty a new toolbox for Christmas. Betty had been with Island Contracting for years and Josie felt it was time for some sort of recognition of that fact. A toolbox with the logo of the company printed on its side was on order at the island's hardware store. "I thought you had figured out some sort of repair."

"Yeah, but that broke too. Oh well, I can live with a broken toolbox, but how are we going to start work on an accessible bathroom when only one roll of mastic was delivered? The entire room will have to be treated as a shower, with backer board and waterproof mastic over everything, right?"

"Yes, and we don't have any on hand in the storage area?"

"Nope. Also, I spent some time studying the plans and I don't think the building inspector is going to approve of the lighting the architect designated for the bathroom."

"Why not?"

"Recessed lights are attractive, but if they're accidentally splashed with water from the shower, they might explode— and no one needs glass raining down when they're naked and wet."

"So we'll change them all to the type of light we install in showers."

"That will mean a change in the plans," Betty reminded her boss.

"And that will mean another meeting with Professor Charming." Josie frowned. "I don't suppose you'll do it again?"

"He wasn't so charming this morning," Betty said. "In fact, he was pretty insulting. He said something about me expecting him to be a happy gimp. God, I was so embarrassed. I wouldn't ever call anyone a gimp! I had no idea what to say."

"That's exactly the problem. He always makes me feel that I've said the wrong thing," Josie agreed. "And I'm trying so damn hard to say the right thing to him. It's impossible."

"Well, now that he doesn't like either of us, maybe we should send one of the new employees," Betty suggested, a twinkle in her eye. "It's just possible that he'll get along with someone else better—and Sandy is the electrician on this project, after all."

"She also seems to be more than a little outspoken."

"You don't think they'll get along?"

"I think I'll ask Layne or Caroline to visit him next," Josie mused.

"Do you think they're rather unusual carpenters?"

"We both know that women carpenters are rather unusual in and of themselves—but you mean something else . . ."

"Poetry. They read poetry." Betty made it sound as though they were involved in some sort of underworld activity.

"To each other?" Josie wondered if there was a budding romance here.

"To anyone who will listen. Last Friday, during our lunch break, when you were involved in your mysterious errand at the hardware store"—Josie had gone over to make sure Betty's Christmas present had been ordered—"they spent the entire time talking about someone named William Williams and a poem he wrote about a city in New Jersey."

"William Carlos Williams, and the poem's about Paterson, New Jersey." Josie remembered an American Lit class her freshman—and only—year of college.

"Yeah, weird. I mean who would write a poem about a town in New Jersey, for heaven's sake?"

"I think he lived there for most of his life. . . . But why do you think it's so weird?"

"They went to college—why did they end up working construction?"

"Who knows? Maybe they like being out of doors. Maybe they like working with their hands. And who knows what might have led them to carpentry? A lot of people's lives end up differently than they planned."

Betty, who knew something of Josie's life, just nodded. "I guess. Nothing ever happens to me."

"Well, if being the sexiest young single woman on the island isn't enough for you . . ." Josie said, grinning.

"But real things. I mean, I date, but I don't fall in love. Not really. Not like you and Sam. And I'm here living in the same place where I grew up, doing what I planned on doing. I guess the truth is that all that makes me different from most people is that I'm pretty lucky."

"You're not knocking it, are you?"

"No, but sometimes I feel like there's something missing. . . ."

Josie realized what was going on. "This is the first Christmas you're not going to be spending with your family, isn't it?"

Betty looked up at her boss. "Yeah. I thought it wasn't going to bother me. You know, I really don't have a wonderful time visiting my parents in Florida—everyone's there, and the grandchildren get most of the attention—and my relatives feel it's just fine to ask me rude questions like why I'm not married. I thought staying around here was sort of a grown-up thing to do—besides, I'll save money, and maybe I'll be able to afford the down payment on a Miata next spring. But it is depressing me a bit. You never spend holidays with your family. Do you ever feel lonely?"

Josie thought for a moment. "Well, I've always had Tyler with me . . ." She had a sudden memory of her first Christmas after her family had thrown her out. Pregnant, broke, scared about her future, she had spent the holiday listening to the radio in her little one-room apartment, eating Ritz crackers spread with strawberry jam, and crying. "I'm glad you'll be eating with us this year."

"I'm really looking forward to Christmas at your house," Betty enthused. "What can I bring?"

"Ah. Well . . . I haven't planned the menu completely."

"In my family, we always have this special crab appetizer on Christmas day. Why don't I bring that?"

"Sounds wonderful." At least part of the dinner would be good.

"My sister usually brings it. I'll call her for the recipe. I've always wanted to try making it," Betty said happily.

So much for reliability. "Great! Are we straightened out here? Do we know exactly what we need to tell the supplier tomorrow morning?"

Betty looked down at the sheets of paper in her hand. "Yup. Do we need to look inside again?"

"Wouldn't hurt. The more we know, the better off we'll be

tomorrow. I don't think the demolition is going to take very long," Josie said, unlocking the front door as she spoke.

She struck the wall switch by the door and two brass lamps glowed in the darkness. "It's a nice house," she muttered.

"But small," Betty said. "Oh, not for you and me, for us it's a mansion. But it's interesting how much room it takes for a wheelchair to get around, isn't it?"

"Yeah, I guess." She hadn't really noticed. She walked over to the tile counter in the kitchen. The entire thing was going to be taken off its base and lowered. That way Professor Sylvester would be able to see over it and his chair would fit underneath. There was even a cutout for the controls on his armrest. The counter on the rear wall would remain at its normal height for the use of the person cooking.

Betty wandered back to the bathroom as Josie stopped to examine a pile of shimmering shells that had caught her attention. She was still there when Betty reappeared. "You know, we may be able to make do with the stuff that's here," she announced, joining Josie. "I remeasured and I think, if we piece together the backer board, we might not have to reorder. We'll use waterproof mastic, so there shouldn't be any leaking. . . . What's so interesting?" She looked at the shell Josie was turning over in her hand.

"Look at this," Josie said, moving it closer to Betty.

"I am."

"What does it look like to you?"

"A sand dollar sprayed with gold glitter and tied with a golden cord. It's a Christmas tree ornament."

"I know that. And you know what?"

"What?"

"I'm going to make dozens of these ornaments to hang on my Christmas tree."

"Uh, Josie . . ."

"It's going to be a perfect, old-fashioned, homemade Christmas." Josie smiled happily, completely ignoring the skeptical expression on Betty's face.

FIVE

DEMOLITION STARTED BRIGHT and early the next morning. One bedroom was being eliminated and a large wheel-in bathroom created in the space. After hanging drop cloths in the hallways to protect the part of the house that wasn't being remodeled, the four women ripped down walls and destroyed doorways, tossing the rubble out open windows onto the ground below as they worked. By coffee break time, they were well on their way to knowing each other.

Sandy was a straightforward worker. When she saw something that needed to be done, she did it. Period. Once in a while she stepped in where she wasn't wanted, but she was always dependable and hardworking.

Caroline and Layne worked hard too. But as a pair, tackling job after job together instead of just looking around to see where one or the other was needed. Josie understood this. It was the way she and Betty worked; it was the way most people worked when they had been together for a long time. By the time they were sitting around, pouring coffee from thermoses and digging into the slab of crumb cake that Josie had picked up at the grocery store on her way home the night before, it was obvious that someone was going to ask about their relationship.

Sandy, direct as ever, asked the question they were all wondering about. "You two a couple?" she asked, waving her coffee cake in the air to indicate Layne and Caroline.

Layne looked at Caroline and laughed. "No. We were married to the same man though—but not, of course, at the same time."

"That should answer the question you didn't quite ask. We're not gay either," Caroline said.

"No. On the other hand, it might just be easier if we were. Think of all the dumb men we've dated."

"True, but then what would we have to talk about?" Caroline asked.

"You were married to the same man? Not really! Is that how you met?" Betty asked.

"Sort of. You see, Caroline and Ben were married and built a house on the hill where I was living with my boyfriend—this was in Maine, in the back country up north, not the ritzy area on the ocean down east. Since we were neighbors in a rural area, we became friends."

"And when Ben and I broke up, I left for a few years . . ." Caroline continued the story.

"And while she was gone, my boyfriend and I broke up, Ben and I fell in love—or that's what I thought at the time—and we got married, and I moved into the house that Ben and Caroline had built."

"And Layne added on to that house—she almost made it a new house, in fact. And when she broke up with Ben, she stayed there. I came back to visit the house, found out what wonderful things she'd done to it, and we just picked up our friendship where it had left off. . . ."

"Except that we had this wonderful new hobby—trashing Ben."

"And carpentry," Caroline added. "We both learned a new trade while we were working on that house."

"Then you weren't carpenters before—before you moved to Maine," Betty asked.

"Nope. Students. I was a fine arts major in college. I planned on painting to make a living—as well as getting a job in some chic gallery in New York City. I was more than a little naive when I was young," Caroline explained. "But Layne is a poet. She wins awards and everything."

"I've won one or two minor awards and had poems published in small academic magazines," Layne said. "I earn my living building houses."

"Not many people make a living writing poetry," Josie said, pouring more coffee into the top of her thermos.

"True. I thought about teaching for a while—in fact, I always assumed I'd go back to school and get a graduate degree to prepare myself for teaching, but then I got into carpentry and the problem of earning a living sort of took care of itself."

"You're telling us that you two not only married the same man, but you both built and lived in the same house?" Sandy cut to the chase.

"Yeah, great house," Caroline said, stuffing the last of her coffee cake in her mouth.

"Truly," Layne agreed. "Caroline designed the original house."

"It was small," Caroline explained. "Two rooms and a bath. When I left Ben, we had begun work on a studio loft to go over the living room."

"Which I enlarged when I moved in," Layne took up the story. "In fact, I added another bathroom with a sauna, a sunroom, and another bedroom."

"It's a wonderful house," Caroline added. Both women were smiling now. "Lots of glass and pine and . . ."

"And leaks in the roof and a foundation that's just slightly crooked, and . . ."

"And that horrible loose window frame in the kitchen . . ."

"And the illegal wood stove . . ."

"And that warren of plumbing pipes in the crawl space. I sure hope none of them ever start leaking—tracking down a problem could be . . . could be a real problem." Layne joined Caroline in chuckling over their story.

"I've always wanted to build my own home," Betty said.

"It has its advantages."

"And disadvantages," Caroline said. "In the first place, you know exactly what is wrong with your house. And in the second place, it's damn difficult to leave well enough alone. You see a corner and start imagining a door there leading to another room . . ."

"And another. And another," Layne agreed. "But it is

empowering. You know you don't have to live with anything you don't want."

"Like Ben," Layne said.

"Like Ben," her friend agreed.

Everyone was chuckling by now, and Josie, knowing that workers who got along well made for an easy job, hated to break this up, but it was time to get back to work. She stood up and the other women took the hint.

"Maybe it's time for someone to clean up outside—it's warmer now than it's probably going to be for the rest of the day," Josie stated.

"You just want everything in the Dumpster?" Betty asked.

Josie nodded.

"I'll go out. I could use some fresh air," Sandy volunteered.

"If you need anyone else, I'd be happy to go," Layne said.

"Great. Maybe you'd both better do it," Josie said, peering out the closest window. "It's beginning to look like rain—or snow."

"I love a white Christmas, but can't it just come down on December twenty-fourth and melt on the twenty-sixth?" Betty said.

Chattering about the weather and the holiday, they returned to work.

"When is Tyler coming home?" Betty asked as they resumed work.

"Right before Christmas. He's only home for two weeks—his biology class is taking a trip to the Everglades the last week of winter vacation. In a few years, I guess, he might not be coming home for the holidays at all." She spoke casually, but the pang in her heart was deep.

"He'll be thrilled when he sees the little village you built for the town green," Betty said.

"I've been thinking about that. It would be nicer if it were lit up," Josie said, relieved by the change of subject. "What do you think about running a couple of wires between the buildings and illuminating their interiors?"

"I think it would be great. Do you need my help?"

"I was hoping you'd volunteer."

"Volunteer for what?" Sandy asked, appearing in the doorway, her arms full of broken and split two-by-fours.

"We're going to illuminate the little village down on the town green," Betty explained.

"I saw that. It's cute. If you two need any help, I'd be glad to offer my services."

"For what?" Layne stood in the doorway.

"We're going to illuminate the toy town," Josie explained.

"Need any help?" Caroline stood behind Layne. "We'd love to work on it."

"Yeah, we were just talking about how difficult it's been to get in a holiday frame of mind," Layne explained.

"The more the merrier," Josie said. "Why don't we meet at the office after dinner?"

"We could go over right after we're finished here, order pizza, and eat while we work. Then there might still be some daylight and it shouldn't take too long to finish," Betty suggested.

"Actually, Layne has a big pot of vegetarian chili sitting in the refrigerator that she made last night . . ."

"And Caroline baked a couple of loaves of her whole wheat bread over the weekend . . ."

"Hey, I got a huge box of Christmas cookies from one of my sisters this morning—I'll bring that along," Betty offered, picking up the theme of the evening right away.

"I could grab a six-pack of Mexican beer at Sam's store," Josie said.

"Great."

"Fabulous."

"Sounds like a lot of fun."

"So we'll head home, do our stuff, and meet down at the town square around six," Josie suggested.

"Super."

"Great."

"But first we'd better get this demolition finished," Sandy reminded them all in the straightforward way she had.

They worked hard the rest of the afternoon, actually finishing before five.

"Good day," Josie commented as the women packed up their tools.

"Yeah, but if they'd played 'Jingle Bell Rock' one more time I might have been forced to go down to that radio station and kill someone. . . . Oh, damn it!" Betty knelt down to pick up the things that had fallen from her toolbox as its handle popped off again.

"You could use a new toolbox," Sandy made the obvious suggestion.

"I've already asked my parents to give me one for Christmas," Betty said. "Although I'd much rather have some new clothing—my mother usually sends a bikini or two," she added wistfully.

Betty's parents had retired to Florida after running what had been the only grocery on the island for years and years. Luckily, Josie had their phone number on the emergency information Betty had provided for the company. She would call them and explain why a bikini would be an appropriate and appreciated present again this year. "See you all in about half an hour," she called out, jiggling the lock to make sure all was secure before they left the work site.

The women's cars roared off down the street, but Josie took the time to comb her long hair and smear on some lipstick before she started the truck. After all, she was on her way to Sam's store.

Sam Richardson was out front, pouring salt and sand on his icy sidewalk. He beamed as Josie's truck pulled up.

Josie jumped out and, after a particularly warm greeting, she got right to the point. "I need a few six-packs of Mexican beer."

"You're giving a party and I'm not invited?" he asked with a smile, crumpling up the empty sack of salt and opening the door to his store for her.

"It's my crew. We're all meeting down at the town square to add lights to the Christmas village."

"All of you? Then things are going well, I take it?"

"Fabulously. This is really a nice group of women. We work

together well, and I think this project may turn out to be a lot of fun. I've never had a poet and an artist working for me before."

"A poet and an artist?"

"Layne and Caroline—the carpenters from Maine I was telling you about."

"Poetry and painting are pretty unusual hobbies," Sam said.

"Not hobbies. That's what they were trained to do. They're both college graduates," Josie explained.

"Sounds like this is going to be an interesting job. Did you see your employer today?"

"Nope. And I can't say it makes me unhappy. I'm betting he's going to be one of those people who insists on checking out every little thing. And you know how that can be."

"You've worked for unreasonable clients before. And this guy is apparently worried about things more important than the color of the bathroom tiles."

"Yeah, I suppose. Sam . . ." Josie started and then stopped. She just didn't know what to say. It was the holiday season. She had a good new crew and a good new job. So why did she feel so uncomfortable?

SIX

O NE OF THE advantages of living in a resort community off season is that it is always easy to find a convenient parking spot. Josie lined up her truck (running now that the day had gotten warmer) behind the battered navy van with Maine plates which belonged to Caroline and Layne. The familiar squeal of the brakes of Island Contracting's old Jeep indicated that Betty was close behind.

Josie pulled two six-packs of beer from the seat beside her. She had stopped at the beach and picked up shells, and they fell on the floor as she jumped down from her truck. She knew they were going to eat and then work—that way the chili would be warm. A cold wind was coming off the ocean and she wondered if, perhaps, a hot drink would have been a better idea than beer.

She and Betty joined the other three sitting on the bulky concrete benches set up near the tiny Christmas town. Layne passed around Styrofoam cups of chili and Josie handed out bottles of beer. The women, too hungry to worry about their manners, dug in. They had finished the alfresco meal in less than fifteen minutes. Then they put everything away, and tool-boxes replaced food. They got down to work.

The town square was located on a large median strip at the end of the long concrete causeway at the north end of the island. Since most of the tourists used this entrance rather than the rickety drawbridge at the southern end, it was a logical spot to place announcements and official greetings. A large billboard had been erected for just this purpose. All summer long it was crammed with notices of bake sales, 5K and 10K runs to benefit the lifeguards' various funds, swimming lessons, sand castle building competitions, and the like. But now it was as empty as the flower beds that outlined the square, stripped of their traditional display of hideous pink and purple petunias. This was the first year it had been decorated for the holidays.

Josie and her workers redirected the power from the light that illuminated the billboard to a wire, which was wound under the sand and from little house to little house. When they were done, less than half an hour later, the windows gleamed cheerfully.

"Great work, ladies," Josie said, bending down to pick up her tool chest. "I . . . What the . . . ?" There was a crash and Josie looked down. There was a handle in her hand. The tool chest was on the ground—it had fallen through the roof of the model of Sam's liquor store.

"Oh, Josie, I'm sorry. That's my toolbox," Betty cried. "I moved yours when I was working on that part of the town." She knelt down. "And now look what's happened to Sam's store!"

"Don't worry. I can fix it," Josie insisted. "I'll even make a modification or two. Sam was wondering why his name was in such small letters on the door. I'll give him a sign to be proud of."

"I can help," Betty offered.

"If you want. But it's getting late. Let's worry about it tomorrow," Josie insisted.

"I'm glad you said that. I'm exhausted," Layne said, picking up her toolbox and preparing to leave.

"Let's all go home to bed. And thanks, ladies. I can't tell you how much I appreciate the help. This would have taken hours without the extra hands," Josie said.

"Hey, we'll do anything for free beer," Sandy bragged, a smile on her face.

But despite their cheerfulness, it was cold, and the women were tired, and they didn't spend a whole lot of time admiring their work. They piled everything in the vehicles they'd arrived in and, within minutes, the place was deserted and the lights of the miniature town twinkled into the night—unappreciated.

The light was flashing on her answering machine when, ten minutes later, Josie entered her apartment. She pulled off her parka and tossed it on the couch, reminding herself that such a gesture would be unacceptable when her son arrived home from boarding school. She headed straight for the machine. She smacked the play button and flopped down on the couch to listen to the four recorded messages in comfort.

"Josie. This is Guy from Island Hardware. Problems with that order you sent in. The wife and I will be at the Girl Scout holiday festival—whatever that is—tonight. Give me a call in the A.M."

She grimaced and wrote a note to herself on the back of a magazine lying by the phone. Maybe the second message would bring good news.

Or maybe not.

"Miss Pigeon. I'm calling from First Island Banking. There's a small problem with your personal account. Nothing major, but we'd appreciate it if you would take care of this as soon as possible. Call me at extension three. Or stop in during banking hours. Oh, and a few of us around here were wondering why our bank isn't represented in your little village down on the green. We handle over 30 percent of the mortgages on the island, you know. And, of course, many of our clients borrow money for major remodeling projects. . . ."

She sighed. What next?

Sam's mother was next.

"Josie, honey. It's Carol. I hope you had a wonderful Thanksgiving. I don't know if Sam told you that I spent the holiday with friends in New Mexico. We had a wonderful time. And the dinner was incredible—turkey with a Southwestern flavor. You know the type of thing, peppers and cilantro in the stuffing; ginger in the cranberry sauce. Wonderful. Which brings me to the reason I called. I wanted to invite you and Tyler over to Sam's house for dinner on Christmas Day. When we talked last Sunday, Sam said that we were already going over to Risa's lovely apartment for a traditional fish dinner on Christmas Eve. So I certainly hope you all still have an appetite left the next day.

"Oh, and I bought Tyler one of the computer games that he wanted. I thought I'd let you know so you don't duplicate the gift. Didn't want him to think he might be getting a step-grandmother some day who thinks underwear is an appropriate present. Toodles, sweetie."

A stepgrandmother? Where had this come from? Was Sam's mother imagining things, or had Sam said something about his own plans for their relationship? Josie decided she would have to think about this later.

The fourth caller didn't have to waste time identifying himself. Josie would have recognized his growl anywhere.

"So, Ms. Pigeon, just how long am I going to have to hang around here waiting for you to return my phone calls? If this is the type of service I will be receiving from Island Contracting, I guess I should have picked another company to work on my house."

Josie sighed again. She knew exactly what had happened. Hugh Sylvester had left a message on Island Contracting's office phone and, when she didn't reply as quickly as he would have liked, he looked up her phone number and called her home. It had happened before. She didn't want to pay for call forwarding; she didn't really want Island Contracting's calls to come to her house, but now she was going to have to go down to the office and get the message. She got up from the couch (where her body seemed to have become incredibly comfortable in a very short period of time), grabbed her coat, and headed out the door.

It's impossible to run down an old wooden stairway wearing heavy workboots without making a lot of noise. Risa, alerted by the commotion, was waiting for her at the bottom of the stairs.

"*Cara,* you're not going to see Sam dressed for work, are you?"

"No, I'm going to the office." Josie didn't bother to inform her landlady that Sam had already been treated to the sight of her worn-out overalls earlier in the day.

"It's so late to be working . . ."

"I'm just going to check the answering machine and maybe

make a few phone calls. I'll be back in no time." She hurried out into the night. If she took the time to argue, it would be too late to call Hugh Sylvester back.

She was actually looking forward to speaking with him. Today's progress just might impress the crabby son of a bitch. Maybe.

Josie lived only a few minutes from her work, and she was in her tiny office quickly. She pulled off her jacket and hung it on a hook by the door, thankful, as always, that she and Betty had spent some backbreaking hours last spring installing insulation underneath the building that jutted out over the bay. The room's temperature could now be comfortable without applying for a bank loan to pay an enormous monthly utility bill—not that it sounded as though her bank would be interested in accommodating her right now.

She walked over to the desk and sat down to listen to her messages.

The first call was from her son. "Mom. You'll never guess what."

"Wanna bet?" she muttered. Tyler had been coming up with harebrained schemes since he could walk. (Actually, before he could walk, come to think of it. His method of escaping from his crib had been remarkably inventive.)

"I've decided I don't want a computer for Christmas. Hear that, Mom? I'm trying to save you money. You know how you're always saying we should try to save money. Well, I thought about this all very seriously and decided that a computer would be—well, redundant. After all, I can use one in the computer lab here anytime I want. And some big donor is going to give the school a bunch of laptops and I'll probably be able to talk someone into letting me use one over most vacations. . . ."

"If you can't, nobody can," was Josie's thought.

"So what I thought, Mom, was that you should get me a motor scooter. Now, I know what you're thinking, but we're not talking about a motorcycle here. Just a tiny little motorbike. And I could make money with it. Maybe get a job next summer making deliveries for the drugstore—or the deli. Yeah, that's it.

The deli. Then maybe I could get all the free hoagies I could eat. Whaddaya think, Mom? Well, got to go. Don't want to get caught cutting class. Bye. Love you."

Josie stared at the phone machine for a moment. She knew exactly who her next caller would be.

"Mom. Me again. I just wanted to explain. I wasn't. I mean, I'm not cutting class. But if I'm too late, it might look like I'm cutting class. See? Gotta go. Bye. Don't forget about the motorbike."

There were two more calls left.

"Hi Josie. Basil here. Just wanted to offer you the very best the season has to offer. I'm almost ready to go to the airport. My flight for Antigua leaves in a few hours. I'm going to drop off a small something for you and a present for Tyler at Sam's house on the way off-island. I bought him that computer game where you can zap your way to the end of the world. I think it's compatible with the computer you're buying him. If not, feel free to return it. Have a very merry Christmas, Josie, my dear. And I'll see you in February. Maybe we can discuss what it might cost to remodel that awful Italian restaurant down at the pier—I understand it might be coming up for sale in 1999."

Josie smiled. Basil owned some of the best restaurants on the island. And he was a good friend. Maybe she would start out the new year with a new job lined up. But her happiness was short-lived.

"Ms. Pigeon. We've . . . no, you've got a problem. Call me immediately."

He didn't bother to leave his name. Perhaps he knew that, as the most obnoxious person Josie had ever met, she was unlikely to mistake him for anyone else. Josie reached for the receiver. She already had his phone number memorized—a bad sign with a new client, she knew.

It rang only once.

"Yes?"

She was slightly put off by the tone of voice. Did he really think one miserable word spoken in a grouchy tone of voice was an appropriate way to answer the phone?

Apparently he did. He repeated himself. "Yes?"

"This is Josie Pigeon, Professor Sylvester. You called and left a message on my machine. Well, actually two messages . . ."

"Yes. I know. It's my spine that's broken, not my brain."

"I didn't mean to imply . . ."

"I don't care about what you mean or don't mean. I just want a good professional job done on my house. And done quickly and with the least amount of hassle for me. I don't want to know what's going on in your life—or the life of anyone on your crew."

"I understand that, Professor Sylvester. So why don't you tell me why you've been calling and I'll see how quickly I can fix whatever is bothering you."

"I just told you what's bothering me—as you so quaintly put it. I don't want to be bothered with anything that is going on in the lives of your crew members."

"I don't understand. When have you seen my crew members?"

"I haven't seen them." He sarcastically repeated her phrase. "I've been getting phone calls for them—stupid phone calls. Some woman who insists on telling me about herself and that it is so very important to talk to someone on your crew. I told her to stop bothering me. And I want you to make sure that she does."

SEVEN

"**A**ND THAT'S WHEN he told me about these phone calls," Josie explained to Betty. She was back at home on her couch and, despite the late hour, had called her friend.

"And he didn't tell you who they were calling for?"

"Nope. Just someone on the crew. Could have been me for all I know."

"Guess it's time for you to give your lecture about receiving personal calls at the client's house," Betty said.

Josie thought she detected a yawn on the other end of the line. "I'm sorry. I should let you get to sleep. It's been a long day."

"I am tired . . ."

"Then go to sleep. I'll see you tomorrow."

Josie hung up. Urchin, Tyler's little dark brown cat, recognized the sign as a time for getting some of the attention she was sure she deserved, and jumped up on Josie's lap. Josie reached out for the television remote control. As a mother, she had spent her share of time yelling at her son to turn off the television and get to bed. So why couldn't she follow her own orders, she wondered, finding an old movie that she had absolutely no interest in seeing again and settling down to watch.

She should shower. She should get into her flannel nightshirt and go to bed. She should . . . She had dozed off before the first commercial could tell her what imported fragrance should be right at the top of her Christmas wish list.

Maybe it was the commercial. Or the time she'd spent

lighting the little Christmas village that evening. Or maybe it was just the time of year.

But she dreamed about her childhood. She was back in her parents' living room. From the hideous cabbage roses on the slipcovers, it was probably around the year she entered junior high school—a time when the English country look was popular. Gifts were piled under the designer Christmas tree her mother preferred—this year decorated with blue and silver ornaments. Josie had loved that tree—it reminded her of being under water in the town's swimming pool. And it was very chic—just like the trees in the ads in *Vogue*. Josie was standing in the doorway, hoping the large white box with the shimmering bow was the portable hairdryer she had put at the top of her Christmas list. All the magazines insisted that the use of this particular dryer, combined with the gigantic wire curlers around which she wound her hair daily, would turn her unruly curls into the smooth swing of straight hair currently required for popularity among the in crowd at school.

Josie walked across the floor toward the tree, painfully conscious of the rubbing together of her chunky thighs. Silver shells hung from the branches, twinkling in the artificial light. They were beautiful, but as she got closer, they began to look more and more like the cheap plastic they were, rather than something born in the sea. Josie reached out to touch a small starfish but a voice stopped her.

"Josephine, those ornaments have been placed in exactly the right spot. Please don't knock them off. You know tonight is our annual holiday cocktail party. You know how important it is to me. You know . . ."

Josie turned around to explain to her mother that she was now grown up, that she had created a life of her own, that she was a mother herself, and, in fact, she didn't give a damn about her mother's elaborate and artificial entertaining. It would be a wonderful moment—painful, but a catharsis. And, in the way of dreams, she woke up.

Urchin was industriously giving herself a bath—smack in the middle of Josie's stomach.

"Time for bed, Urch," Josie insisted, getting up and dumping the cat on the floor.

But she took a moment to compare her current living conditions with those in the house she'd grown up in. This room was a mess. The couch, bought at a Goodwill store years ago, was inadequately covered with an old cotton throw that barely hid its hideous brown upholstery. The rest of the furniture was equally undistinguished and mismatched. The decorations on the walls had been picked up at garage sales on the island and were variations on the ocean scenes so popular with summer residents. The curtains, donated by her landlady, were bright batiks; the rug a cheap sisal from a Pier 1 Imports closeout sale. The effect was warm, even homey. Josie smiled. It might not be chic, but it made her happy.

A smile still on her sleepy face, she headed off to get ready for bed, Urchin at her heels.

After a good night's sleep, Josie was up and ready to leave for work only slightly later than usual. She pulled a comb through her unruly hair, grabbed her parka, and took off, running down the stairs.

Happily, the truck was running smoothly and she zipped along the almost deserted roads to work. Island Contracting's Jeep was parked outside the Professor's home. Betty was on her knees by the back bumper.

Josie pulled up to the curb and hopped out of her truck. "Betty, are you okay? What happened?" She ran toward her friend.

"I'm fine. It's just this damn toolbox. It fell apart again."

"You need a new one," Sandy said, joining the women.

"I know. I stopped on my way home last night, but the ones they had in down at the hardware store were different inside than mine. I'd really like to replace this one with something similar."

"Oh, well . . . you should spend some time looking then," Josie said. "You don't want to end up with the wrong model or something." She made a mental note to check out Betty's toolbox as soon as possible. And she had to talk to the women about accepting personal calls at work—or at their workplace. She sure didn't want to be on the receiving end of another of the Professor's angry calls.

She worried about Betty's present and the Professor's house all morning. She might have worried all afternoon, but by then she had something else to worry about.

Caroline was ill—sick to her stomach. It had started during the morning coffee break. One minute Caroline was eating her sandwich. The next she was choking, spittle sliding from the corners of her mouth. Later, Josie couldn't even remember getting up, finding the phone, and dialing 911, but she must have, because the emergency crew came crashing through the door a few minutes later. She didn't think she'd called Sam, but he must have followed close behind the ambulance, as he was there to hold the door for the EMS crew while they maneuvered their laden stretcher outside.

"I'll go to the hospital with her." Josie heard herself speak. She might be needed. There would be things to do. Insurance forms to fill out and the like.

"No, you'd better stay here. Betty can go in the ambulance. She can answer any questions admissions might have, and I'll give her my cellular and she can call you if there's any change in . . . in . . . in her condition."

"Caroline. Her name is Caroline," Josie said.

"I'd like to go too." Layne spoke up for the first time.

"Yes. They're good friends," Josie agreed. "It will be nice for Caroline to have a friendly face around. You know how hospitals are."

Sam looked over at Layne, a less than friendly expression on his face. "Well . . . I don't suppose it will hurt. But there isn't room in the ambulance for more than one person—if that. Why don't you follow in your car," he suggested.

"I can go if . . . if there's some reason for Betty to stay here." Sandy spoke up.

"Maybe that's a good idea," Josie said. She had no idea if it was or not.

"Why don't we let Betty go." The words were noncommittal, but Josie realized that Sam's tone of voice didn't allow for disagreement.

"Yes. Betty should go," she agreed.

"And she'd better hurry," Sam added as the ambulance's siren cut through the air.

"I have to find the keys. . . ." Josie searched through the numerous pockets in her overalls.

"Don't worry. I'll take the Jeep," Betty insisted.

Layne, looking worried, hurried Betty out the door.

"She's going to be okay, isn't she?" Josie asked.

"Well . . ."

But Sandy didn't let Sam finish. "Didn't look good to me," she said in her flat way.

"What do you mean? How serious could this be?" Josie began to run her hands through her long hair. They needed every crew member right now. How were they going to get this job done before Christmas if Caroline was really sick?

"Josie . . ."

An even more terrible thought struck her. "You don't think we all ate it, do you? You don't think we're all going to be sick? Wouldn't the rest of us be ill by now if we had been exposed to food poisoning? I promised . . . And that man isn't going to accept any excuses. . . . And . . ."

"Josie! Josie!" Sam grabbed her shoulders and held her tightly.

"You think that was food poisoning?" Sandy looked down at the remains of their snack still sitting on the floor.

"I don't know. Could it have been a heart attack?" Josie asked no one in particular.

"Did she have any heart problems?" Sam asked.

"I . . . Not that I know about. Of course, she might not have told me, since she wanted this job . . ."

"She was in excellent health," Sandy said. "She was a health nut, in fact. Was always bragging about how little animal protein she consumed. Didn't eat junk food. Exercised every day. You know the type."

Everyone looked down at the remains of the food on the floor. "Health food?" Sam said the two words with a puzzled expression on his face. There were two bags of crullers, a box of decorated Christmas cookies, a carton of tiny gingerbread men, a tin of thin Moravian ginger hearts, two Tupperware containers, and a shaker of salt. "Looks more like a Christmas cookie exchange to me."

"We all brought something. And you know how appealing all the holiday treats look in the grocery these days," Josie said.

"We brought the cookies. But Caroline brought some sort of health food stuff," Sandy explained. "In this plastic thing probably." She kicked a Tupperware container with the toe of her workboot.

"I don't think you should touch anything," Sam said in his I'm-the-lawyer-here voice.

"You think she might have been poisoned by someone?" Sandy looked up at Sam with her eyebrows raised.

Josie looked at the two of them. "What are you two talking about? You can't give someone food poisoning. Food poisoning just happens. Accidentally," she added, in case they didn't understand.

"If it was food poisoning," Sandy said flatly.

"Do you know of anyone who would want to hurt her?" Sam asked.

Sandy shook her head no. "We only met a few days ago. She's known Layne for a while apparently, but they seem to be best friends. . . ."

"Sam, what's going on? If you think this is so serious, shouldn't we all be going to the hospital?" Josie looked around at the mess, torn by conflicting demands on her time. "I mean, we need to work, but . . ."

"I think we should all wait here." It was a statement, one that left no room for discussion.

Josie noticed the searching look Sandy gave him, but didn't say anything. What was going on?

"Look, I know you don't know me from Adam. And you sure as hell have no reason in the world to trust me. But if"— she glanced over at Josie before continuing—"if something happens and the police get involved, is there anything special I should do?" Sandy asked.

"Why would the police get involved? Because we called an ambulance? Is that it?"

"Josie, it's possible that Caroline was poisoned."

"I don't get it. Why don't you think it's just food poisoning?"

"Well, I don't know, but . . ." Sam began in the slow and methodical way Josie usually found comforting. This morning, however, it was irritating as hell.

"But what? Why do you think she was poisoned? And why, if she was, would anyone choose to do it in front of a bunch of people? Tell me that!" Somewhere inside, Josie knew she was being unreasonable, but she didn't seem to be able to help it. These two people were acting as though she were a child and they understood something that she was incapable of perceiving.

"She has a point," Sandy said.

Sam merely nodded. "To answer your question," he continued talking to Sandy almost as though Josie hadn't interrupted them, "there's nothing you should do. If the police end up involved in this, we'll let them do what they have to do."

Sandy looked back down at the mess on the floor. "You don't think we should . . ."

"I don't practice anymore, but I'm a lawyer. In fact, I was a prosecuting attorney before I moved here."

"So you're saying you're on the side of law and order." Sandy wasn't sneering, but she didn't make it sound like a compliment either.

"Yes. Although the two don't necessarily go hand in hand on this island."

"Sam's talking about our police chief and his son," Josie explained. "They're the island's police force in the winter. In the summer, extra officers are hired straight out the state academy. They get something to put on their résumés and we get a good-sized police department right when we need it—when all the tourists and summer people are around."

"But surely not all the crime happens in the summer," Sandy said.

"No, but we year-rounders like to think it does," Sam answered sadly.

Josie felt her patience running a bit thin. "I know there's just the two of us, but we really should be getting back to work. I'd hate to lose the entire afternoon."

Sandy picked up on her suggestion and the two women headed back to work. Sam frowned, wrapped his jacket around his shoulders and, propping himself against a wall, stared off into space, a thoughtful expression on his face.

He was still there an hour later when a police car rolled into the driveway.

Mike Rodney, the closest thing the island had to a mounty, had arrived. He was wearing old, tattered clothing and, from the smell of him, he hadn't changed since his last fishing trip. Josie, hearing the car, came out to see who had arrived.

"So, Miss Pigeon, I understand there's been some excitement around here today."

Josie didn't answer.

"So, aren't you going to say hello?" he asked.

"I'm waiting for your father to appear so I don't have to do it more than once."

"Then you're gonna be waiting for a while. Dad's in Florida. Getting in some deepwater fishing."

"When is he due home?" Sam asked quickly.

"On or about Christmas Eve. I expect to have solved this murder by then, and I'll just hand it to him with an extra-big bow—sort of for a Christmas gift."

"So she's dead?" Sam asked.

"Yup. Didn't even make it to the hospital. One of the guys on the emergency squad is some sort of true crime freak— amateurs! But he seems to know something about poison. Thought this was cyanide. . . . Or did he say strychnine? No, digitalis. Yes, digitalis, I'm sure of it."

"Well, it was nice of you to come by and tell us this, but I think maybe Josie'd better be getting over to the hospital . . ." Sam began.

"Excuse me, Sam, but this has become a murder investigation, and I'm in charge of it. I think I'd better be the one telling people where they ought to go and what to do when they get there, don't you?"

"No. In fact, it's against the law to hold people for questioning—as you well know."

"Of course I know that. I know that as well as the next guy. Now what I'm really interested in doing is looking around the crime scene. This is where it all happened, I gather?"

"Yes . . ." Josie began.

"This is where Caroline was when she became ill," Sam interrupted. "If she actually was poisoned—and I'm not saying I agree with you about that—it might have been done anywhere."

"I thought some of these poisons are fast-acting?"

"And some of them aren't."

Josie didn't see where any of this was getting them. "Sam . . ."

"Josie. I think we should leave this young man here to . . . to do what he has to do," Sam said, taking her hand. "I think you were saying something about getting back to work?"

"Yes. Yes, we should do that." Josie took the broad hint that Sam had just dropped. "Why don't we go back to the hallway and get going on that roughing in," she suggested to Sandy.

The other woman shrugged. "Hey, you're the boss."

As they left the room, Josie glanced over her shoulder. Mike Rodney was kneeling on the floor, looking through the bags of half-eaten food in an aimless fashion. She felt a sharp nudge in her side. "Hey!"

"Shh! Get going. I want to talk with you before that young idiot figures out that he needs to do something and starts blundering around," Sam hissed in her ear.

"You two probably want to talk alone," Sandy said, and disappeared in the direction of the bedroom.

"We . . ."

"Thanks," Sam said, grabbing Josie's arm and pulling her into the bathroom. He turned then and looked around at the large hole in the wall. "Where's the door?"

"A special door is being ordered."

"Well, I suppose we can talk quietly. It might look suspicious if we go any farther."

"Sam, everything's happening so fast. Shouldn't we insist on going to the hospital?"

"No. Who has the beeper?"

She felt her pockets. "I do. Why?"

"I was just hoping you'd had the sense to give it to Betty before she left. Then we could call and find out exactly what's going on at the hospital—like that young idiot is probably doing," he added, as sounds outside indicated activity on the two-way radio hanging from the cop's hip.

"Who's talking to him?" Josie asked.

"A dispatcher. Someone at the hospital. Who knows? But we may not have a long time alone. So listen to me. I don't suppose you know more about these three women than you usually do when you hire people?"

"No. Not more than they tell me—and we haven't been working together very long."

"And Mike's alone for this one." Sam frowned.

Josie smacked her head with her hand. "Sam! Caroline must have been killed by someone she knows! And the only person she knew before coming here was Layne. Oh, God, what am I going to do? I'll never finish this project on time short two workers!"

"Yeah. . . . You're gonna have a real difficult time without Betty, I'll bet."

Sam and Josie looked up at Mike Rodney, framed in the unframed doorway.

"Betty?" Josie repeated the name. "What does Betty have to do with this?"

"I'm arresting her for murder."

EIGHT

"**B**ETTY! I CANNOT believe that asshole arrested Betty for murder! It's crazy! It's insane! It doesn't make any sense! Sam, you've got to do something!"

"Josie . . ."

"You've got to stop him! Just because he's a policeman doesn't mean he can do anything he wants to do or arrest anyone he wants to arrest. He's probably mad because Betty would never go out with him! You know what an idiot he is, Sam. You have to do something!"

"I . . ."

"And you know what really pisses me off? He did this because he hates me and he knows I need Betty to stay in business." Josie's red hair was flying out in all directions as she paced back and forth through the debris of demolition that littered the floor. She clenched and unclenched her hands, and she knew she wasn't making much sense. The holiday, the project, Betty—Betty, her best friend, a person she had been relying on for years . . . The thought of Betty being arrested for murder was absurd! "Sam, it's insane!"

"I know. And I'm not arguing with you, am I? But wait a minute. I think she's leaving." Sam walked over and peered out the window into the street.

"Who's leaving?"

"Sandy. She drives an old black van, doesn't she?"

"Navy. Yes, I told her to go ahead and leave early." Josie joined him at the window. She looked up at the handsome face she loved. "You were waiting for her to leave, weren't you? That's why you've been letting me ramble on and on."

He smiled down at her. "I also knew you had to get a lot out of your system. This has been a pretty shocking day."

"You don't trust Sandy?"

"Well, she practically suggested we contaminate the crime scene. And I'd sure like to know why."

"Sam, now that there's no one here, we could look around, couldn't we? I mean, we could just look."

"As long as we're careful not to bother anything, I don't see any reason why not . . ."

Josie had dashed from the room before he finished speaking.

The crime scene didn't reveal much. They stared at it for a moment or two.

"The plastic thing was Caroline's?" Sam asked finally, bending down to peer into the container. The top was off and a fork had fallen handlefirst into the middle of the . . . "What is that stuff?" he asked.

"Looks like vomit, doesn't it?" Josie grinned. "That's what we all thought when we first saw it."

"So what is it?"

"Something called TLC. Or TCP. Or something like that. It's a meat substitute. It's made out of soybeans or tofu."

"Tofu is made from soybeans."

"Whatever. It looks gross, doesn't it? Caroline ate that stuff for lunch a few times—mixed with different vegetables, rice, and spices and things. It's fat free and completely nutritious or something like that. But it made the rest of us with our hoagies and burgers and pizzas feel pretty guilty. Not enough to commit to a diet of that stuff, though."

"I thought you were on your coffee break when Caroline became ill, not eating lunch."

"Yes, we were." And she was selfish enough to wish she'd had time to eat a bit more before Caroline had been poisoned. She was starving! "Do you think anyone would notice if I ate just one of those little gingerbread cookies?"

Sam grabbed her hands. "Don't even think of it! Who knows what might have been tampered with. Just because Caroline died doesn't mean she was the intended victim. Or that the poison was in her food. She might have taken a cookie or something else, right?"

"Oh . . ." She looked down at a particularly large—and innocent-seeming—piece of crumb cake and sighed. "I guess so. And I guess Caroline did eat things that she didn't bring—we all did."

Sam frowned. "She must have been a dedicated fan of this stuff if she ate it for lunch as well as on her coffee breaks."

"She didn't usually. She sometimes brought along carrot sticks or celery or radishes—some sort of raw vegetable for breaks. In fact, she did today. But she gobbled them up quickly and then started her lunch. Apparently she and Layne got up late and missed breakfast this morning."

Sam thought for a moment. "Layne is the other carpenter she lived with?"

"Yes."

"And did Layne eat this stuff?"

"Not all the time. We talked about it, of course. But just casually. I think Layne may have been a vegetarian at one time. And I got the impression that they ate vegetarian meals at home at night. They brought a vegetarian chili when we were lighting up the little Christmas village last night and it was really good. But Layne wolfed down the same junk we did during the day."

"Did you taste this stuff?"

Josie looked down at her nonexistent waistline. "Just a bit. It wasn't as bad as it looks. But it wasn't what I would call tasty either. It's probably very good for you."

"Food doesn't have to taste bad to be good for you," Sam said absently. He was slowly circling the edge of the room. "I wonder what sort of logical—or illogical—thought process Mike used to convince himself that Betty was guilty. Was she sitting next to Caroline?"

"Let me think." Josie looked around the room where all the women had been relaxing and chatting only a few hours ago.

Josie and her crew had pushed a large floral covered sofa against the long wall and dumped a wicker coffee table on top of it. Three wicker basket chairs were precariously stacked nearby. A rolled rag rug, four cheap brass lamps, beginning to corrode in the salty air, and an old console television were jumbled together. All of this was covered with drapes of clear plastic sheeting. The accessories—truly ugly woven wall hangings, plus huge Italian pottery pieces—had been stored in one of the empty bedrooms.

The crew had covered the floor of the cleared room with canvas drop cloths, and two old-fashioned wooden sawhorses were set up. Besides the paper bags and food containers, their open toolboxes were another indication that they had been interrupted midday.

Josie answered slowly. "Not next to her. More behind her, in fact. Betty was perched up on that sawhorse and Caroline was sitting in front of her, on the floor."

"And you were where?"

Josie reached out and touched the sawhorse closest to her. "Right here. Well, most of the time I was right here."

"Most of the time? Did you get up and move around?"

"We all got up. We had a delivery during our break. Those guys at the hardware store promised us the stuff yesterday. But the blues are running late this year, and they were all out fishing. You know how it is."

"I've learned." But Sam wasn't interested in trading stories about the complexities of life on the island. He was studying the scene carefully.

"And Professor Sylvester's aide, Nellie, came through. In fact, the homemade cookies in that tin were brought by her."

"Hmm. That was nice of her." Sam was concentrating on the problem at hand. "So any one of you could have brought the poison with you this morning in your toolbox."

"Yes, but it would have to have been put in the food—if it was put in the food—pretty quickly. No one was alone in this room for long. The supplies were carried through here to the back bedroom—we're using that for storage."

"How long did it take to carry in the delivery?"

"Maybe fifteen minutes—only one or two trips per person."

"And you were all split up then?"

"Not really. Those things are long and awkward. We worked in pairs."

"So . . ."

"So if someone was trying to pull poison from their toolbox and pour it over Caroline's lunch, they sure wouldn't have had long to do it. Besides, Sam, couldn't it have been done earlier? Or even before Caroline arrived this morning?"

"So you think Layne did it?"

"Sam, for all we know, Caroline spent last night with someone—someone not connected to the crew—and that person poisoned her food."

"Was she involved with a man?"

"I don't have any idea. I was just pointing out that it's a possibility."

"I'm not arguing with you. Tell me, did anyone from the hardware store come inside the house?"

"I . . . I don't think so."

"Did you know the men who made the delivery?"

"Oh sure. It was Hank DeMilo and his nephew Jeremy. Jeremy's home from his first semester of college. We chatted a while." Jeremy's enthusiasm for his classes and his newfound freedom had unexpectedly brought Josie an uncharacteristic moment of regret for decisions she'd made long ago. She frowned.

"Did you just think of something that might indicate who killed Caroline?" Sam asked, misinterpreting her expression.

"No. It's not that." She paused for a moment. "I know you went to Penn to get your law degree, but where did you go to college?"

"For my undergraduate work?" He was obviously surprised at the turn this conversation had taken.

"Yeah."

"Northwestern. Why?"

"What did you major in? Or could you just be prelaw or something?" she asked, realizing she was woefully unprepared to ask even the simplest question here. One year as a floundering—and then pregnant—freshman at college almost fifteen years ago was her entire collegiate experience.

"I started out in American history. I was thinking maybe I'd teach. But the law bug bit in my sophomore year, and I switched. Does this have something to do with Caroline's death?"

"No. I was just thinking about Jeremy and college and . . . and everything. And I realized I didn't know where you'd gone to school. I'm sorry. I don't know why I'm talking about this now."

"Because you're exhausted and it's been an upsetting day." He placed an arm around her shoulders and squeezed gently.

"We're going to do it again, aren't we?" Josie asked quietly, surprised to feel tears coming to her eyes.

"Do what?"

"Investigate. Snoop. Whatever you want to call it. We're going to have to look into the background of everyone on my crew."

"We don't want Betty convicted of a murder she surely didn't commit."

"No, of course not." Josie looked down at the floor.

"What are you thinking?"

"Just that this is the third time this has happened since Noel left me Island Contracting." She grimaced. "Maybe I need to change the employment forms. I could add the type of question we always seem to end up asking."

"Such as?"

"Oh." She considered. "Is there anyone you'd like to kill? Does this person live on the island? Is this person currently involved in any way with Island Contracting or one of Island Contracting's projects?"

Sam chuckled. "Actually . . ."

But Josie was on a roll. "Do you own a gun? Can you use a gun? Would you use a gun on someone you know? Can you cook? Can you cook with poison? Do you know how much strychnine it would take to kill a healthy, middle-sized carpenter . . . ?"

"Josie . . ."

"Yes, Sam. Maybe you'd better let your girlfriend know I'm here before she goes on with whatever she was saying." Mike Rodney had returned. "And it was digitalis, Josie. Not strychnine."

NINE

J OSIE GOT HOME earlier than usual that night. She knocked on Risa's door as she passed, but apparently her landlady was out. Sam had gone off to the police station, promising to call as soon as he knew anything. She'd wanted to go along, but he'd talked her into letting him handle the situation alone. Now she regretted that decision. She needed someone to talk with, something to do while she waited.

She trudged up to her apartment, tired and depressed. There was a pile of books toppling over on the mat outside her door. Cookbooks. Who would have thought the world needed so many cookbooks? There was note stuck to the one on top.

"*Cara*. I got these from the library for you. If you insist on cooking Christmas dinner, they may help you to plan. —Risa."

Josie picked up the books. She had other things to worry about... . But a letter from her son had been shoved through her mail slot and it put a smile on her face for the first time since Caroline's collapse. She used her foot to pull the door closed behind her, dumped the books on the couch, and ripped open the envelope.

Tyler had learned to type last year and, while she missed his spiky handwriting, his letters, written in his school's computer lab, were much easier to read now.

He was doing well in school. (He always did.) He had been chosen treasurer of the music club and was thinking that maybe he wanted a guitar for Christmas. (A guitar?) Did his mother want a food processor for Christmas? One of the guys on his floor (a suitemate, actually, Mom) had a mother who sent him cookies every single Friday, and she had a food processor. She said it saved lots of time in the kitchen. (Oh, fine, now her son was giving her cooking advice.) And another guy in his suite didn't have anything to do the week before Christmas. And Josie was always telling him that she wanted to meet his friends from school. Could this guy come home with him for a few days? He wouldn't expect much in the way of cooking. Tyler had already explained that Josie was happier with takeout. That his mother worked hard. And they could share a room and practice their music at night. (Apparently this kid had already been given a musical instrument or two.) Please, Mom.

Josie smiled. Well, why not? She did want to be more connected to her son. She knew she would find out things from being with his friends that he might not reveal if they were alone together. She was going to be doing some special holiday cooking, so the more guests the merrier. She glanced down at the magazine which topped the pile of dirty dishes, unpaid bills, and papers from work on her coffee table. HOLIDAY HOSPITALITY MADE EASY! the headline on the glossy pages promised. COOKIES! CAKES! CHRISTMAS GOODIES MADE EASY! DECORATE YOUR TREE THE OLD-FASHIONED WAY!

Well, she wasn't going to solve a murder sitting here. She might as well do something else, she decided, flipping through the magazine. EASY! QUICK! DO IT YOURSELF IN JUST ONE EVENING! A photograph spread across two pages caught her eye. CHRISTMAS IN CONNECTICUT CREATED BY A CHARMING HOSTESS! Josie skimmed the article. It seemed the housewife featured in the article was known for her holiday parties and food—every little bit created by herself at home. " 'I've had no formal training. I just picked up a cookbook and taught myself to do all this,' says the elegant brunette, surveying the spread laid out in her formal dining room. 'Believe me, anyone who can follow directions can do this. It just takes time and work—and lots of enthusiasm.' "

Josie had worked for this woman years ago—and remembered her large and well-equipped kitchen. "Well, Mrs. Henshaw, I'll give it a shot. But I wonder if you've ever had to do all this stuff, run a business, and solve a murder at the same

time," Josie muttered while flipping her son's letter over and
starting to write furiously on its reverse side. Food. Decorations. Parties. Presents. She had filled that sheet, one other, and
was in the middle of a third when the phone rang.

"Hi. Josie, are you feeling better?"

"Oh, Sam! I'd forgotten. I was thinking about . . . about
something else. Are you at the police station? Is Betty all
right?" Visions of sugarplums dancing in her head were
replaced by an image of Caroline's red and terrified face
peering up from the gurney as the paramedics rolled her away.

"I'm in the phone booth outside the police station. I was
wondering if you were done with your shower and ready to go
out. We need to talk, and the sooner the better."

Josie glanced down at her clothing. "I . . . I had a few other
things to do. I can be ready in ten minutes."

"I'll be right over." Sam hung up without giving her time to
protest.

Josie dropped the magazine on the floor and dashed for the
bathroom, shedding clothes as she went.

She was wrapped in a thick terry-cloth robe and searching
for her hairdryer when Sam walked in the door. It was a sign of
how distracted he was that he didn't even comment on her near
nakedness. "I need to use your phone," he announced, and
headed over to the counter that divided the kitchen from the
rest of the room.

Josie frowned and resumed her search. Apparently Sam had
to make more than a few phone calls. She had discovered her
hairdryer, dried her hair, gotten dressed, and put on mascara,
blush, and lipstick before Sam was free to talk.

"How is Betty financially? Does she have much in the way
of savings?"

Josie shrugged. "Probably not. I pay her a fair wage, but it
isn't an awful lot. We've been working steadily for the last
year, but she moved to a bigger apartment at the end of last
summer and now she needs a new car. Why?"

"Because I just called a friend of mine. He's a criminal
lawyer—one of the best—and he doesn't come cheap."

"Sam, don't you think you're overreacting? Just because

Mike got it into his head to arrest Betty for some stupid reason . . ."

"It isn't a stupid reason. He insists that Caroline accused Betty of poisoning her right before she died."

"You're kidding!"

"No. And I can't imagine any reason why he would lie, can you?"

"He's asked Betty out and she's refused . . ." Josie stopped talking. She could hear how silly she sounded. "He wouldn't arrest her just because of that."

"I doubt it. Most of the women on the island would be under arrest if that were true."

"Yeah, I guess." She thought for a moment. "Do you know exactly what Caroline said?"

Sam pulled a folded sheet of paper from the back pocket of his pressed chinos. "I didn't want to take notes in front of him, so I waited until I was outside to write this down, but I think I got the words right." He pushed his horn-rimmed glasses up on his nose and read slowly. "There were two medics in the ambulance. A Gertrude Knox and a kid named Lee something . . ."

"I think I recognized him. It's Harris, I think. Redheaded kid? Lanky? Late teens?"

"Sounds like him."

"Yeah, I heard he was helping out the paramedics on the island."

"You know him?"

"Slightly. His younger brother is a year older than Tyler and they were in the same cub scout troop for a few years. Lee helped the parents with various fund-raising projects—selling candy and junk like that. He seemed like an okay kid. A little immature maybe. He went off to college last year, but I heard that didn't work out and he was back on the island living with his parents."

"What do you mean, 'didn't work out?' "

"I suppose it could mean anything—maybe he didn't like college, maybe he flunked out. I didn't have any reason to pay attention. But I was down at the drugstore around Labor Day and there was a poster up for classes in CPR. Some people were standing around talking about the courses and someone mentioned that Lee was teaching the course—and that he had joined the volunteer ambulance corps."

"He doesn't get paid, does he?"

"Not that I know of. I mean, they are volunteers, aren't they?"

"So he probably has a job."

"I can't imagine that his parents would let him live at home and not work. His father is one of the only men on the island who still makes a living fishing—he takes tourists out on day and night fishing trips on his boat. His mother works taking money on the dock. The kids used to help out in the summer, but I don't know what they do in the winter. Why are you asking me all these questions?"

"I'm just trying to find out if he's a reliable witness. Because if we are to believe what Lee said, Caroline's last words were to accuse Betty of murder."

"What?"

"This is pretty much an exact quote. 'My food. My food. Something in my food. Betty.' "

"Isn't that rather out of order? It would make much more sense if Caroline had said, 'Betty put something in my food.' "

"Yes, but she was choking on her own phlegm and vomit at the time, as well as being in a lot of pain. I don't think we should blame her for being less than articulate."

Josie tried to ignore the image his words created. "But don't you think it might be misinterpreted?"

"Yes, you could certainly argue that she refers to someone other than Betty, and that she was going to tell Betty who when she stopped speaking."

"So . . ."

"And I'm sure that's exactly what any good lawyer will argue. But there are two important things here. The first is that Mike Rodney has arrested Betty, and therefore is probably not out looking for any other suspects."

"But we can do that," Josie said eagerly. "We've solved murders in the past. We can do it again."

Sam looked doubtful. "Maybe," he conceded. "But there is something else."

"What?"

"Betty is refusing to talk."

"But that's smart. She shouldn't talk to anyone except a lawyer—isn't that the advice you would give her?"

"She's not just refusing to talk to the police—which in this case is not just the correct thing to do, it's the only thing to do, considering who the police person is—but she's refusing to talk to anyone."

"You mean you."

"Me and the public defender who even Mike had the sense to call right away."

"Just because she doesn't want to talk with anyone doesn't mean she's guilty."

"I'm perfectly aware of that. But it isn't helping her get out of jail. And it's not going to help us investigate this crime. Think, Josie, there must be some reason why she's clammed up."

"She'll talk to me."

"She might and she might not."

"Sam, of course she'll talk to me!"

He sighed. "Yes, maybe she will. But more importantly, she might listen to you. And you need to convince her to cooperate with her lawyer."

"She will," Josie assured him. "She didn't kill anyone. So why wouldn't she do everything possible to get out of jail?"

"I sure wish I knew the answer to that one," he mumbled to himself, following Josie down the stairs.

TEN

"**S**HE REFUSES TO see you."

Josie could tell from the huge, shit-eating grin on Mike Rodney's face that he was thrilled to be passing on this message. "That's not possible. She's my best friend."

"It's the truth, Josie. I guess sometimes we just don't know some people as well as we think we do, now do we?"

"We know some people just fine and . . ." She realized she was becoming confused. "Just tell Betty I'm here to talk to her. That it's important, damn it."

"What Josie is trying to say . . ." Sam began.

"I know just what she's trying to say. But she's not listening to what I'm saying. Betty refuses to see her. Betty refuses to see anyone. I can't make her have visitors, now can I? You lawyers would probably claim that I was violating her precious civil rights if I forced the prisoner to have visitors, wouldn't you?"

Mike Rodney's grin was getting bigger and Josie was getting madder.

"Why don't you write Betty a note?" Sam suggested. "Officer Rodney can deliver it and we'll be on our way. Betty may feel better after a good night's sleep."

As Sam was tugging on her belt in a way that couldn't be ignored, Josie decided there was nothing to do but agree. "Look," she said, trying to sound reasonable, "I haven't had anything to eat since . . . since our break this morning. Why don't we go out and get something and I'll write a note then. We can drop it off later and Mike can give it to her."

"Excellent idea." Mike Rodney said. "I guess you've found out by now that this little woman sure likes to put on the feed bag."

Sam grabbed Josie's arm and pulled her out of the police station before she could respond to that.

"Sam! What the hell?"

"We're here to help Betty. Fighting with that young idiot is not going to help Betty," he hissed as he pushed her toward his car.

"Mike's probably back there laughing his head off," Josie insisted, stretching to look over her shoulder.

"He's not important. Betty is." Sam swung her around and stared straight into her eyes. "Josie, you have to listen to me. Just because you can't believe Betty would kill anyone doesn't mean she is going to be able to convince a jury of that. . . ."

"Sam . . . you don't think . . ."

"I think we need to marshal our forces. Your idea of going out to dinner and writing a note to Betty was genius . . ."

Josie didn't get a chance to bask in the glow of his approval. ". . . but then you ruined it by getting angry when Mike goaded you."

"But that's just it, Sam. He goaded me. He wanted me to be angry."

"So maybe you shouldn't give him the satisfaction of getting what he wants," he answered gently, opening the door of his antique MGB for her.

"Yeah. I know you're right. But . . ." she added, turning to him with a scowl on her face, "I don't particularly like to be told about it."

"It's been a terrible day, Josie. You're holding up remarkably well. And you will feel better when you've got something in your stomach."

Josie chuckled quietly. "Anyone ever tell you you sound like your mother?"

"Actually, no. I'm just trying to take care of you. . . ."

She reached out and squeezed his thigh, taking the time to appreciate its firm muscles. "Thanks. I'm sorry I'm acting like an idiot."

"Most people would be after a day like you've had. But it's probably going to get worse before it gets better, so . . ."

"So let's go get dinner and write that note and you can tell me what we need to do."

"Great. Seafood or Italian? Or we could go down to the Shanty."

The Shanty was a bar that served burgers, fries, and greasy chicken wings. There were only two other restaurants open year-round on the island. One served seafood, fried or broiled. The other was Italian. The menu was more likely to offer spaghetti with tomato meat sauce and lasagna with three cheeses than wild mushroom risotto or polenta with peppers, but Risa provided Josie with plenty of the real thing, and she decided she could do with something filling, spicy, and red. "Italian."

Sam turned the car around and stepped on the accelerator. "At least we don't have to worry about getting a ticket for speeding tonight."

"Nothing like having only one policeman on the island," Josie commented.

"If Mike is smart—okay, if he's at all competent, and I think we'd agree that he is that at least—he'll call for some help from the state people."

"Yeah, but they won't be setting up speed traps."

"They can do pretty much what they want, but I think we're safe for now," he agreed, steering his car into a spot right in front of the restaurant.

"Hmm. Smells like garlic bread." Josie sniffed the cool night air.

"Probably made with margarine rather than butter," came his voice as he followed her into the dark, wood-paneled restaurant.

Josie knew he'd eat his share, despite what she thought of as his New York City fussiness. True, he'd taught her to recognize the taste of real ingredients as well as synthetic, but she saw no reason not to appreciate both—and in large quantities.

"We'll have a bottle of the house red," Sam said, as they sat down.

"And I'd like the lasagna and an order of parmesan garlic bread," Josie added, getting right to the point.

"And I'll have the linguine with white clam sauce—and a few more of these paper place mats. We need to do some writing while we wait for our meal."

"You're going to be able to get Betty out of jail right away, aren't you?"

Neither Sam nor Josie was surprised by their waitress's question. Not only did news travel fast on the island, but Betty was that unusual thing, a native, born and brought up here. There were going to be a lot of concerned people when they heard what had happened.

"We're sure as hell going to try," Josie answered.

"Protein. That witch who used to teach health at the high school was always going on and on about how you needed protein to think. I'll make sure someone in the kitchen puts extra cheese on your garlic bread. . . ."

"Great." Sam flipped over the place mat and pulled a ballpoint from his pocket. "Let's start with the events of the day that led up to Caroline's death. Anything unusual happen?"

"Nothing. Not that we've gotten into a routine yet. I mean, we're not really into this job, and the crew is new at working together. You know how it is at the beginning of a new project."

"So you started the day on time. And took your break at the usual time."

"I guess. We may have been a little late starting, and our break may have been early. . . ."

"And there was a delivery in the middle of the morning, right?"

"Yes. . . . Do you think one of the guys from the lumber company could have killed her?"

"Do you think it's possible?"

"I suppose. They weren't in the house for long. The truck had one of those cranes that put everything on the ground. But then we carted it all around through the backyard and into the house. I only pay for stuff to be unloaded when I want the delivery company's insurance to take a risk I'd rather not assume for Island Contracting. It's something I learned from Noel," she explained, referring to the former owner of Island Contracting. "When a delivery is complex, and stuff has to go in through second- or third-floor windows, or heavy metal beams are to be unloaded, I pay for delivery. Because those guys know what they're doing. And I don't need one of my women getting hurt and then some idiot at the insurance company complaining that a man would have done the job without an accident."

"Good point. How about other delivery people? You didn't get a food delivery, did you?"

"Nope. I'd stopped at the grocery on the way to work and so had Betty."

"And Caroline brought her own food."

"Yup. And then Nellie gave us those cookies. We had lots to eat."

The waitress returned with their wine, a plastic basket overflowing with bubbling bread, and messages of support from the people in the kitchen. Betty, they discovered, had dated both the chef and the restaurant owners' son and everyone was concerned about her well-being. In fact, there was a large basket of food from the restaurant being delivered to the jail right now.

Josie bit into a large piece of garlic bread, grimacing from the pain as it burned her tongue, then smiling as her taste buds did a little dance of thanksgiving.

"You said you all started your snack, were interrupted in the middle, and then returned to your food. And that's when Caroline was poisoned."

"Yeah. But she might have eaten the poison earlier, then gotten ill after we sat down again."

"Not likely. And definitely not if it was cyanide or digitalis—they both work pretty quickly." He sipped his wine and frowned. "That is, they work quickly if mystery novels are to be believed. I've never prosecuted a poisoning case. In my experience, most people who want to kill someone either smack them over the head with something very, very hard or else shoot them. Although I once prosecuted a strangler . . . ugly way to die."

Josie looked down at her food and took a deep breath. On the other hand, it wouldn't help anyone if she didn't eat, would it? She reached out for another piece of garlic bread. "So what shall we write to Betty?"

"Well, what do we want to accomplish with this note?"

"We want to get her to see me!"

"Not only that. Because if she won't see you now, she might decide not to accept notes from you. I think we should consider the possibility that this may be the only message we get to Betty while she's in jail."

Josie stopped eating. "Do you really think that could happen?"

"I have no idea. But it's not like Betty to refuse to see you— or to refuse help, for that matter. I just get nervous when people begin to act in an uncharacteristic manner." He took another sip of his wine. "I really think we should consider what we write very, very carefully."

"You're saying that the point of this isn't to try to get her to see me."

"No. We need to convince her to see a lawyer—preferably my friend, who should be driving across the George Washington Bridge as we speak," he added, glancing down at his watch.

"He's driving down tonight?"

"Yeah. I thought it was important that we get Betty's defense going. And he . . . uh, sort of owes me a favor."

"It must be a big favor if he's as important a person as you say he is."

"He is, but our relationship isn't important now. We need to figure out how to convince Betty to see him tomorrow morning."

Josie frowned. "So we've got about two hours before this lawyer friend of yours gets here."

"John. His name's John Jacobs. And I'd guess three hours tops. I caught him at his desk after a long day. He'll probably stop for a meal on the way."

And if he was anything like Sam, he wouldn't stop at

Burger King, Josie knew. "So this guy's really good. Now what do we do?"

"Write the note. So, how do we start? What exactly do we need to tell her?"

"That we know she's innocent and she has to see this lawyer because Mike is such a jerk and isn't out searching for the real killer—and that we'll find the murderer, so she shouldn't worry. And that she shouldn't worry because this lawyer, this John Jacobs, is really, really good. But maybe we shouldn't say that, because if she thinks we think she needs a good lawyer, maybe she'll think we think she's guilty. And she needs us on her side now. And we know she's not guilty." She stopped and took a deep breath.

Sam repeated his question gently. "So how do we start?"

ELEVEN

THE NOTE HAD been a work of art. Josie and Sam had gone through a pile of place mats, changing and correcting draft after draft until they were sure they'd created something which would cause Betty to respond.

They'd been wrong. According to Mike Rodney, she had read the note, shaken her head, and turned around to face the wall.

Sam had driven Josie home, and by mutual if unspoken agreement, the two of them had gone their separate ways.

Josie tramped up the stairs and, not inclined to be neat at the best of times, had no trouble ignoring the mess of magazines and cookbooks spread across her couch, and headed to her bedroom. Usually exhausted, she frequently fell asleep as soon as she got into bed. Tonight, however, she expected to lie awake, staring at the ceiling, worrying about Betty . . . about Island Contracting . . . about Professor Sylvester's house. . . .

When the phone rang at five A.M., her first thought was surprise that she had gone to sleep so quickly. Her second was that someone had a lot of nerve to wake her up so early. But by the time her hand was on the receiver, she felt little beyond panic. Her heart was beating so hard surely the person on the other end of the line would hear it.

But Layne was crying too hard to hear anyone's heartbeat.

"I'm so sorry to bother you, but I just . . . I just . . . I just don't think I can keep going, and I don't know anyone else around here. I . . . I don't have anyone else to talk to. I always . . . Caroline and I . . . she was my best friend. . . ."

"Layne, maybe you shouldn't be alone." Josie sat up and

switched on the bedside light. "Why don't I come over to your house? Or you could come over here. Or we could meet somewhere. . . ." Josie had no idea what, besides the police station, was open at this time of night, so she was relieved when Layne agreed to her first suggestion.

"If you could come over here . . . " Layne sniffled loudly. "I know it sounds stupid, but I just can't stand being alone anymore."

"I'll be there right away." Josie hung up without saying good-bye and climbed out of bed and into her clothes.

Layne and Caroline had moved into a house just a few blocks away from Josie's, and she was knocking on their door before much time had passed. It had been easy to find. On a block of rental properties deserted in the off-season, it was the only house with a cheerful evergreen wreath on the front door.

But Layne's face was anything but cheerful. Splotchy, tearful, she displayed every bit of the misery she felt. Her first words surprised Josie.

"Want some coffee?"

"I suppose . . ."

"See. Look at me. Ever the good hostess. If Caroline were here, she'd be giving me all sorts of crap." Layne smiled weakly. "Sorry. I seem to be getting punchy. Come on in. It's freezing out there." She stood back from the door and allowed Josie to enter.

This house, like the one they were working on, was furnished in the manner typical of beach rentals. The living-room floor was covered with beige industrial wall-to-wall carpeting. Two Naugahyde dark brown couches, a heavy mahogany glass-topped coffee table, and matching end tables completed the room. There was also a massive stone fireplace. But everything, even the prints of soaring gulls on the walls, was overlaid with Christmas cheer.

There was a large, decorated Christmas tree. Fresh green boughs were mixed with pinecones on the mantel. Sprigs of holly perched on top of picture frames and were tucked around knickknacks on the coffee tables. "You . . . you and Caroline brought all this stuff with you?"

"Yeah. We've both collected ornaments for years and years and we just picked out the ones we didn't want to be without and brought them along. We bought the tree and the greens here, of course—and I was just starting to bake cookies that we were going to decorate and use to fill in any empty spots. And Caroline was still making tree ornaments. She was just stuffing those little felt stars last night."

Josie looked at the ornaments on the tree and wondered if perhaps these two women weren't just a bit compulsive—to spend time making more ornaments when the fir was almost drooping from the load it already held. But Layne was tearing up again—and asking a question.

"There are people to call—Caroline's fiancé should be the first, don't you think?"

"I didn't even know she was engaged, but . . . but, yes, of course he should be called. Unless she has other family? Brothers and sisters? Parents?"

"Yeah, you're right. I guess I need to make a list." Layne wandered aimlessly around her living room.

For the first time, Josie realized there was one glass and one Scotch bottle on the coffee table—one empty Scotch bottle.

Layne saw what she was looking at and apparently felt the need to explain. "I thought I'd be in less pain if I got drunk. But it didn't work."

"You still feel terrible . . ."

"I couldn't seem to get drunk. Normally I'm one of the world's cheapest drunks. I stagger around after two glasses of wine. Tonight nothing seems to faze me. . . ."

"You've had a terrible shock." Trite but true.

"Yeah. And it's really not tonight anymore, is it? It's almost morning. Caroline's been dead for a day. I . . . I should start making those calls."

"Maybe you should wait until daylight. It's only a few hours away, and there's no real reason to wake anyone up immediately, is there?"

"No . . . I guess not."

"Why don't I get a paper and pencil, and we can make a list of people you need to call. I'll write."

"Yes. That would be easier." Layne sat down on one of the large couches and closed her eyes.

Josie frowned and headed toward the kitchen. There was a phone hanging on the wall. Surely there'd be something to write on nearby.

She found a small notepad and a pen. But of slightly more interest was the coffeepot nearby. Layne was still sitting quietly. Josie opened cupboards until she found a bag of beans and some paper filters. Sam loved good coffee, and she had learned to make the brew to his specifications—strong. In a few minutes, she carried two steaming mugs back into the living room, the notepad and pen tucked in one of the ample pockets of her overalls.

"Here. This might make you feel a little better." She put the mug down on the end table within Layne's reach. "It's coffee," she added, when Layne didn't respond.

"I guess I can drink it now without feeling guilty."

"Why would you feel guilty about drinking coffee?" Josie asked. Layne seemed to feel better when she was talking, and Josie was more than willing to listen. Perhaps she'd discover something that would get Betty out of jail.

"You know how Caroline felt about coffee. She called it poison."

"She did?" If she had mentioned it during a coffee break, Josie probably had been too intent on getting to the jelly doughnuts to notice.

"Yeah. She was very careful what she ate. She had been a vegetarian for over six years."

"And she thought everyone else should stop eating meat too?"

"Not everyone, just me."

"Why?"

"Well, it's sort of a long story . . ."

"If you want to tell me . . ."

"Yeah . . . I don't mind." Layne closed her eyes again and, for a moment, Josie thought she wasn't going to speak. But then . . .

"You see, I'm the person who talked Caroline into adopting

a vegetarian diet in the first place. I started eating like that in college. God, college days . . . We all thought things would be so easy back then, didn't we?"

For Josie this certainly wasn't true, but she was interested in what Layne was going to say as well as anything that might relate to the murder. "Things were certainly different."

"Yeah, I remember when I really believed I was going to take the literary world by storm. Give readings in coffee-houses. Get published in *The New Yorker*."

"That's right. You were a writer. . . . You are a writer," Josie added, realizing she might be stepping on a wounded woman's toes.

"I wanted to be one. But no, I don't write much anymore. Being a poet isn't something I can do part-time. It takes too much dedication and concentration."

"I can understand that," Josie said, having no idea if she could or not, in fact.

"Most people can't. Most people seem to think writers write in the hours of the day when others—mere mortals—need to sleep. It's a convenient belief—then they can be imposed on and their time not valued. . . . I'm getting on a hobbyhorse. Sorry."

"I didn't mean to offend you."

"You didn't. It's just that you brought back a lot of what psychologists used to call baggage. You reminded me of Ben, in fact. He seemed to believe I could work part-time, build a house part-time, take care of all the laundry, cooking, and cleaning—and those three things are three full-time occupations when you don't have modern appliances—and then sit in the shade of the old chestnut tree and reel off a poem or two. He could be a real idiot."

"You lived without modern appliances?"

"I lived without running water, electricity, or indoor plumbing for almost two full years. Ben and I were at the tail end of the back to the land movement. Urban kids who thought it would be romantic to homestead up in the middle of the woods in Maine."

"You hated it."

"No, I loved it." For the first time that day, Layne smiled. "I really, really loved it. Although I loved it more after we had a toilet. And turning a switch for heat instead of filling a pellet stove was a nice luxury, but it was wonderful from the beginning. And I learned so much. Let's face it, being a poet is a license to starve, but being a builder is a pretty good life. I get to work outdoors and I like the different jobs. It might not always be fun, but even when it's boring, it doesn't stay that way for long."

"Yeah, I know what you mean. Did Caroline feel the same way?"

"Sure did. She was better prepared than I was. She graduated with a fine arts degree, and she'd taken a few sculpture and three-dimensional art courses along the way. So building wasn't quite as new an experience for her as it was for me. On the other hand, she and Ben did the difficult part of building the house. They dug out the basement and put in the foundation . . ."

"By themselves? Without modern equipment?"

"No, they hired a few unskilled people and a man with a backhoe. Actually, the guy I was living with at the time was one of the men who helped. They all did a damn good job, in fact. Build a good foundation and everything else is a lot easier. As we both know."

Josie merely nodded. She was more interested in the story than she was in discussing construction. "So you all knew each other while Caroline and Ben were married?"

"Yup. We were isolated, you see. Isolated in two different ways."

"What do you mean?"

"Well, we were living in the middle of the woods—there just weren't many people around geographically. And we were isolated culturally as well."

"I don't understand." The coffee was good and Josie was beginning to wake up.

"There were three types of people living in the area at that time. There were the natives, the summer people, and a few people like us—the natives and the summer people called us hippies, but we really weren't. We weren't political. And no one was involved in drug use to any great extent. We could probably best be described as trying out an alternative lifestyle—without the drugs or promiscuous sex." She giggled unexpectedly. "Caroline used to say without anything to make it interesting."

Josie smiled. "You two shared a lot of history."

"The best years of my life," Layne sniffed.

"She moved to the area before you did?"

"Yup. But only about three months earlier."

"And you were close immediately."

"No way. We hated each other at first. Ben used to kid about that. He used to say that if one of us was found dead, all the police had to do to find the murderer was locate the other one and lock 'em up."

TWELVE

"**Y**OU HATED EACH other?"

"Yeah. Well, that might be putting it rather strongly. But we didn't hit it off from the first. I thought Caroline was a flake and she thought I was a pseudointellectual snob."

"You're kidding! But you seemed so close."

"Well, we became very close. You see, there were two old hunter's cabins—shacks really—in this valley. They were in such bad shape that the natives wouldn't have anything to do with them. Most of the wood was so rotten that it couldn't even be salvaged for another building project—but, being completely ignorant, we had no idea about any of these things. And neither building was near a pond, or a stream, or anything to attract people looking for a summer home. So some enterprising person put an ad for them in a bunch of the New England college newspapers—and Ben and Caroline bought one, and then, just a few weeks later, I bought the other."

"I thought you went up there with a boyfriend of some sort," Josie said, interested in the story now.

"Yeah. His name was Aaron and, if I'm telling the complete truth, he's the reason I bought that cabin. I thought that if I had a place to live, he might be interested in moving in with me. And I was right. I have no idea what he's doing now, but I sure hope he's developed some initiative over the years.

"I really didn't know him all that well. We'd been together in some classes and had dated a little. I had a crush on him, but he sure didn't feel the same way about me. On the other hand, Aaron was convinced that he was a gifted artist and that, as

80

such, he deserved to be supported by the rest of us mere peons. I was the first sucker he found willing to do just that."

"So you told him you had a place to live . . ."

"And he suddenly discovered that I was one of the most attractive women alive."

"Nice."

"Not," Layne agreed. "But I was stupid. On the other hand, so was he. His vision of a bucolic life in a natural environment didn't even last through the first gentle rain, which fell ever so ungently through the roof and onto our bed." She giggled for the first time. "He was pissed. And he didn't have enough money or sense to leave before winter arrived, and that was a hell of a lot worse."

"And was the same thing happening to Caroline and Ben?" Josie felt it was time to get back to the main story.

"Nope. They were smarter and more energetic than we were. Besides, Ben had grown up in a family of do-it-yourselfers and Caroline . . ." She appeared to remember for the first time that Caroline was gone. "Well, Caroline was wonderful. She started designing a new house after the first week. And they had dug a foundation and built one weather-tight room before the first snows came. That's probably why we all became friends. Aaron and I visited them a lot that first winter—just to stay warm. The only other alternatives for almost a hundred miles were neighbors we didn't know, the general store where we owed an ever-increasing amount of money, the post office which was too small for more than two people to squeeze into at one time, and the town hall and the library, which was the same place and only open every other Wednesday."

"Wow. That really is rural."

"Yup. That's probably one of the reasons Caroline and I got on each other's nerves so much in the beginning. We were forced to spend time together and, at first, we just didn't click. It was really my fault."

"Why?"

"Because I was so stupid and defensive about Aaron. I was completely infatuated with him. And at that time I thought that being in love with someone meant I had to think he was perfect. So I was not only defensive about him, but I worked twenty-four hours a day pretending our lives were perfect. Like an idiot, I didn't climb up on the roof and install shingles to keep out the rain. I specialized in cooking perfect little macrobiotic meals to keep us alive so we could freeze to death. It was no wonder that Caroline was disgusted with me."

"But you became friends."

"Yes. You see, the ingredients I needed weren't available locally, so Aaron and I mail-ordered most of our food. The house—Caroline's house—was closer to the main road and sometimes our things were delivered there. Once when I stopped by to pick up some packages, I found her crying. She and Ben had had a fight.

"It sounds stupid now, but I was amazed then that they weren't a perfectly happy couple. It wasn't just Aaron that I thought of in terms of being completely perfect or completely rotten.

"Well, we started talking, sharing our true feelings about our lives and . . . and we became friends." Layne smiled at the memory.

"So how did you end up marrying Ben?"

"Caroline left. She wasn't just unhappy with Ben, she was unhappy with her entire life. She couldn't get over the feeling that if she didn't try to make it in the art world while she was young, she'd never get a chance. So she took off for New York City right before Thanksgiving the next year.

"Ben and she got a divorce that winter. And Aaron and I broke up. I was so lonely. I missed Caroline more than anything. I think, in my confused way, I thought that by getting involved with Ben, I would be getting a bit of Caroline back." She glanced over at Josie. "I was a pretty immature person back then."

"We all make mistakes," Josie said, knowing how true it was.

"Yeah, well I moved in with Ben the day the divorce was final. And we were married less than a month later—more because of an incorrect home pregnancy test than anything else."

"You weren't pregnant."

"No, but I thought I was and, as usual, I rushed in where any sane person would fear to tread."

"How long were you married?"

"Almost two years. And I regretted every single minute of it—as did Ben probably. But I loved the house. I spent every spare minute working on that house. Caroline was shocked when she came back and saw it."

"She said you did wonderful things to it."

"I did," Layne said. "Working on that house kept me sane. I was suffering from rather low self-esteem. After all, I had failed to become a writer, twice chosen the wrong man, and I was stuck in an almost uninhabited corner of Maine. My life seemed to be going nowhere. Except that I was teaching myself to be an excellent carpenter. And I was loving every minute of it. When Ben left . . ."

"He left you?" Josie was slightly embarrassed to hear how surprised she sounded.

"Yup. Moved right in with one of the daughters of a local family. She hated Maine and they moved to the Southwest almost immediately. They had one child and another on the way, last I heard."

"And you stayed on in the house. Wasn't it lonely?"

"Not for long. Caroline came back for what I thought was a visit and, after admitting that her time in New York and then Boston had been something less than a smashing success, she moved in."

"And you two live there still?"

"Just for part of the year. We usually go south in the winter to work and we both take vacations, of course. My father's ill and I'm going to be taking a few weeks off and going to see him in early January. Besides, the area isn't so isolated now—especially in the summer. But that's mainly because of the workshops we give. . . . We gave . . ."

Josie got up for more coffee and to give Layne time to

collect herself. The workshops were one of the things which interested her the most, and she sure hoped Layne would continue.

And she did. "The workshops were Caroline's idea. She had noticed, when she was living in New York and Boston, that a lot of her friends—especially women—were fascinated by her tales of house-building. In fact, she had done some remodeling of a friend's loft in Tribeca to earn a living when she first got to New York. And she had taken some courses in women's studies and things like that. The idea of a workshop for women to learn to build their own living spaces was a logical combination of the two."

"And that's what you do in the summer?"

"We have for the past six years. The first year we had six students and we set them to work building a ten-bed bunkhouse—killing two birds with one stone, Caroline said. After all, they learned while they built and, at the same time, they built a place for other women to come in the future."

"How did you get students?" Josie asked, momentarily diverted. Maybe she could do something similar to tide Island Contracting over through the lean times.

"Mainly word of mouth that first year. We put ads in some college newspapers and a few feminist rags, but I think all but one of the students at first were women Caroline had known during the time she was out of Maine." She yawned, leaning back on the couch and closing her eyes. "I think that's true. But I'm feeling very tired. . . . Do you think it would be okay if I took a short nap?" And, without waiting for a response, Layne began to snore gently.

There was an afghan draped over the back of the chair where Josie had been sitting, and she tucked it in around the sleeping woman, admiring the pattern of angels, stars, and Christmas trees as she did so. Layne certainly deserved to be exhausted, and Josie was willing to wait while she slept off some of her shock and sadness and Scotch, but she thought she might as well use the opportunity to look around a bit.

She started with the Christmas tree standing in front of the picture window by the front door. It didn't give her any clues as to who might have wanted Caroline dead, but it did say a lot about the women. In the first place, they had been wonderfully creative. Wood scraps exactly like the ones she had been paying to have carted away for years had been fashioned into tiny moons and bells and sprayed with gold and silver enamel. Tiny birds and stars had been cut from brightly colored felt and embroidered with silk thread. Strips of tin had been fashioned into icicles and shimmering whirligigs. Moons and planets had been cut from sheets of copper and tied to the tree with bright red ribbons. Interspersed between these was a collection of ornaments which told something of these women's lives. From a crabby-looking hag dressed flamboyantly in red calico with a straw broom in her hands, to a ceramic lobster with *Bar Harbor* printed on it, to the very skirt tucked underneath the lowest boughs and embroidered with the saying, *Friendship is the best gift of all.*

But she had learned more about them as individuals from what Layne had told her. Josie glanced at Layne. She appeared to be enjoying the deep sleep of the exhausted. Would it be so awful if she just took this opportunity to glance into their bedrooms? Would anyone know?

Getting up before she had the chance to change her mind, Josie tiptoed across the room and down the hallway. There were five doors and three were open.

One was a bathroom, hideously decorated with bright yellow and bilious green tiles on the walls and floors. The white towels, printed with brown and green moose, told of the different tastes of the renters. Josie decided to wait to check out that room. After all, it was always possible to find an excuse to go into someone's bathroom.

The bedrooms the women had chosen were almost identical. Furnished with inexpensive pine bedroom sets, each contained twin beds with a nightstand between, a large dresser, and an old-fashioned dressing table. A whatnot shelf hung on the wall in one room. An incredibly ugly painting of a conch shell, magnified to ten times its normal size, hung above the bed in the other. But what really distinguished the rooms was the attitude of their occupants.

One room was left pretty much as it had been rented. On the whatnot Josie noticed two birds, a tiny castle, a panda bear, a kitten, a pagoda, and three anatomically incorrect other creatures made out of seashells. Here the beds had been covered by the hand that chose the bathroom color scheme. Quilted nylon, decorated with garish bull's-eyes of pink, green, and turquoise had been made into matching bedspreads. But both beds were so covered with tossed-off clothing, books, magazines, and towels that it was difficult to tell what sort of shape they were in. There were, in fact, now that Josie could concentrate on the mess, more towels here than in the bathroom. Every doorknob held some article of clothing and the amazing thing about the pile of books toppling to the floor off the nightstand was not that it displayed a serious enthusiasm for reading, but that the owner of those books, in town for such a short time, had managed to accumulate them.

She resisted the urge to look in closets and drawers, and crossed the hall to return to the other bedroom.

Night and day. As different as night and day. She could almost hear her mother speaking the words. And it certainly was appropriate in this situation. This bedroom was not only spotless, but care had been taken to make the occupant's personality felt. White seersucker covered the beds, and pillow shams embroidered with ivy made the hard headboards more inviting. A bag of knitting sat on the floor between the beds, and a pile of notebooks stood on the nightstand, but everything else was put away neatly. On closer examination, Josie realized that even the artwork had been personalized. Someone had taped a tiny sprig of holly in the pelican's mouth. She would have loved to investigate further, but Layne's voice pulled her back to the living room.

"Did you call?" Josie asked, idiotically. What would this woman think about her wandering around the house while she was asleep?

"Were you in the bathroom?" was the question Layne asked.

"Yes."

"I have another question. . . ." Layne rubbed her eyes. The

short nap had done her little good. She looked more exhausted, if anything.

"What?"

"When do you think the police will be coming to arrest me?"

THIRTEEN

"I DIDN'T WANT TO leave her alone, so I called Sandy and we all met at the office. But I've got to get over to the work site, Sam. Professor Sylvester left another message this morning. He's going to be there early and wants to talk. He's probably been told by now about Caroline's death and I'll bet he's going to fire Island Contracting. I sure don't want that to happen, and I've only got a few minutes. . . ."

"Then tell me again what happened when you told Layne that Betty had been arrested. You said *nothing*, but . . ."

"I said *nothing* because there was no reaction. Nothing. She didn't shrug her shoulders, but she might as well have. She just said something like, 'Oh.' "

"That's all? Didn't she do anything else?"

"Nothing. Really. I was tired, but that doesn't mean I wasn't paying attention. She didn't do anything."

"Did she seem less distraught? Less upset over Caroline's death?"

"Maybe. A little. But she had perked up a lot before then. There is a limit to how long a person can cry continuously. And the alcohol had finally had some effect. But I told you that already."

"Yes, but . . ."

"So I helped her make a list of people she needed to call about Caroline—it turned out to be pretty short. After all, she could call one family member and that person could call the rest. And then I left her."

"Yes, but . . ."

"Sam. I have to hang up and get over to the house. I just

88

stopped at home to change. I absolutely have to be at the work site by eight. . . ."

"It's almost a quarter after, Josie."

"I . . . What? This damn watch!" She didn't even bother to say good-bye, hanging up and dashing off, the door slamming behind her.

Hugh Sylvester was waiting. And the scowl covering his face wasn't a surprise either. Josie started to explain before the door swung closed behind her.

"I'm sorry. My watch seems to be slow . . ."

"Just because I can't walk doesn't mean I have all the time in the world to wait around, Ms. Pigeon."

"I never thought . . ." Josie began, then stopped. "Look, I didn't mean to be late. But it doesn't have anything to do with you or your . . . your disability . . . that I am. Okay? The problem is my watch, Professor Sylvester. Just my watch."

"And apparently you have so few resources that finding out the correct time is an impossibility."

"I didn't say that."

"How else should I interpret your actions? Perhaps you don't care whether or not you're prompt. In which case, I probably should have chosen another contractor."

Josie's temper went with her hair. "If you care so much about your time, why are you wasting so much of it discussing something that's over and done with?"

"She has a point there." His aide had joined them.

"Nellie, why is it that you always interrupt me when you're not wanted and I can never figure out where the hell you are when I need you?"

"I am always within shouting distance and you know it, Professor! I was just getting some coffee for your guest and some juice for you. . . ."

"She's not my guest. She's my employee. Just like you are."

"Then I think I'm safe in saying that she and I both wish you'd treat your employees with a bit more courtesy." Nellie plunked down the tray she carried on the nearest pair of sawhorses and stalked off.

"It's damn hard to find competent help," Hugh Sylvester growled.

Josie didn't see any reason to suggest that a little considera- tion for others might be an asset. There was a mug of steaming coffee on the tray and a glass of juice with a straw sticking out. She was exhausted and was probably on the verge of losing a job; without thinking, she picked up the coffee and took a sip. Then she realized she was the only one drinking.

"Would you like the juice?" she asked politely. Should she offer to hold it for him? Would he find it embarrassing?

Hugh Sylvester apparently didn't find the situation unusual or anything to be concerned about. "Yes. You'll either have to hold it or call Nellie back to do it for me."

"I'd be happy to hold it." She picked up the glass, and prayed she didn't spill it on him.

"Bend the straw."

"What?" She stared stupidly at the plastic tube with the perky stripes.

"It's a bendable straw. The type of thing kids use. Bend it. If you don't bend it, you'll have to tilt the glass too much and I'll end up covered with cranberry juice."

"I'll . . . I'll be careful. I haven't fed anyone in a long time. My son is fifteen. . . ." She bit her lip and shut up. Just what sort of insensitive person did he think she was?

But to her surprise, he chuckled. "Well, I think I'm a bit easier to feed than your average baby. After all, I can't run away and I have better manners than to spit food at the person feeding me. Most of the time, that is."

Josie smiled and held the straw to his lips. Maybe he wasn't going to be the employer from hell after all. "You wanted to talk about Caroline's death," she began.

"I did? Do I know this Caroline?" He pulled his head back and a drop of juice dribbled down his chin.

Josie looked around for something to wipe it off with. The handkerchief she found in her pocket was filthy. She held it about a foot away from his face and frowned. "It's dirty," she explained when he merely stared.

"I can see that. Why don't you use the napkin Nellie left on the tray?"

"Oh, yes. I didn't see it there. . . . I'm sorry."

"This Caroline. The dead one. She isn't the same young woman I met with your crew the other day? The one with the long blond braid hanging halfway down her back?"

"Uh . . ." There was no way she could lie. He'd certainly find out sooner or later. "Yes. She died yesterday."

"She seemed to be enjoying good health when I met her. I assume it was an accident?"

"Her death?"

"Yes, her death. It was an accident?"

"I'm not sure. The police . . ." In for a penny, in for a pound. She took a deep breath and continued. "The police think it was murder."

"Why?"

"Why what?"

"Ms. Pigeon, are you dim or something? Why do the police think it was murder? Because she was found with a knife sticking out of her back, or something even more obvious?"

"No, she was poisoned. We thought it was food poisoning at the time," Josie continued, the words coming so fast that she was running them together. "She was nauseous and she doubled up like she was in pain. Then she fell to the floor. We thought . . . We all assumed it was food poisoning," she repeated. "Why would we think of murder, after all?"

"Why indeed? On the other hand, why not? What do the police say?"

"That it was murder."

"Not by food poisoning, I assume?"

"No. Plain poison. You know, real poison. I mean, digitalis." She decided to abandon all hope that he might leave this conversation thinking she was something other than an idiot, and offered more of an explanation.

"You see, when she fell over, we just thought it was food poisoning. . . . I know, I've already said that, but I thought you might want to understand. So we called the paramedics and they took her to the hospital. Layne and Caroline are—

were—best friends, and Layne was very upset, so Betty followed the ambulance and drove Layne to the hospital. In her car, that is. But then she died—Caroline, that is, not Betty or Layne—and the doctors said it wasn't food poisoning, it was digitalis poisoning. And so the police said it was murder, and they arrested Betty right there at the hospital. . . ."

She snapped her mouth shut, realizing what she had just said. Betty and Layne had gone to the hospital together. If the police had arrested Betty there, how come Layne hadn't known about it? And how, in fact, had Layne gotten home last night?

"Ms. Pigeon?"

"Huh?" Josie looked down at Hugh Sylvester. "I'm sorry, I just thought of something. You see, Betty was arrested and . . ."

"If Betty is the young woman with the huge chest, I can see how the young men on the island might be in mourning, but I hardly see how it interests me. In fact, you seem to have omitted the only part of your sordid tale which might be of interest to me."

"I . . . What part?"

"Where, exactly, did this take place? At your office?"

"No. . . . No, she died at the hospital." Josie frowned. She might as well get it over with. "The police think she was poisoned here. In your house. Here," she repeated stupidly. "In this room, in fact."

"Why did I have a feeling you were going to get around to telling me that very thing eventually?"

"Ah . . . I don't know what else to say," Josie said and shut up.

"Where?"

"Here. . . . Oh, you mean, where was she sitting when she was poisoned?"

"Yes, that is exactly what I mean."

"Right over there. On that sawhorse," Josie nodded across the room.

"Really." He was silent for a long moment. "Funny, isn't it? How much we're influenced by the mass media no matter how much we deny it?"

"I don't understand."

"I was just thinking. There's no yellow tape. You know, that *Police Line, Do Not Cross* stuff."

Josie didn't say anything.

"Maybe the policemen on the island don't have much need for that particular item."

"The tape, you mean," Josie said slowly.

"Yes, perhaps it's only on television that the police drape it around the crime scene."

"No. No, they usually use it here. I mean, I've seen it in the past. Around auto accidents and stuff like that," she added quickly. Since he hadn't fired Island Contracting immediately, there was little reason to remind him of her familiarity with such things.

"Yes, I guess you know more about this type of thing than a lowly professor. When my colleagues want to kill someone, they usually remember the axiom 'the pen is mightier than the sword' and do their skewering with a Mont Blanc."

"I don't believe Betty killed anyone. I've known her for years and she's not a murderer."

"Very trite, Ms. Pigeon. That's always being said about murderers."

"She's not a . . ."

"Understand, I appreciate your loyalty. And I appreciate the position you find yourself and your company in. But I wonder if you appreciate mine."

"I . . . I don't understand."

"I cannot live anywhere. Or, at least, not comfortably. And so I contracted with your company to remodel a home to meet my specific needs. And then I find that I am likely not to be in my new home by Christmas, that I have inadvertently become involved in a murder investigation . . ."

"No, you're not . . ."

"My property is, then."

"Yes, but if the area isn't cordoned off, we can still work. . . ."

"You seem to be two workers short, Ms. Pigeon. One is dead and the other incarcerated."

"I know. But believe me, that won't make any difference. Betty won't be held long on this stupid charge. In fact, a very famous defense lawyer is due here today. He might already be here for all I know. Betty could be released from jail and showing up for work any minute now." *If there is any work,* she wanted to add. "I can always fill in with someone else anyway," she was inspired to add. "There are one or two people on the island who are well qualified and would love to work with us." It was a lie, but how the hell was he to know that?

"You're telling me that you'll be able to finish on schedule. And without sacrificing quality."

"Yes. Absolutely. Without a doubt. Ah . . . yes, sir." She snapped her mouth shut, feeling a fool.

"Then I will give you one more chance, Ms. Pigeon. But if I see any yellow tape around here keeping you from your job . . ."

"You won't. Don't give it a second thought. Believe me, nothing like that is going to happen here."

"Then I won't waste any more of your time." And without saying good-bye, Hugh Sylvester placed his hand on the ball at one end of the armrest, moved the instrument a quarter of an inch and, his wheelchair swinging in a circle, headed for the back of his home and his aide.

Just in time, too. Out the front window, Josie could see Mike Rodney walking up the sidewalk, a large roll of yellow tape in his hand.

FOURTEEN

"**M**IKE. HI. YOU'RE just the person I wanted to see," Josie lied as enthusiastically as she could, as Mike Rodney tramped up the temporary ramp covering the front steps.

"I have work to do. You wanna talk, you're gonna have to do it while I work." He waved the crime scene tape in the air to illustrate his point.

"Well, yes. I can see you have things to do, but I . . . I think you might want to see something. . . . Something that has to do with the murder," she improvised.

"What?"

"Well, I don't know exactly what to call it." Not especially surprising since she had no idea what *it* was. "I mean, it's sort of a clue. At least I think that's what it is."

He looked skeptical. "Just where is this clue right now?"

"Down at the office. At Island Contracting's office," she elaborated. "It could be very important. You know how your father is always saying to leave no stone unturned in a murder investigation." She was beginning to feel quite proud of herself. This making up things was much easier than she would have suspected. "And . . . and I don't know how much longer it's going to be there," she added.

"At your office?"

"Yes. Yes. It won't take more than a few minutes to get there and then just a few more to show you, and then . . ." And then I'm going to have to think up some other reason to keep you from hanging that damn yellow tape all over this house, she thought.

"Just a few minutes?"

"Yes. Really." Josie crossed her fingers behind her back like she had when she was little.

"And then we can get right back here?"

"Yes. Definitely."

Mike appeared to be considering her suggestion very carefully.

"You can follow my truck . . ." Josie began.

"You will go with me in my police car. And we'll go now."

"Yes. Yes. Of course." Josie had a terrible feeling that she had just done something very stupid. Layne and Sandy were still at the office. And she had no idea what she might show Mike. On the other hand, she sure didn't want another run-in with Hugh Sylvester this morning. He was still more than capable of firing her. She followed Mike Rodney to his car.

Or, actually, to his father's car.

"I see you're using the police chief's car."

"My father and I believe it is of utmost importance for there to be an official police chief presence on the island at all times," he answered pompously.

Josie had no idea what 'an official police chief presence' might entail, but she was glad for any conversation she didn't have to contribute to. She mentally inventoried the contents of the office, wondering what she could come up with that might interest Mike—or be in any way remotely connected with Caroline's death.

The drive was too short to find an answer that didn't exist, but she was relieved to discover the office unoccupied. She didn't have time to worry about what that might mean; Mike opened the car door for her (and he was probably the only man she knew who could make this old-fashioned chivalrous gesture into a hostile act), and, before she knew it, she was unlocking the door to her office.

What was she going to show him? What might interest him? What might distract him? What . . . ?

"What the hell is this?"

"I . . ."

"What in heaven's name do you call this?"

"I . . ."

"Josie, what is going on here?"

"I have no idea." She sure hadn't planned on being honest. But what choice did she have? She really had no idea what the huge box filling most of the floor space in her office could be. She walked over to it.

"Boy, it must have taken some maneuvering to get this thing through the door."

She nodded, staring. "Another inch wider and it would still be outside."

They circled the box together. It was slightly taller than Josie's head, almost as wide as the doorway, and about four feet long. It appeared to have been delivered by air freight.

"Wonder how much it costs to ship something like this?" Mike said.

"Good question. . . . Hmm." She squinted at the shipping label. "Do I know anyone in Great Barrington, Mass?"

"How the hell would I know?"

"It was a rhetorical question," Josie explained. "That's where the box was sent from." She squinted again. "I can't quite make out a name."

"Well, there's just one way to find out." Mike reached up to rip a hole in the cardboard.

"Don't do that!" she screamed, smacking his hand. "Don't touch that!"

"Hey, Josie, what the hell? Do you want to be arrested for assaulting a police officer?"

"Do you want to lose your badge for illegal breaking and entering?" she retorted.

"Illegal breaking and entering? You don't know what the hell you're talking about, Josie. You let me in. You asked me to come here, in fact. There's nothing . . ."

"I didn't ask you to open my Christmas present though, did I?"

"Christmas present? This huge thing is a Christmas present? That's just wishful thinking on your part."

"It is not! Look what it says. *Do Not Open Before December 25th!* Right there! Read that!" She pointed to the large black and white sticker over the shipping label. "Why would it say that if it weren't a Christmas present? Tell me that!"

"I don't give a damn if it is a Christmas present or not. Is it or is it not what you brought me here to see? You did say there would be something that had to do with the murder, didn't you?"

Josie opened her mouth and closed it again. She had, in fact, said that very thing. She had gotten so involved in the surprise package that she had forgotten what she'd said. "I . . ." She looked around the small room as though expecting another large package to rise from the floor.

"Well, Miss Pigeon? What sort of game are you playing exactly?"

"Are you badgering Miss Pigeon, Officer Rodney?"

"Sam." Josie was so relieved to hear his voice that she felt slightly faint for a moment. "What are you doing here?"

"Right now I'm trying to find out what Officer Rodney is doing here," Sam answered, his voice still stern.

"Your wacko girlfriend invited me here. She said she had something to show me. Something that had to do with the murder," Mike added.

"Josie?"

"Yeah, that's what I told him," Josie admitted. "Mike came by the house I'm working on to . . . what were you going to do there?" she asked.

"String some scene of the crime tape," he answered, his old arrogance returning. "As an old prosecuting attorney, surely you know how important it is to preserve the crime scene in a pristine state."

"When was Caroline poisoned?" Sam asked quietly.

"Yesterday."

"When yesterday?"

"Around eleven in the morning."

"And you're just getting around to preserving the scene of the crime, Officer Rodney? What exactly are you trying to preserve? The changes that have been made since the time of the murder?"

"What changes? Who said anyone changed anything?" Mike was loudly indignant.

Sam continued his questions, soft and insistent, and Josie realized why he had been such a successful courtroom lawyer. She didn't know about Mike, but he was intimidating the hell out of her!

"Exactly who took photographs of the crime scene? And when?"

"Well . . . You know, Sam, this isn't exactly any of your business. Just because you were some big deal hotshot defense lawyer in New York City doesn't mean you have anything to do with this case . . . unless you're defending Betty Patrick?"

"I spent my career as a prosecuting attorney, Officer Rodney."

"You . . . You're saying you were on the side of the cops? Of law and order?"

"I am a firm believer in law and order," was Sam's only response.

Josie was intrigued that he had managed to imply that such were not Mike Rodney's interests. She was just wondering when Mike would realize he was losing this battle of wits and call it quits when he did just that.

"I don't have time to hang around here. I have a murder to solve. And if you're interested in showing me something again, it had better be real, Miss Pigeon. Or else—and I think Sam will agree with me here—I'll charge you with obstruction of justice and haul you down to the police station."

Josie waited for Sam to defend her—in vain. He stood silently, apparently interested only in the large box in the middle of the room.

Mike, seeming to realize that no one was about to argue with him, spun on his heel (leaving, Josie noticed, a large black mark on her nice wooden floor) and stomped from the building.

No one spoke for a moment. Then, "Do you know what's in

it?" Sam asked, giving the side of the box a poke with his fist. It didn't give way.

"I don't know. A Christmas present apparently." She realized she was smiling. "A Christmas present for me."

"It was shipped from Massachusetts. Do you know anyone in Great Barrington, Massachusetts?"

"Not really. But it is addressed to me. I mean, I think it must be for me, don't you?" A worried expression crossed her face. "You don't think someone made a mistake delivering it here, do you?"

"No. The address is just fine. Aren't you going to open it?"

"It says not to open until Christmas day." Josie pointed to the label with these directions for the second time in less than half an hour.

"And you're going to wait just because someone you don't know put instructions on the outside of the box?" Sam sounded incredulous.

"Yes, I am. It will be more fun to wait. It will make my Christmas better."

"Josie, are you all right?"

"Of course. Why?"

"It's just that waiting for things isn't exactly your style."

"Sam, how can you say that?"

"Because I've lived through one Christmas and four birthdays with you—yours as well as mine—and you can't even wait to give away presents. And when it comes to getting them . . ."

"Sam, this Christmas is going to be special. I . . . I really don't know who sent this present, but I'm going to do whoever it is the courtesy of waiting to open their gift. There is just one problem though."

"What?"

"Where am I going to store it? Too bad there aren't any basements on the island." She looked up at Sam with what she hoped was a beguiling smile on her face. "I don't suppose it could stay in your garage for a few weeks?"

"Josie, it's winter. You know my car doesn't do well in cold

weather—it's old like its owner, and it needs special attention."
He leered at her, but Josie was busy staring at her gift.

"But . . ."

"But I know where we can put this thing. I'm keeping an eye
on my next-door neighbors' house while they're in Florida for
the winter months. I'm sure they wouldn't mind if your gift
spends the next few weeks in their kitchen."

"Sam, that's fabulous!"

"But how will we get it there? Is it heavy?"

"I don't know." Josie put her shoulder against the box and
shoved it gently a few inches across the room. "It doesn't seem
to be." She patted the side of the box gently. "Imagine
someone sending me a Christmas present all the way from
Great Barrington."

If Sam had a puzzled expression on his face, she was too
pleased with her gift to notice.

"Why was Mike here anyway?" he asked.

"I asked him to come. I told him there was something here
which might be a clue to solving this murder. I wasn't thinking
of anything. I was trying to keep him from putting up that
stupid yellow tape."

"I can see that to do it now is a little like closing the barn
door after the cows get out, but I don't see why you care.
Unless you're afraid Island Contracting won't be able to work
after he sets it up."

"Exactly. Sam, there really isn't any reason for him to do it
now, is there?"

"Probably not legally. I mean, in court any decent defense
lawyer would point out the foolishness of preserving something that already could have been tampered with. But Josie,
I'm not sure Mike is thinking ahead that far. I get the impression that he's more interested in impressing his father than in
getting a conviction."

Josie frowned. "Yeah, but would it be illegal for me to move
the tape—or work behind it?"

"Yes. You could get in big trouble and that won't help you
get the job done either. Look, why don't I see if talking to Mike
will help?"

"That would be super, Sam. I don't think Professor Sylvester is going to accept someone blocking off half of his living room—and no matter who strings that tape, I'll get the blame."

FIFTEEN

"**S**O WHAT EXACTLY is going on? There's no one working today and I would have thought, if you planned on finishing the job on schedule, that there wasn't a lot of time to dawdle around. This morning you assured me that my house would be remodeled despite the murder and arrest. You know, if Island Contracting can't handle this job, maybe I should hire someone else." The message on the answering machine ended without the caller identifying himself, but Josie had no problem guessing his identity. She picked up the receiver and dialed Hugh Sylvester's number. His answering machine was on.

"Professor Sylvester, this is Josie Pigeon. You've done nothing but threaten to fire Island Contracting ever since we came on the job. What I'd like to know is why, if you thought Island Contracting was so incompetent, did you hire us in the first place?" She slammed down the receiver.

Then she had second thoughts and picked it up again. "And you will find that any contractor you hire will frequently be doing some of the construction off-site." She hung up more gently this time, hoping she hadn't just hung herself. After all, a college professor surely had the brains to realize that they had to finish the demolition before beginning any construction—on- or off-site. She put her hand back on the phone—would three calls be one too many?

Fortunately, the decision was made for her. The phone rang.

"Josie? This is Sandy. We're going ahead with the demolition like you ordered."

"I . . ."

"We just wanted to be sure that you had picked up the stuff and were coming over here right away."

Josie frowned. Obviously someone was listening in on the conversation. Probably Hugh Sylvester. Sandy was trying to account for Josie's absence. And most likely trying to tell her to get her butt over there and bring . . . Here she was stumped. Bring what?

"Okay. See you in a few minutes." Apparently Sandy thought she had given Josie enough hints, and hung up the phone.

So for the second time that day, Josie looked around her office, hoping to find something appropriate to drag over to the Professor's. Absolutely nothing struck her fancy. Finally, deciding that something was better than nothing, and something unidentifiable better yet, she grabbed a large manila file folder full of brochures, tucked it under her arm, and took off.

The hightop van was parked in front of the house, so Hugh Sylvester was still there. Josie sighed, took a deep breath, and jumped down from the cab of her truck. She grabbed her toolbox and the bulging folder, then stomped up the walkway with as much confidence as she could muster.

There was no one in the living room. And no scene of the crime tape either. Maybe Sam had been successful. Or maybe Mike was on his way. Oh well. There was nothing she could do about it now. A loud noise told her where Sandy and Layne must be working, and she headed off in that direction.

Now, at least, she knew what a narrow escape meant. She barely missed a collision with Hugh Sylvester's wheelchair. He, of course, didn't appreciate the dexterity it took for her to avoid him. All his attention was focused on the pile of papers which dropped into his lap as she fell against the wall.

"What the . . . Well, well, well, does this indicate a bit of unexpectedly creative thinking on your part, Ms. Pigeon?"

"I . . ." Was there a compliment hidden in there? What was he talking about? She looked down at the open Kohler catalogue in his lap. A goosenecked faucet sparkled like a diamond in the photograph. The plumbers were provided with different catalogues, full of pages of black and white drawings, and specs. This was for the consumer, and the general impression left was that everyone could have a bathroom which was a work of art. There was no indication that anyone would ever use the room for anything other than the most refined purposes—and a drop of water would never dare leave a spot on any of the carefully lit surfaces.

"The top moves, right?"

"Ah." She looked at the photograph which was getting so much attention. Thankfully, she had used a larger version of the same appliance in the last kitchen remodeling she'd done. "Yes. Not only does the spout move, but it can be turned 360 degrees." She suddenly realized the source of his interest. "In fact, it can be moved with just a gentle push. It's very well designed and very well made. You can add the faucets with wings, which can be pushed on and off. And the entire set would be a perfect match for the slanted sink which Kohler recommends for handicapped use."

"Hmm. Do you have any thoughts about how we might regulate the temperature of the water so that while just pushing and pulling these things around I can keep from burning myself? Just because I can't feel anything doesn't mean my skin can't burn."

"I . . . uh . . ."

"You know, you might want to install that little device under the sink which beauty parlors use."

Josie turned around to see who had made this suggestion and was surprised to find a young woman she didn't recognize. "I helped install some just the other day," the young woman continued, glancing over at Josie and then immediately glancing away.

"What exactly is this device, and is it going to add major dollars to the cost of the project?"

"Ah . . . it sounds like you're more familiar with this than I am," Josie said to the younger woman.

"It's cheap. Almost every beauty parlor and salon in the country has them on their sinks." Well, whoever she was, she sure could be an authority on beauty parlors—Josie could count six different hues of dye in her shoulder-length hair.

"The architect who designed the modifications on this house didn't include anything like that, did he?" Hugh Sylvester asked Josie.

"No. In fact, he specified a very expensive European system to control water temperature. This system would probably be much cheaper." Josie hoped like hell this young woman knew what she was talking about.

"We wouldn't be recommending it if it weren't better and cheaper," the young woman stated flatly, and then had the grace to look over at Josie and blush to the dark roots of her hair. What a nerve this person had to be acting as though she were a part of Island Contracting!

"Well, it looks to me like you and this lady have proven Island Contracting's competence at last," Hugh Sylvester said, smiling for the first time since he and Josie had met.

"I . . . Thank you." She didn't know what else to say.

"What is the name of this young worker?" he asked, looking at the girl with multicolored locks.

"My name is Pamela James. Pam."

"Well, Pam, I want to thank you for renewing my faith in the company for which you work."

"I . . ." Again Pam glanced at Josie. "Yeah, thanks."

"What Pam means is we'd better get to work," Josie suggested.

"And I have to leave. Mind if I take these things with me? There might be something else of interest in them." He glanced down at the brochures in his lap.

"Of course not."

"Then maybe you would be so good as to put them in the backpack hanging from my chair," he suggested, once again leaving Josie feeling like a fool for not seeing the obvious.

But she had other things to worry about. Who was this Pam James and why did everyone seem to think she was a member of Island Contracting's crew?

As soon as the women were alone again, she asked those questions. It was Layne who offered an explanation.

"Meet Pam James," she said, an embarrassed expression on her face.

"You are going to explain a little better than that, aren't you?"

"You see, I dropped by to see Layne and Caroline this morning," Pam began.

"She's on her way to spend Christmas at her parents' home in North Carolina," Layne offered.

"Actually, at my brother's home in South Carolina," Pam corrected her.

"Oh. Well, we knew Pam back in Maine. In fact, Pam was trained by us up there. She was one of the first women to actually build her own home after taking a few of our classes," Layne said.

"And then I found out that Caroline had died," Pam continued.

"And we do need another crew member, what with Betty and Caroline not here," Sandy added.

"So you offered her a job?" Josie was shocked by the presumption.

Apparently the two women were shocked that she might think they were so presumptuous.

"No."

"Of course not."

"We would never do anything like that."

"We certainly had no right to even consider such a thing . . ."

"So why did Hugh Sylvester think you were an employee?"

"He thought that right away," Sandy explained.

"You see," Layne began, "Professor Sylvester came in while we were working. And we all felt just a little awkward about having a visitor . . ."

"And I really didn't mean to cause any embarrassment," Pam interrupted to insist.

"But Professor Sylvester just assumed she was a worker he hadn't met before," Sandy added.

"And we didn't think it would be a good idea to disagree with him."

"Or give him the idea that you were entertaining friends at his home while you were supposed to be working," Josie stated flatly.

"Uh . . . yes."

"This is really all my fault," Pam insisted.

"No, it's mine," Layne said.

"We all . . ." Sandy began.

"Are you qualified to work with us? Are you looking for a job?"

"I . . ."

"We . . ."

"She . . ."

All three women looked at Josie. Then Sandy and Layne turned their attention to Pam to see how she would respond to Josie's question.

"Yes. And yes."

"You mean you want the job?" Layne asked, sounding surprised.

"What about your brother?" Sandy asked. "Won't he be disappointed if you're not there for the holidays?"

"I do want the job. And I'm qualified. And my brother couldn't care less if I'm there or not. His wife will probably be thrilled that I'm not. She's one of these compulsive women who wants her house just so. Watches Martha Stewart religiously and is always making things out of felt and stuff. The last thing in the world she wanted was a guest sleeping on the foldout couch in their family room—I don't blend in with her beige and taupe color scheme," she added, tugging at a fuchsia lock of hair.

"And you won't mind being away from your family for the holidays? This job is going to run right up to Christmas Eve—if we're lucky enough to finish it," Josie added.

"I'll miss my nephews. They're great kids. Tyler and Trevor. Eight-year-old twins. I haven't seen them since summer . . ."

That settled it as far as Josie was concerned. "My son's name is Tyler too," she said, feeling that somehow the fact that they both cared about a boy with the same name created a bond. "It's been a while since he was eight, but he'll be home from boarding school in a week."

"I'll need a place to stay," Pam mused.

"You can stay with me—there's a bedroom that neither Caroline or I used. You can stay there if you like," Layne offered.

"It wouldn't be an imposition?"

"It would be a relief," Layne answered. "I closed the door to Caroline's bedroom, but frankly, I was dreading going home tonight. There's so much of her in that house. I . . . I think it will be easier if you're there. Unless it would bother you?"

"No. I don't think so. Caroline and I were good friends, but never close like the two of you. What did Ben say when you told him about her death?"

"I . . . I haven't told him. You know Caroline hadn't spoken with her family in years and years, but I did call her parents. They were . . . well, they were awful. Crying and hysterical. You know. I didn't have the nerve to tell them it wasn't an accident. And then they wanted to claim the body, so I had to tell them about the autopsy. They didn't ask more questions, but they will eventually. I . . . I got so upset that I didn't even talk to Ben. I just came on over to work. I thought maybe you could help me," she said to Josie. "I really don't know what to do."

SIXTEEN

I T WAS AT that point that Josie interrupted the women and suggested they might talk and work at the same time. The paperwork required to put Pam on the payroll could be filled out later. (She had no trouble at all guessing what Sam would say about this plan, but they had to get on with the job. Period.)

Almost immediately she felt confident about the decision to hire Pam. The young woman was not only a good worker, but she knew what she was doing, and, as she related the story of her life, it was evident that she fit right in with Island Contracting's philosophy of hiring. Like many of the women Josie hired, like she herself when she was hired so many years ago, Pam needed a fresh start on her life.

The story Pam told wasn't all that unusual. Involved with the wrong man, she had dropped out of college only a few months short of graduation, following him to live in the back-woods of Maine. Only to find that, even in the wilderness, some men manage to find the perfect other woman. Unwilling to admit that her family and friends had been right, she had looked around her for a way to make a living—and a life.

Caroline and Layne's school was located in the next town. She headed there, got a job in a nearby restaurant, and started taking classes. Two years later, she was a carpenter on vacation traveling down the coast when she stopped in to find her old friends and mentors—and discovered that one of them had died.

Pam's story didn't interest Josie nearly as much as hearing more about the school for women builders that Caroline and Layne had created. Layne, she realized quickly, had been modest in talking about the school. It was a real school, not just a collection of random workshops. And apparently, it was now thriving with a waiting list of students for spring classes, but getting it to this point had been a real struggle.

Pam had heard about the school when it was two years old. It was still in danger of closing at that time. The first round of pupils, culled from women Caroline had known in Boston and New York, had departed to use their newly acquired skills, and had not been replaced by more pupils. Caroline and Layne, after trying to get jobs in the area and not succeeding, had moved down to the suburbs of Boston for a winter of working for any company that would hire them. They had met Pam almost immediately after their return to Maine for the summer session.

The third year of the school, the year Pam attended, had been critical to its success. There was no money to advertise, little cash available for supplies, and no need to build yet another bunkhouse for students who didn't appear. And then, Pam explained, a benefactor was found, a few new students appeared, and the future was assured.

"You mean someone gave a whole pot of money just to keep the school going?" Sandy had stopped working to ask the very question that was bothering Josie.

"Yes. That's right."

But Josie thought she heard some hesitation in Layne's voice. "I don't suppose this wonderful person would be interested in investing in a contracting company, would they?" she asked, half in jest.

"I don't really know."

"Do you get money every year, or was it just one big donation?" Sandy persisted.

"I don't know that either." Layne made a face and continued. "If it sounds like I don't know very much, it's because I don't. The donation actually went to Caroline—I mean, it was for the business, but the money went to her and she handled everything about it. It sounds strange, but I never really thought about it until now."

"Caroline got this donation to keep your school going and

you not only don't know who gave it, you don't know if it was given yearly or just the one time?" Josie was amazed. Up until now, Josie would have sworn that she herself was the most casual businesswoman in the universe. Apparently she was wrong.

"Yes. You see, he or she wanted to remain anonymous. And Caroline did all the bookkeeping—had always done it," Layne explained, a deep frown on her face. "I guess it will be my job from now on."

"Don't worry. It's not as difficult as you think it's going to be," Josie assured her, interpreting the expression on the other woman's face as dread.

"I don't know if I'm going to have anything to do. I can't imagine the school without Caroline. It will probably close down."

"But you can't just abandon the school!" Pam cried. "Think how much it's meant to so many women! I don't know what I would have done without it. How could I have earned a living? To say nothing of my self-respect!"

"That's what Caroline used to talk about the most. Self-respect. She always said nothing builds your self-respect more than building yourself a house."

"Yeah, I remember the first time she said that to me. I thought she was nuts. All I wanted was a place to live—and some way to keep a roof over my head. I sure didn't expect to learn everything there is to know about two-by-fours and why penny nails are called penny nails. I didn't even think I was capable of learning stuff like that."

"You sound like you weren't really interested in being a student at the school," Josie said.

"It sure wasn't my first choice—it was my only choice. I didn't have money to leave the state and get started somewhere else and I didn't want to borrow from anyone. When Caroline came to me with the suggestion that I become a student . . ."

"Caroline came to you?" Everyone in the room heard the surprise in Layne's voice as she asked the question.

"She didn't actually come to me. I was waiting on her at the diner one morning—serving her breakfast. There was a lot of general talk about how the restaurant was going to close for the winter and whether or not it would be opening again in the spring. And who was going to be doing what. You know. And Caroline asked me what I was going to do. I told her I had no idea—that I didn't even know where I was going to be living. (I lived in an apartment above the restaurant and that was going to be closed up for the winter as well.) She said the school was going to be open year-round and that, if I wanted to study to be a carpenter, I was welcome to spend the winter with you all." Pam shrugged. "It was sure the best offer I'd had in a while."

"I thought you weren't open in the winter months," Josie said.

"We were for two winters." Layne paused. "Right after the donations started coming in, in fact." She frowned. "I guess I should have been more involved in the day-to-day running of the school."

"Not necessarily. You had someone to share the work with—why duplicate efforts?" Josie said. "If I had someone else running Island Contracting with me, that's probably just the way I'd be."

"At the time it made sense. In fact, I never even thought about it. But now I keep thinking of how little I really under-stood about the foundation of the school. I'm a good teacher and I was pretty good at making sure the people teaching elec-trical skills and plumbing were doing their jobs, but that's it really. I guess I'll miss Caroline for a whole lot of reasons."

Josie and Sandy went off to work in another room then, leaving Pam to comfort a sobbing Layne. Josie noticed that there were tears in Pam's eyes too. She had a lot to think about and she worked alongside Sandy in silence.

The demolition would be done before they left tonight. And tomorrow they'd start framing in the new doorways. She should spend some time back at the office checking on the status of their orders, but assuming things came in on schedule, they might actually end up only a day or two behind. Of course, it would help out more than a little if Betty were out of jail and back on the job. Josie frowned and thought for a moment before speaking.

"You know, I need to run back to the office for a few minutes. Do you think you guys can go on without me?"

"Sure. Don't worry about a thing. Someone can always call you if there's a problem, right?"

"Yes. I won't be long. I just have to check a few things."

"If you don't mind me asking, is Betty one of them?"

"Yes."

"I understand she won't talk with anyone."

"Well, she won't talk with me. But I'm hoping it's just me— if you know what I mean."

"You hope she's talking with other people."

"Yeah." She was going to call Sam first thing. His lawyer friend should have gotten through to Betty by now. Maybe he would have some idea when she was going to be released. She was fairly comfortable hiring Pam to replace Caroline—it almost sounded as though Caroline had arranged this somehow for her protégée. But she sure didn't want to have to hire someone to replace Betty.

Certainly there were more than a few people free this time of year, people who would be glad of the work and the opportunity to make some extra money right before the holidays. She might even take the time to call around and see who was free while she was back at the office, she decided on the drive there.

But when she arrived, she discovered a distraction. A box on the front porch did not appear to be a Christmas present, and on closer examination, her worst fears were confirmed.

"You poor thing," she said to the cat lying curled up in a tight ball, trying to stay warm. "Imagine being abandoned two weeks before Christmas."

She hurried to unlock the door and get the animal into the relative warmth of the office. Island Contracting was known as a place where strays would be taken care of, but usually at this time of year, the need for animal shelters was minimal. And while dropped-off kittens were a fairly common occurrence in the late spring and early summer, a full-grown cat was a rarity. Usually people just drove a good distance from home and dropped the cats from the car—hoping, she assumed, that someone would pick the poor things up before it was too late.

"But you sure look as though you've been well cared for," she said, putting the box on the floor and leaving the cat to become acquainted with her new surroundings. The large tiger didn't waste any time. She stood, stretched, and jumped from the box to the desktop in almost one movement. There she stayed, surveying her new home as she washed off the dust of her trip. "Well, you're certainly the princess," Josie said, pulling open the bottom file drawer and pulling out a box of dry cat food and two bowls. "I just hope you're not a fussy eater. The selection around here is rather limited right now."

She yanked an already filled litter box from the bottom of the only closet in the room, hoped the cat was sophisticated enough to get the general idea, and started on her phone calls. Sam first, she thought, dialing the familiar number.

"Hi Sam. How is everything? Did your lawyer friend get here? Is Betty out yet?"

"Yes. No." Sam's replies were short and to the point.

"Yes he's here?"

"And no, she's not out yet. In fact, she refuses to talk with him."

"She won't see him?"

"Oh, she'll see him all right. She will even sit in the same room with him for almost an hour. And she did. But she won't talk to him."

"Is she listening? I mean, he's not just sitting there saying nothing, is he?"

"Are you kidding? For the money this guy charges, he should be speaking in verse. And he can only assume she hears him. Apparently she's not responding at all."

"At all? Are you sure? Isn't she smiling or frowning? Or anything?"

"Look, Josie, he's right here. Why don't you talk with him? That way you can get your answers directly from the horse's mouth—so to speak."

She heard rustling as the phone was passed from one man to the other, and then the defense lawyer came on the line.

"Ms. Pigeon? This is John Jacobs. It's nice to be talking with you at last. Sam's told me a lot about you over the years."

"Really? How nice." She hoped it was nice.

"I spent the afternoon with your employee . . ."

"She's my friend."

"Your friend and employee then. And I explained the situation she was in to her as I saw it—I've spoken with the local police, but at that time, I only had a rough idea of the facts in the case—and I told her what I knew of the law which would apply to her situation. And then I waited for her to answer me. And she didn't. I waited over half an hour."

"And that's it? You're not going to help her?"

"I didn't say that. I told her I would expect an answer to the question of whether or not she wanted me to represent her in the next twenty-four hours. If she didn't answer me directly by five P.M. tomorrow, I would assume the answer was in the negative, and leave town."

"And that's how you left it?"

"Yes. I can't represent someone who doesn't want to be represented."

"And she didn't say or do anything? Anything at all?"

"Well, I thought . . . perhaps . . . just perhaps . . . that I saw a slight smile as I entered the room."

There was more rustling as the phone once again changed hands. "John's being modest, Josie." Sam's voice came over the line. "He's one hell of a slob. But women seem to find him irresistible—there aren't many women who don't automatically crank up a smile when he walks in the room."

"Then let's just hope there's a female judge assigned to Betty's case," was all Josie could think of to say.

SEVENTEEN

"SHE SMILED WHEN he came into the room. That's all. Just a smile. John is a professional. He was merely reporting what happened."

"But don't you think it's a good sign? That she reacted? I mean, it indicated a connection to life. Sort of like she cares about something." Josie picked up a ball-peen hammer and balanced it in her hand. She and Sam had stopped at the hardware store on the way home, and she had taken the opportunity to do a little Christmas shopping while checking on the Corian countertop that she had ordered.

"All I'll say is that it's likely that in Betty Patrick the sex drive will be the last thing to go." Sam grinned.

"Sam. I'm serious. Don't you think this is a good sign?"

"Josie, you're asking for an assurance I can't give you. I'd like to. I'd give anything to make you feel better, but I just think you're making a bigger deal out of this than it is. Betty smiled—slightly. That's all John said. That's all she did."

Josie frowned. "Yeah. I know I'm hanging on to threads, Sam, but I don't know what else to do. I can't believe Betty refuses to see me! I just want to understand what's going on."

"Have you learned anything yet about Caroline's past that might connect her to Betty?"

"Nope. But I've learned a fair amount about Caroline and the school she and Layne ran. One of their students appeared here today." She paused and thought for a moment before continuing. "In fact, I'm thinking about hiring her."

"I'm glad to hear you're only thinking about it. In the past, you probably would have hired her on the spot. If you've become a bit more cautious, at least you've learned something from all this."

"Sam . . ." She started to protest, then realized she would just have to invent another lie.

"I'm sorry. I didn't mean to sound so condescending. You know the respect I have for you and the way you've made Island Contracting a thriving business."

Josie suspected that he would have liked to add *despite all the stupid mistakes you make* to his statement, but she figured she shouldn't complain.

"So tell me about this student. How did she find out Caroline was dead?"

"Oh, she didn't know. She just stopped by to visit on her way down the coast. She was—is—on her way to her brother's house in the Carolinas, and wanted to say hello to Caroline and Layne on the way—and maybe get a place to crash for the night," she added. "She was shocked to find out about Caroline, of course. And she and Layne have been doing a fair amount of reminiscing."

"So she stayed around while you worked?" Sam gave Josie a suspicious look.

"Yes. To comfort Layne as much as anything," Josie added quickly.

"Sounds like a nice young woman . . ."

"That's what I thought too."

"So what did you learn? Anything interesting?"

"Sort of. I had the impression that Layne and Caroline taught some workshops irregularly. But it wasn't like that at all. Apparently it's a real school. And it sounds wonderful, Sam. They were really doing a service for their students. They even got a big donation to stay in business because their work was so significant."

"Sounds impressive. How is Layne taking Caroline's death? Has she called Caroline's family?"

"Yes, earlier."

"But there doesn't seem to be a bevy of relatives and friends flocking to the island to mourn Caroline—or support Layne."

"But would there be? This isn't really her home, after all."

"You know, Josie, Betty may have been arrested, but Layne is the only person on the island who has any sort of history with Caroline. She really is the logical suspect."

"But she was so upset."

"If she killed Caroline, surely she would know that not showing remorse would be a sign of her guilt."

"So you think it's all an act."

"I didn't say that. She might even have murdered her friend and been genuinely upset about it at the same time."

Josie dropped the hammer she was holding to the floor. "You're right. I hadn't even thought of that."

"Which doesn't really help us with our immediate problem."

"Getting Betty out of jail," Josie agreed, picking up the last hammer on the display.

"Josie, what the hell are you doing? Planning on twirling one of those things like a baton?"

"Checking out the balance. Everyone has their own way of doing it. This is mine. I'm thinking of buying hammers for the crew for Christmas. No matter how many power tools you have, hammers are used the most. And they're always getting lost. Do you think this is a good gift? My only other thought was something dull like bath oil."

"Do you usually buy Christmas presents for everyone who works for you?"

"No. Usually, of course, we don't have a job at Christmastime and, except for Betty, I just send cards to everyone who has worked with Island Contracting in the past year. . . . Damn. I forgot that. Would you mind if we stopped at Knight's on the way home? I need to pick up another box of cards. And I need to go to the grocery store. I'm going to make plum pudding for Christmas Day and it's important to start soaking the raisins and . . . and other things as soon as possible. Did you have any idea that raisins were the plums in plum pudding?" she asked, standing up and stretching.

"Yes I had an aunt who brought a plum pudding to dinner every year. We used to take pieces as small as possible, slather hard sauce on them, and wash them down with egg nog."

"You don't like plum pudding?"

"Not particularly. And I'm sure it takes lots of time. My aunt did nothing but play mah-jongg, write nasty letters to the *New York Times*, walk the dumbest little bullterrier in the world, and bake elaborate desserts that no one needed or wanted. Josie, you're in the middle of this project, Betty is in jail, Tyler's coming home . . ."

"He's bringing one of his suitemates."

He looked at her and frowned. "Okay, with a friend. You're planning this elaborate Christmas dinner. And now you're giving gifts to everyone on the crew—one of whom very well could be the person who killed Caroline. You're going to be a wreck before Christmas. Why don't you just let my mother . . ."

"Don't even say it, Sam. I have invited everyone to dinner at my apartment on Christmas Day. And everyone is going to be fed a wonderful meal, see a beautiful tree, have a wonderful time, and . . . and . . ."

"And God bless us all, said Tiny Tim. Josie, no one in their right mind tries to re-create fictional holidays. . . . Oh, wait a second." He reached down to his belt.

"Since when do you wear a beeper?" Josie was so surprised by the discovery that she didn't protest his last statement.

"It's not mine. It belongs to John. He was going to beep me if he heard anything from Betty. Let's just hope this is good news."

"There's a phone near the cash register. No one will mind if you use it," Josie said, pointing him in the right direction.

"If he's using it to help get Betty out of jail, he can call Alaska—or Singapore—or wherever—and talk all night." The store's owner appeared by their side. Josie wasn't surprised by the comment; just another example of the locals supporting their own.

Sam picked up the phone and dialed the number flashing across the top of the pager. Josie and the store owner stood quietly by, each hoping for good news.

"Hi. It's me. Yes. Yes. Yes. Okay. Listen, why don't we meet for dinner. For seafood. Yeah, it's not the best food in the world, but they actually have a wine list and we can always get some single malt Scotch there. Okay. How about an hour? Okay."

By the time he put down the receiver, Josie was ready to strangle him. "Dinner? You're making plans for dinner before you tell us what's going on? Sam . . ."

"Betty called and asked to see John," he interrupted her.

"Oh, Sam, that's wonderful!" She was astounded by how relieved she felt.

"It's not quite as wonderful as it sounds. She saw him. And all she said was that he could act as her lawyer. But she wouldn't tell him anything about the murder other than that she didn't do it."

"But that's good."

"It's not bad. But John says that's all she would say. She said her piece and then just refused to talk anymore."

"Doesn't sound like Betty. That young woman was born talking—ask anyone on the island." The hardware store owner looked concerned.

A horrible thought struck Josie. "Sam, you don't think she's being abused in jail, do you?"

"Josie, Betty is in one of the two holding cells on the island. There are no other prisoners. She might not be getting the best food . . ."

"You don't have to worry about that. Some of the women on the island got together and are cooking for the jail in shifts. Last I heard, my wife was making her special sea scallops for dinner this evening. I was looking forward to closing up the store and getting home to see if there were any leftovers."

Sam grinned. "What an island. Betty's probably going to be eating better than anyone else as long as she's incarcerated." He put his arm around Josie's shoulder. "Let's get out of here so this man can head home for his dinner."

"Do you think she would be allowed to have a CD player? I could bring one over to her . . ."

"She has the tape machine which used to be down at the diner. And my wife's sister brought sheets and is making sure she has fresh towels each day. And Mary down at the drugstore supplied a bunch of free shampoo samples and stuff."

Sam chuckled. "Who provided the Christmas tree?"

"The women's circle from the Methodist church," came the serious answer to the sarcastic question. "The circle leader used to be Betty's Sunday school teacher. She's also the children's librarian, and sent over a bunch of books on tape."

"And you were worried about her," Sam said, putting his arm around Josie's shoulder and leading her toward the door. "We'd better get going."

"I'll decide about the hammers later," she called over her shoulder.

"We gift wrap." The words floated out the closing door behind them.

"Gift wrap. I haven't bought gift wrap yet!"

"Just put the word out that Betty wants some to wallpaper her cell and you won't have to shop. Every woman on the island will be bringing her some."

They got into Sam's car and sped off toward Josie's apartment.

"You're only going to change, aren't you?"

"Hmm."

"I might just stop in and say hello to Risa if you're not going to be long."

"Fine."

"I have a few things to say to her. You're not listening to me, are you?"

"I was thinking about . . . about Christmas. You know."

"I do. And I won't repeat my suggestion."

"What suggestion?"

"That you let my mother do it all. Josie, she would love to. It's been years since any woman I went with allowed my mother to cook a holiday meal. And you know how much she likes you," he added quickly, realizing what he had just said.

But Josie wasn't paying much attention. "I can do it," she muttered automatically as they arrived at her home. So all those women in New York City had wined and dined Sam Richardson in the manner to which he had become accustomed, she thought, walking up to her apartment.

She took a deep breath and looked around. Magazines and cookbooks were scattered across the couch. Dirty dishes filled the sink. There wasn't even a sprig of holly in sight. And a strange smell seemed to be coming from somewhere near her refrigerator. "I just love Christmas, don't you?" she said, grinding her teeth.

EIGHTEEN

THE RESTAURANT SAM had chosen was offering a seafood casserole as the dinner special, and Josie had no trouble picking it as her entrée. The men from New York spent what she considered an enormous amount of time inquiring into the contents of each dish before settling on broiled salmon, salads, and rice pilaf instead of the buttery potatoes Josie had chosen for a side dish.

"This will be edible," Sam assured his colleague. "The fish here is fresh. But there's really wonderful food on the island in the summer. There's a man named Basil Tilby who owns two restaurants, and they're both exceptional. In the winter, your best bet is to look hungry and hope Josie's landlady takes pity on you and invites you to dinner. She's an absolutely fabulous cook."

"And now that Sam has increased the selection of Italian wines that his store carries, Risa loves him to death. If you're a friend of Sam's, you won't have any trouble at all being offered a few meals. In fact, I'm surprised Risa didn't invite us all over tonight. You were down there when I was changing, weren't you?"

"Yes, but she was busy cleaning shrimp. She's going to make one of her Tuscan specialties for Betty's dinner tomorrow night. If Betty's not careful, she's going to have a weight problem when she gets out of jail."

"But she is going to get out, isn't she?" Josie leaned across the table to John Jacobs. He was an interesting-looking man. Younger than she had imagined (closer to her age than Sam's), he had longish blond hair, high cheekbones underneath smooth tanned skin, and deep blue eyes. In his plaid flannel Ralph Lauren shirt, he looked a lot like a preteen boy nervous about his first date. He had been disappointingly quiet about Betty and her situation.

"I'll do the best I can."

"But what are you going to do? What did she tell you?"

John frowned as the waitress poured wine in his glass.

"Oh, I'm sorry. Did you want something else?" The young woman asked, misinterpreting his expression.

"No, this is fine. Thank you." The smile he sent in her direction almost knocked the woman over. Josie wondered if he could possibly not realize the effect he had on the female population of the world. It wasn't that he was sexy as much as that he was charming. "I really can't tell you exactly what she said. Confidentiality and all. But the truth is that she didn't say anything other than that she would accept me as her lawyer. I've spent the afternoon wondering if we should think about hiring a detective of some sort to look into the case. I'll do as much as I can, of course, but it would be nice to know something about what happened."

"I've been talking with my workers. Getting some background on Caroline's—the dead woman's—life, and who might have wanted to kill her."

"And have you found anything?"

Josie thought she detected a certain doubt in his voice.

Sam must have heard the same thing, for he interrupted the conversation to increase Josie's credibility. "It's not the choice I would make for her life, but Josie has already solved two murders since I've known her."

"Really?" John looked at her intently. "I thought Sam told me you were a contractor."

"I am. But there have been two murders connected with the jobs I've worked on in the past few years. I know it sounds a little strange, like I'm some sort of Jonah or something, but it's just the way it's happened."

"Believe me, nothing shocks a trial lawyer. But I am a bit surprised that you've been involved in solving these murders."

"You've met Mike Rodney, I presume?" Sam interrupted.

"Well, if anything, he's slightly more competent than his father."

"He's just not as lazy as his father," Josie suggested as an alternative explanation.

"You're saying that if I want to kill someone and get away with it, I should do it on this island—as long as Josie isn't around at the time."

"That's one way of looking at it."

Their salads arrived, Josie's covered with blue cheese dressing, the men sticking with oil and vinegar. They got down to work eating, Sam explaining the circumstances of Josie's past involvement in crime and Josie waiting to hear any suggestions John might have as to how she could help Betty.

She ended the meal thinking that she might as well join those who were cooking for her old friend. John not only didn't know what she could do, he didn't know what he could do.

"I'll visit each morning and each afternoon and then again in the early evening. But if she doesn't talk to me, I don't see how I can help."

"But if she accepted your services, doesn't that mean she wants your help?" Josie asked.

"It may mean that she would rather have me hanging around than the court-appointed defense attorney that she would surely get when this thing goes to court."

"How long can you remain on the island?" Sam asked.

"As long as necessary. I may have to dash back to the city for a day or two, but I think I'll be able to manage to keep in close enough contact for anything essential. There may be more crime over the holidays, but there's a lot less court time. And I really want to help this young woman. I'm not sure she has any idea what sort of trouble she's in. There's nothing worse than an incompetent police department when it comes to convicting the wrong person."

"But you won't let that happen," Josie cried.

"I'll do my best. Believe me, I'll do my best. Betty Patrick is not going to go to prison if I can help it."

"Go to prison! Sam, she's not going to go to prison! I want to get her out of jail. I never even considered prison."

"Josie, don't worry. We're all working together. With the three of us behind her, Betty will be just fine."

Josie wished she could be so sure.

She and Sam had come in his old MGB, and after repeated reassurances from John, they left him at the restaurant and drove home together.

"You know, I could come in," Sam suggested gently as he stopped the car in front of her house. "In just a few days my mother will be here, and then Tyler. We're not going to have many opportunities to be alone together."

"Yeah, I guess," Josie replied absentmindedly.

"Not that my mother would be upset if we spent the night together. She's a woman of the world and all that. And she's crazy about you. She'd probably start to plan a wedding if she thought we were sleeping together."

"Yeah, she's like that."

"She might go as far as to get a shotgun and force me to marry you."

Josie didn't notice the grin on his face. "Yeah. You know what I think?"

"I know you haven't been paying attention to a word I've said."

"Oh, yes. I'm sorry." And she was, really. "Sam, you know, I wonder if we've been going about this all wrong."

"In what sense?"

"You know how I've been hanging around with my crew and asking questions about Caroline and her school and all."

"I got the impression you weren't having to work very hard to hear about any of that."

"No. Well, it was logical that Layne would spend time reminiscing when her friend had just died. And I suppose the same is true of Pam James."

"Who just happened to show up two days after Caroline was killed."

"You think that's more than a coincidence?"

"It sure sounds like more to me. But you know, these things do happen. They sound suspicious, but they're perfectly innocent."

"You don't think this one is."

"Who the hell knows?"

Josie looked over at Sam, sitting in the driver's seat, just staring out the window. "You don't seem very optimistic."

"Josie, John looks like a kid on his way to the junior prom, but he's the best there is. On the other hand, if Betty refuses to talk to him, there's only so much he can do. You haven't discovered any connection between Betty and Caroline from Caroline's angle. Maybe it's time to start thinking about what Betty's been doing. Has anything changed in her life lately? Any new loves?"

A stream of cold air was seeping through the seal around the MGB's convertible top, and Josie shivered. "I'm cold. Do you want to come up and have some decaf and we can talk?"

Sam chuckled. "It's not exactly the offer I was hoping for, but sure."

Josie, still lost in her own thoughts, almost slipped on her mail, which had toppled to the floor from the table in the hallway, where Risa had placed it sometime earlier in the day.

"Christmas cards?" Sam said, picking up the envelopes and handing them to her.

"Maybe a few. Probably more bills."

"Here's one from someone named Patrick in Sarasota, Florida. Isn't that where Betty's parents retired to?"

"Sure is. They're such sweet people. They always send a card and a long chatty letter. Her father always tells me about the largest fish he's caught all year. And her mother reports on her volunteer work at the local hospital and nursing home. Those are two people who really know how to enjoy their retirement."

"Why don't you open it now?" Sam suggested, using his key to unlock her apartment door.

"Yeah. Maybe they know something that has to do with Caroline's death."

"I don't think we should get our hopes up, but . . ."

Josie was too busy ripping open the envelope to listen to discouraging words.

Sam took the rest of her mail from her and placed it on the

only available spot on the coffee table. He had grown accustomed to her messiness, and she had grown accustomed to him straightening up when he was over. But tonight Sam was aimless, walking around the room, picking up Urchin, and putting her back down without even bothering to scratch under the feline's chin. There was a large cardboard box labeled GAMES in the middle of the floor, and he flipped open the top as he passed by. It seemed to contain Christmas ornaments and wrapping paper. He wondered what the one labeled CHRISTMAS ORNAMENTS might contain. A Tasha Tudor Advent calendar hung on one window, days one and two opened to reveal an improbably cute mole baking cookies and a raccoon knitting a sweater. He took the time to update the calendar, discovering more dressed-up animals than he had seen since reading *The Wind in the Willows*, then moved on to the kitchen and stooped down to search the cupboard for decaf beans.

Josie, meanwhile, was studying the two-page letter from Betty's parents with a frown on her face.

"Something interesting?"

"Well, Betty's mom broke her ankle while jumping between two floating docks and spent a few days in one of the hospitals where she usually does volunteer work. And the bonito are running unusually small this year. But other than that, nothing of note. Do you want to look?"

Sam, who had found the beans and the grinder, put them down on the counter, took the letter from her, and read it through. "Okay, does Betty's mom usually make comments like these?"

"Asking if Betty and I are going to remain single forever? Yes. Always. Although I think I'm included automatically. She really wants Betty to get settled—and start producing grandchildren. She adored Tyler—used to baby-sit for him when he was a baby and I had just started at Island Contracting. Betty was still in school then, of course—her biggest concern back in those days was who to pick to go to the prom with."

"She's always been popular, hasn't she?" Sam said, looking around for clean mugs.

"Can you imagine anyone who looks like Betty being anything else? And you know how much she likes men."

"Hmm." He had given up the search and was washing a couple of the mugs left filthy in the sink. "But has she ever been serious about anyone?"

Josie thought for a moment. "Once about two years ago she talked about getting engaged to someone she was seeing. To tell you the truth, I don't remember who he was."

"Was he from the island?"

"I'm not really sure. You know, I could find out. I could call her parents. Her mom loves to talk about the family."

"But does Betty always confide in her family?"

"Of course not. But her mother has long antennae and tends to pick up information whether Betty wants her to know about it or not. It is, of course, a small island, and you know how everyone here cares about Betty. On the other hand . . ." She paused.

"What?"

"How am I going to tell them that Betty has been arrested?"

NINETEEN

THE PHONE RANG.

It was late. Josie's mind, as always in this situation, flashed between worst-case scenarios: Tyler was ill, injured, dead. The office had burned down. Hugh Sylvester had found a reason to fire Island Contracting. Another member of her crew had been killed. Or arrested.

But it was Betty's father. And, when she could get a word in edgewise on the extension, Betty's mother. And they were very, very upset.

"We were out all day. First our annual holiday golf tournament down at the club. Then the awards banquet . . ."

"I told him it was time to come home, but did he listen? No, just one more drink with his friends, he said. If we had come home earlier, we'd already be on a plane to Kennedy. We could have been on the island before midnight."

"I keep telling her there's no reason to rush. I'm sure this is just a mistake. Something that can be solved with just a phone call or two."

"Are you out of your mind? Our daughter is in prison. She's incarcerated. She's . . ."

"She's . . ." Josie started.

"That's why we're calling, Josie. We got almost a dozen calls on our answering machine. . . ."

"More. It was filled. More people than that could have called."

"I know, but . . ."

"Josie, we're more than willing to get on a plane immediately. You know we would do anything for our daughter."

"Poor Betty. Locked up. And she was always a young woman whose freedom meant so much to her. Even as a child . . ."

"Maybe if she had cared a little less about her freedom and gotten married . . ."

"What? You want her to have married the wrong man? To be miserable and unhappy?"

"Dear, we're not making progress. We haven't even told Josie why we're calling."

"I can tell you that she's okay," Josie reassured them as soon as she could sense an opening.

"Everyone has said that. In fact, the first two callers reassured us before we had any idea what had happened to her," Betty's father explained.

"She's not okay. She's in prison. Locked up," Betty's mother interrupted for the fourth time.

"We're not telling Josie why we're calling," her husband said gently.

"I can tell you that she really is going to be okay. . . ."

"We're looking for Sam Richardson." Betty's mother continued to interrupt. "Betty's always saying that he spends more and more time with you. We've left a message on his machine, of course. That's one of the first things we did when we realized what was going on."

Josie didn't even bother to respond. She merely handed the receiver to Sam and picked up a mug of coffee.

"Sam Richardson here." He listened without interrupting for at least five minutes. Josie hoped he was hearing a more coherent story than she had gotten—and that he had something comforting to say to these poor people when they finished speaking.

Apparently he did. "We've never met, but you should know that I'm always honest with clients," Sam began in a calm voice. "I was a prosecuting attorney for years and, in those years, one of the things I learned to do is judge defense lawyers. And I've found your daughter one of the best. We all know she's innocent, but she still needs John Jacobs. You don't have to worry about her legally. And frankly, I don't think you have to worry about her welfare while she's in . . . ah, while she's locked up. Your friends on the island are taking exceptionally good care of her." He stopped talking and accepted the mug of coffee Josie passed him. "Yes. Yes. Yes, I don't think I would bother if I were you. Yes. At my house. Anytime. I'm pretty busy at the store—the holidays, you know. Well, please do. Do you have the number? Good. Yes, I'll tell her. Nice talking to you. Please, feel free. Really. He'll call you first thing tomorrow morning. Definitely. Yes. Yes. Good night." He hung up.

Neither of them spoke for a few minutes.

"Well . . ." she said finally.

"Yeah, well."

"It's better if they don't come up here," Josie added.

"Yes. But we still don't know if they know anything about any relationships Betty's had that might bear on all this. And it's going to be difficult to call and ask any questions without sending those poor people into a panic."

"True. So what are we going to do?"

"Can you ask around on the island?"

"Tomorrow?"

"As soon as possible."

She frowned. "Okay. I can probably ask a few questions while running errands. And during my lunch hour. I'll do what I can."

"Great. Now why don't you sit down here and relax. We should take advantage of these free moments. Who knows what will happen next."

They didn't have to wait long to find out. The phone rang again while his statement was still in the air—and before, much to Sam's regret, he and Josie had started to snuggle. She reached out for the receiver, assuming the Patricks would be on the other end of the line.

It was Tyler. The one time she didn't panic, worrying that he was in the middle of some sort of crisis, it was her son. And there was a crisis.

If you considered his school closing a week early for

Christmas vacation to be a crisis. (And at this point, Josie certainly did.)

"The boiler broke in the school's power plant. Apparently the classrooms had power, the library, the chapel . . . but only one of the dorms. So the decision was made to close the school a week early," she explained to Sam after hanging up. "The kids who can't be sent home on the spur of the moment will be moved into the dorm with power. And Tyler and his friend are going to take the train to New York City and a bus from there. I told him I'd call first thing in the morning and let him know which bus we'd meet . . ."

"No."

"No? What do you mean, no?"

"I mean that there's no reason for them to take the bus. My mother would love to meet the train and then drive them down here."

"I didn't think she was coming until next week," Josie said. And she had thought she would have time to clean her apartment and decorate a bit before then.

"She calls every day thinking up reasons to come down early. I think picking up those boys and bringing them here is a good idea. And she'll be thrilled."

He reached out for the phone. "I should call her right away. If I know Mom, she'll spend every minute cooking and shopping from the time I call until she leaves to get Tyler and . . . what's the other boy's name?"

"Uh, I don't think Tyler told me. There are six boys in his suite and I keep getting them confused. Oh, Sam, I was going to sit down and write this boy's parents and assure them that he was welcome to spend the holidays here. They'll probably be worrying about him. And I don't have his address or anything."

"Well, you'll just have to make do with a call when he gets here. He'll probably want to call home anyway. Why isn't he spending the holidays with his family?"

"You know, Tyler never told me that either."

"Well, my mother will have his entire life story by the time they arrive here tomorrow."

"Good. Then we can set her to work finding out about Betty."

"We'd be better off if she just stuck to cooking."

"You mean you'd be better off if she didn't start poking around on the island."

"I love my mother, but you know how she can be."

"Yeah, like a mother. A good mother." Josie, accustomed to censoring any painful thoughts on this particular subject, got up. The mood had been lost.

Sam seemed to feel it also. "I guess I'd better get going. Anything I can do to help you get ready for Tyler?"

"Grocery shopping? Laundry? Cleaning up around here?"

"Look, Mom will be tired from the drive down tomorrow. Why don't I take you and the boys and her out to dinner—we could even go off-island, if you want."

"That's a good idea."

"And I'll call my mother and tell her to bring the guys to my house. I'll drive them over to the work site and then here. How does that sound?"

"Like a plan." She raised her arms in the air and stretched, suddenly tired.

"Look, I'll call you in the morning as soon as John sees Betty."

"Make sure he tells you everything she says."

"Josie, there's no way he's going to do that."

"Well, whatever he tells you, promise you'll tell me."

"Okay. I'll call tomorrow. Be sure to bring your cell phone to the work site."

"No problem," Josie muttered, already thinking of what she was going to serve two teenage boys for the rest of the week. And what she was going to serve for Christmas dinner. And how she was going to discover something—anything—that would free Betty.

Sam gave her a quick kiss and left her to make plans. Josie loved making lists. She just wished she didn't always lose them. Sometimes she would find a list long after the completion date for everything on it had passed. She was always amazed by her own good intentions, her excellent planning skills, and her apparently boundless optimism. Rarely had she accomplished half of what she set out to do; frequently just half would have been a miracle.

Ignoring all of the above, she started out to make three lists. The first was easy. Groceries. Food to feed teenage boys: Hot dogs. Ground beef. Makings for tacos. Lots of ice cream, chips, cookies, milk, and orange juice. Bags of Tyler's favorite frozen waffles for weekend treats. Jumbo boxes of cereal. Tyler's letters were frequently full of complaints about school food. Josie knew she wasn't much of a chef, but her son, at least, enjoyed her cooking. Remembering his comments about his friend's mother's cookies, she flipped through one of the magazines she'd been reading. There had been a recipe in that article about Susan Henshaw, the housewife in Connecticut. . . . She found what she was looking for, added the ingredients to her grocery list, and turned to the next task.

Christmas dinner. She knew she had to get organized or else Sam's mother would insist on taking over. She flipped through magazine after magazine. There just seemed to be so many options. Turkey. Ham. Turkey and ham. Duckling. Standing rib roast. Prime rib. When she was growing up, Christmas dinner had been a repeat of their Thanksgiving meal. Except for dessert. Instead of pies there had been cookies and that store-bought plum pudding. Trying not to think about those times, she stared down at the two-page spread open in front of her. Evidently this woman in Connecticut had devised her own holiday menu, "a combination of all the various traditions we love." Josie looked at the pictures. She looked at the recipes. And, with a broad smile on her face crinkling up her freckles, she started to make a second grocery list.

By the time she'd finished the second list, she was tired and, despite the huge dinner she'd eaten earlier, hungry. She headed for the refrigerator. Her dreams of garlic mashed potatoes, wild mushroom pie, and a thick fillet of beef vanished as she opened the door. Two cartons of pineapple yogurt (she had thought they were peach when she pulled them off the shelves in the refrigerator cabinet at the grocery store) and a bag of mixed lettuces (rather old and squishy) awaited her perusal. Well, she didn't need the extra calories. And she still had one more list to make before she hit the pillow. A shower was in order.

The shower woke her up, and she realized how easy the third list was going to be. She had to work tomorrow. Almost as important, she had to appear to be working whenever Hugh Sylvester was around. Betty was a carpenter and a local. All Josie had to do was ask questions as she made her normal rounds. If Betty was dating anyone new, the word would have gotten around. This last list began with the hardware store and continued on through the standard suppliers Island Contracting had come to depend on over the years.

Josie knew she would sleep well that night. She'd worked hard all day and she could look forward to accomplishing a lot tomorrow. And, best of all, Tyler would be home!

TWENTY

JOSIE WAS A carpenter, an independent businessperson, a friend of many, a lover to Sam Richardson, but first, last, and always she was a mother. And Tyler was coming home for Christmas! Anticipation kept a smile on her lips all day long.

And that was quite a tribute to the strength of her maternal feelings. Because it was turning out to be quite a day.

This day began like the day before. The phone rang. Before Josie was fully awake, Sam's mother was on the line, asking questions which required answers. Answers which she didn't have.

"How will I recognize them? I haven't seen Tyler since last summer. Are you sure he hasn't grown a lot? Cut his hair? Grown a beard? Will he and this other boy be wearing some sort of school uniform?"

Josie hated to admit how little she knew of her son's daily life, but she did know the answer to that one. "No. The kids dress pretty much the way all teens dress."

"I know what you mean. Like slobs."

Josie wouldn't argue with that. "I'm sure Tyler will recognize you if you just stand someplace where you can be seen."

"Yes, you're probably right. I'll be sure to wear something bright."

Well, that wouldn't surprise anyone. Carol Greenbaum's fondness for brightly colored polyester clothing was well known to anyone acquainted with her.

"There is something else . . ."

Josie heard some hesitation—and it was not typical of this woman. "What?" She steeled herself for the answer.

"I've been talking with Sammy about Christmas . . ."

Josie thought she knew what was coming. "I . . ."

"Now, honey, listen to me for a moment. I'm very ecumenical in my approach to life. I've been married to men of various religious convictions."

"So . . ."

"But I have always insisted on a traditional Christmas celebration. Not many people have managed to create a traditional Christmas dinner while maintaining a kosher kitchen, but I like to think that was one of my most successful gooses—or geese."

Goose? She had changed her mind. She had decided on beef! "I . . ."

"And Sam says there's been another murder of someone on your crew."

"No, there's never been a murder on my crew before. It's true that I've been involved in murder investigations, but no one on my crew has ever been murdered before. . . ."

"You surely don't need to cook a big meal on Christmas Day."

"I promised Tyler that I would cook for him."

That seemed to stop her. Middle-aged women's fascination for Tyler was legend. If he wanted something, they would see he got it. Carol took a deep breath and started on a different tack. "Then Christmas Eve. We could all get together on Christmas Eve . . ."

"We will. At Risa's apartment. She always creates a wonderful Italian fish dinner. I know she is looking forward to you being there."

That stopped her. During Carol's frequent visits to the island, she and Risa had come to a standoff. The only way they could exist equally was to share the care and keeping of Sam, Josie, and Tyler. They had a common goal—to see Sam and Josie walk down the aisle together. If that ever happened—and Josie wasn't sure if it would for a lot of reasons—she knew they would fight over the privilege of selecting her dress and making refreshments for the reception.

"Well, I think spending Christmas Eve with Risa should be

lovely. Perhaps it will remind me of the wonderful night my second husband and I spent in a tiny villa in Arcidosso so many years ago."

"Maybe." It wasn't like Carol to give up so quickly when she wanted to do something. Josie wondered what Sam's mother was planning. "When do you have to leave to pick up Tyler and his friend?" she nudged gently.

"In just a few minutes. His train doesn't come in for hours, of course, but I have so much to do before then. In fact, there's the buzzer. I told that new doorman to let me know immediately when my delivery was here, so you mustn't keep me. Ta ta, Josie. See you sometime in the late afternoon. Give my love to my son."

She hung up before Josie had a chance to tell her that Sam had spent the night in his own home.

There was a lot to do, and Josie didn't have time to dawdle around in bed. She got up, relieved to find clean overalls hanging in her closet. She wanted to go to the beach to pick up some shells. And if she hurried, she'd have time to dash through the grocery store before going to the office. Sam might be taking them all out for dinner, but Tyler would head straight for the refrigerator as soon as he walked through the door. And he wouldn't be interested in making a meal of pineapple yogurt and wilted lettuce.

And Sam had said he was going to call right after John spoke with Betty; she wanted to be free to take that call. She needed to check in with the cat at the office too. She grabbed her watch off the end table by her bedside and put it on. She had to be at the work site in a little over half an hour; if she hurried and everything went smoothly, she'd make it on time.

As if everything could possibly go smoothly this time of the year. One thing about living on an island is that there weren't any of those holiday traffic jams other cities had to suffer through. On the island, the jams took place at the checkout counters, with fewer employees on the job and more people around to spend the holiday in their second home. There were two registers open at the island supermarket. At one the checker was discussing what she was going to buy her mother for Christmas and why she really hated this time of year with a customer who was vigorously nodding her head in agreement with every word. At the other, the customer was wondering what to buy her young daughter ("She has everything, just everything!") for Christmas and bragging about an imminent family vacation to a few of the more prestigious Virgin Islands which her husband was giving to them all. That checkout girl (old enough to be Josie's grandmother) looked suitably jealous.

Josie, arms overflowing with Oreos, orange juice, milk, frozen waffles, hot dogs and buns, catsup, and two giant boxes of corn flakes, stamped her left foot impatiently, not interested in hearing the joys awaiting this obnoxious snob in the warm waters of the Caribbean, attracting the attention of the woman behind the register.

"Josie Pigeon. I was going to call you during my coffee break today. If you have a moment, there's something I need to tell you."

The shopper in front of her took the hint and, possibly realizing that to stand chatting in the grocery might imply a life with more spare time than was enviable, announced to anyone who cared to listen that she was busy, busy, busy. And, shoving her cart before her, she headed to the door.

"I hear Tyler is on his way home," the checker said, running the groceries across the scanner.

"Yes. Today."

"Isn't that a little early?"

"Almost a week. But there are some problems with the heating plant at school. Apparently closing his dorm was the only answer."

"Well, it will be good to have him back. I'll tell Ed to check our stock of hot dogs. Never forget how he ate over a dozen in one sitting at the island picnic last Labor Day.

"But Josie, I really do need to speak with you." Her voice lowered, she added "About Betty."

"She's in good hands," Josie said, seeing the concern on the other woman's face. "Sam's friend—one of the best defense lawyers in New York City—is here to help. And I'm . . . uh, beginning to look into things."

"Excellent. But what no one understands is why she was arrested in the first place. We know Betty. She wouldn't kill anyone. . . ."

"Of course not," Josie agreed.

"And there are other women on the crew. Women new to the island." The latter was said accusingly, as though Josie were personally responsible for a local crime wave.

"I know. You said you wanted to talk. Do you know anything that might help here? Anything that might get Betty out of jail?"

"The word around here is that she won't talk to anyone—not even that lawyer friend of Sam's."

"He's going to see her again this morning and . . ." Josie glanced over her shoulder, aware of the interest of the shopper behind her.

"I saw that big Mercedes he drives parked in front of the police station on my way here," the woman behind her said, the fuzzy magenta knit hat she wore falling over her forehead as she nodded vigorously.

"Sounds like he's prompt at least."

"Sam says he's the best," Josie insisted.

"I heard he's sort of cute," the checker said.

"That's our Betty. Always did get most of the good-looking men available."

"Has she been dating anyone recently?"

The shopper and the checker both frowned and seemed to seriously consider the question.

"There was that lifeguard last summer," the shopper said. "Too young for her, of course."

"Too dumb," the checker insisted. "He was in his sixth year of college."

"Well then, maybe not too young."

"That must have ended in the fall. Surely she's been dating since then."

"Not that I heard about."

"Me neither."

Josie frowned. She'd known Betty for years. The possibility of her spending weekend nights alone in front of the TV (where Josie had frequently found herself before Sam arrived on the island) was almost unthinkable. "Are you sure?"

"Yup."

"No one that I know about."

Well, Sam had said to look for anything different in Betty's life. Being dateless for months at a time was about as different as it got.

"Heard she was thinking about putting a note on the bulletin board at the hardware store offering her services for baby-sitting," the checker said, cinching the discussion.

Josie had the hardware store on her must-see list. She'd be sure to stop at the bulletin board that hung by the door.

"I got an early Christmas card from the Patricks. Got the impression that they were a little concerned about Betty being alone this holiday. She usually goes down there around now doesn't she?"

"Island Contracting isn't usually working on a job this time of year," Josie muttered, wondering if that was the only reason Betty wasn't planning to visit her family.

"Good point. . . . Twenty-eight forty-seven."

"Excuse me?"

"Twenty-eight forty-seven. You still haven't paid for your groceries."

"Oh, of course." And Josie rummaged around in her pockets for the correct change.

"Give that Tyler a hug for me," the checker insisted.

"Me too."

Josie made a promise that she suspected she wouldn't be able to keep. Tyler, the most affectionate of children, had recently become much more reserved.

"I'll tell him to stop by. He's old enough to pick up his own hot dogs when we run out," Josie said as, with a wave, she pushed her way out of the store.

She was running twenty minutes late. And she'd forgotten to

buy cat food. "Damn." She pulled open the truck door, tossed her groceries over to the passenger's side of the seat, and scrounged around in her pockets for her key chain. That found, she drove off toward her office, wondering what Betty's lack of dates might mean.

If anything.

TWENTY-ONE

THE FLASHING LIGHT on her machine alerted her to the phone calls which had come into her office early. (Probably while she was on the phone at home.) She pressed the button, hoping Sam had . . .

"Ms. Pigeon, I've been thinking over those plans for the kitchen and the seating arrangements, and it occurred to me that maybe we're making a mistake. If you could get here a little early this morning, maybe we'd have time to go over the plans again."

Josie looked at her watch. It was too late for her to get anywhere early. She rummaged in the snack cabinet and found two cans of tuna. As the new cat swirled around her ankles, she dumped the tuna in the bowl and tossed the empty cans in the garbage.

The next message was from Sam. John Jacobs had gone to see Betty early this morning and been refused a visit. He had called Sam to explain his intention of waiting at the police station until his client changed her mind. Sam would call Josie when he heard from John again.

The third message was from Tyler. Unfortunately, that was all she was able to discover. "Hi, Mom, it's me" was followed by a high-pitched whine, static, and a loud click indicating that they had been disconnected. She didn't have time to worry about it now. She had other problems. Like where had she dropped those damn keys when she came in?

Fifteen minutes later, cursing herself for her repeated absent-mindedness, she was parking her truck behind Hugh Sylvester's van. She didn't know whether she was glad he was still around or not. As usual, he didn't give her a lot of time to think about that—or anything else.

"Ms. Pigeon, I've been waiting for you!" The power chair zipped up the sidewalk. Apparently her employer had been getting some fresh air.

"I'm sorry I was late. I had to run some errands before checking in at the office this morning." Why was it always necessary to apologize when they met, she wondered, as she tried to smile confidently. "You said something about a problem with our design. I've got the blues in the truck." She actually kept them in the truck, but how was he to know that she hadn't made a special trip to pick them up? "Are you thinking of major changes?"

"No. Well, I don't think so. I know I accepted the plans as is, but I saw an interesting photograph in a magazine and I was wondering if it would be possible to do something different with the island which separates the kitchen from the living and dining area."

He actually sounded apologetic! Josie was astounded. And worried. How many times had she gotten halfway through a remodeling project when her employer had insisted on changes which took time and money? And how many times had these same employers insisted on blaming Island Contracting for cost and scheduling overruns?

"What magazine?" she asked. He didn't seem like the type of person to spend his evenings perusing *HG* or *Architectural Digest*.

"*New Mobility*. You wouldn't have heard of it—it's a magazine that addresses issues and needs of the physically handicapped. It's not exactly sold at every corner newsstand."

"I guess not. Where . . ."

"It's in my backpack. If you'll just get it out once we're in the house. It's more than a little cold out here."

"Great." She followed his chair up the ramp. A worn leather pack hung from the back. Books, magazines, and notepads bulged out of the top and through a ripped seam in the side. She was trying to read some titles when he stopped abruptly.

"Oh!" She walked straight into his headrest.

"I can't open the door."

"No, of course you can't. Do you want me to do it for you?"

He sighed loudly. "Well, I suppose we could stay here and freeze. Someone will come out eventually."

"I . . . I'll just open it." She hurried up around him and did just that, holding it open until he had passed though.

"Nellie, can you make some hot chocolate?"

"Now, you know you're supposed to be watching your weight." The pleasant woman's head popped up from behind the kitchen counter. "Why don't I make you some tea with artificial sweetener?"

"I want . . ."

"It will go better with these." As a clincher to her argument, Nellie pulled out a large red platter of gigantic cinnamon rolls from under the counter. They were still warm enough to be melting their sugar frosting, and the scent filled the room. "There's enough for everyone," she added as Layne and Sandy tromped in from the back of the house.

"It's a little early for our coffee break . . ." Layne started, but like everyone else in the room, she was looking hungrily at the food.

"So you'll make up the time later. Eat."

"Please eat," Professor Sylvester insisted politely. "Or else she'll start to sulk."

"Maybe I can find that article and look at it while I eat," Josie suggested.

"Maybe you can."

Josie frowned and started to rummage around in his pack. She found the magazine he was talking about amidst scholarly psychology journals, textbooks on subjects she had never heard of, and three mystery novels. She smiled; his apparent affection for blood and gore made him seem a bit more human.

"It's pretty much in the middle there," he explained, seeing the magazine in her hand. "It's the spread about accessibility in the home."

Josie flipped through it and found the article. Seating herself on the floor, a cinnamon roll in one hand and the magazine in the other, she started to read.

"It's the photograph at the top of the page. The . . ."

"The countertop," she said, seeing what he was talking about immediately.

"I thought we could add one on this side of the island. It would be out of the way when I needed to travel by the island, but useful for eating . . ."

"And for spreading out papers when he's working," Nellie added. "I know you. There won't be a clean surface left two days after we move in here."

"It's an elegant solution." Josie nodded her head. "This isn't propped up with braces, it slides in and out under the counter on the other side. One movement instead of a few, and there's no way any bracing can slip and fall. Really elegant."

"Can we do it?"

"Yeah. The Corian counter is already on order, but we'll just slip that up half an inch or so and slip this down . . ." She recognized the scowl beginning on his face and changed what she had been going to say. "I mean we can slip the counter on the other side up as far as necessary to make sure your chair can glide underneath on the room side."

"You're capable of learning. Good."

Josie scowled. And noticed Nellie grinning at her.

"I'll be on my way then. Don't have all day to hang around here and gab. Coming?" He turned his wheelchair in a half circle and headed out the door that Josie leapt up and opened for him.

"In just one minute," Nellie called out. "Don't you worry about him one minute, young lady," she added to Josie. "He used to run one of the biggest and most prestigious psychology departments in the country before his accident. It's not easy to live without moving, and he has a lot of frustrations. I know he tends to take them out on the people around him. But he's fair when he's had a chance to think things through. You just have to get used to him—and not act so scared. His only weapon is his mouth—and I don't mean that he's going to bite you."

Josie smiled. Then it occurred to her that this woman was pretty observant. Perhaps she had seen something the day of the murder that might clear Betty. "Do you live with the Professor?" she asked.

"No. I work the day shift six days a week. He has a male nurse who comes in around eight P.M. and stays until midnight. Then another aide sleeps next door to him. I come in at eight and stay 'til eight. It's a long day, but the work is easy. And I've learned to do things before he asks. Fix food that can be cut up small for him to eat. Put straws in his glasses before he asks. Even move things around so that he can always make his way across the floor. After a while it becomes automatic. And I like taking care of people. Took care of my husband for three years until he died."

"Was he paralyzed?"

"Partially. He had a stroke on his forty-first birthday."

"So young!"

"Sure was. But life isn't always easy. You gotta learn to go with the flow. About a month after his death, I discovered that I had very little money and only some domestic and nursing skills. Professor Sylvester had put an ad in the paper and was looking for an aide at the same time I was looking for a job. We've been together three years now. And it works." She chuckled. "Except that I'm too good a cook—the man is always having problems with his weight."

"You were here the day Caroline died, weren't you? In the morning? Early?"

"Yes. And I've been worried about that. I did, after all, make those Christmas cookies. Wondered exactly what poisoned her."

"I'm not sure," Josie commented, making a mental note to see who had this information. "But it couldn't have been those wonderful cookies. We all ate them as soon as we sat down. They were fantastic."

"Thank you. I like to cook, but I love to bake."

"Did you see—?"

"Josie! Phone! It's Sam and he says it's important!" Sandy yelled from the back of the house.

"And the Professor is out there cursing in three languages.

He wants me to find out why the hell you're still inside. He has some sort of problem." Pam appeared in the doorway.

"Where have you been?" Josie asked Pam, suddenly realizing how late it was.

"Sorry, I got sort of a delayed start this morning. I'll stay late to make it up." Pam grabbed a cinnamon roll as she walked by the counter and headed back to work, her toolbox swinging by her side.

Josie frowned. She expected her workers to be prompt. But Noel, the man from whom she had inherited Island Contracting, had taught her that criticizing workers in front of employers didn't increase confidence in the company. She would talk with Pam later. And with Sam too, she decided. "Tell Sam I'll call in a few minutes," she called out to Sandy and, without waiting for an answer, she hurried out to the Professor.

"I thought we were done," she said. It wasn't tactful, but it was honest.

"I wanted a private moment. As you probably know, the local police have spoken to me about the murder."

"But you weren't here."

"It happened in my house. That boorish young man seemed to think that was significant."

"Oh. I'm sorry you're involved. I never meant . . ."

"I was assuming that you never meant for one of your carpenters to be murdered during a coffee break."

"No. No, of course not."

"Well, I just thought you might want to know that that idiot policeman seems to think that Betty was jealous of the woman who died. That apparently is what he considers motivation."

"Oh." She realized he was trying to help her. "Jealous over a man?"

"I couldn't tell you. I think his exact words were that us men knew how violent a woman could become when she was scorned. I got the impression he thought it was a compliment to me that he would think a woman could be interested in a gimp."

"I . . ."

"Don't try to step in and say something encouraging. My private life isn't as dull as some people think."

"Oh." She didn't know what she was supposed to say. "Thank you for telling me. I'm looking into the murder."

"So I understand. I'm something of a mystery novel fan myself, and I'm constantly amazed by the convention in that genre that an amateur can succeed where a professional fails. But having met the police on this island, I must admit that you shouldn't have much trouble pulling it off."

"Thanks."

"You can thank me by finishing up my house in record time."

"I . . . We'll try." She heard Sandy calling again. "I'd better go."

"Please do."

She waited for Nellie to come out of the door, ran back to the rear room (soon to be a bathroom), and took the receiver from Sandy. "Thanks. Hi, Sam, what's up? Oh. Oh. Oh. Oh. Well, then, bye." There was a long pause between each syllable, and by the time she pressed the button to disconnect, there were three women standing nearby, nervously awaiting a report.

"Well, what's happened?" Sandy asked.

"It's John Jacobs. He called Sam. He says . . . He says . . ." She took a deep breath and finished the sentence she couldn't believe was coming out of her mouth. "He says Betty is going to confess to killing Caroline."

TWENTY-TWO

THE NEWS SPREAD across the island. Everywhere Josie went there was talk about Betty's confession.

There were so many islanders standing around the cash register at the hardware store that she couldn't see if the notice Betty was supposed to have put up was still hanging among announcements of Christmas bake sales, holiday fairs, seasonal school performances, and the date Santa Claus would arrive on the island (on the back of the fire company's ladder truck, tossing candy and tiny gifts to the screaming children who ran behind). She found the owner in the office at the back of the store.

"Have a few minutes?"

"Sure do. No one is interested in doing any work today."

"Everyone's worried about Betty Patrick," Josie guessed.

"Damn right. Josie, I've known that young woman since she was just a sprout. There's not a mean bone in her body. She'd never kill anyone. Not for any reason. . . . Well, maybe if someone threatened her parents—she's always been real close to her family—but no other reason."

That was something Josie hadn't thought of. "Is that possible? Could there be some connection between her family and Caroline?"

"Not that anyone knows. We just think that's the only reason we can imagine Betty getting mad enough to kill anyone. If she did. Which she didn't."

Josie frowned. "Did she put a notice advertising her services for baby-sitting on your bulletin board?"

"Yup."

"Didn't that surprise you?"

"Nope. She said she thought it was time she grew up. My wife's been saying that for years."

" 'Grow up'?"

"Yeah, stop all that dating different men. Get married, you know."

"Betty was going to get married?" And Josie didn't know anything about it? "To whom?"

"Hey, no reason to get excited. I didn't say she had found someone to marry, just that she was telling people it was time to get serious about her life. Stop dating every available man on the island. Not that she said anything about it to me, mind you. But my wife is friends with Betty's next-door neighbor, and apparently Betty and she signed up for the same aerobics class last fall, and Betty's in such good shape—well, anyone who sees her running on the beach in the summer knows that. . . ."

"Yes." There weren't many women who could look sexy jogging while wearing only a bikini, but Betty was one of them.

"So it seems that Betty can talk and work out while this neighbor can only listen or something. And Betty's been working on changing her life—getting more serious may be the term my wife uses, but that's the point. You know, more work and less play."

"Hence the baby-sitting."

"I guess." He shrugged. "When I told her to go ahead and hang up that notice, I never thought the changes she was planning in her life would lead to a confession of murder."

"A false confession," Josie corrected him and got, in return, the first smile she'd seen since she entered the store.

"You're damn right. A stupid, goddamn false confession. What could she have been thinking of? Who could she be protecting?"

"I don't know. But you're the second person who has suggested that today."

"Betty's a warm and generous woman. We all know she wouldn't kill anyone. What other reason would she have to confess?"

"I have every intention of finding out," Josie assured him as she left the office. "Just keep her toolbox for me. I still plan to give it to her for Christmas—even if I have to buy a large file to put in it so she can break out of jail!"

"Way to go, Josie!"

She walked through the store, ignoring the array of tools and equipment on the shelves. She had justified this visit by claiming to be checking up on Island Contracting's orders. But she wasn't going to take the time to do that now. These people were professionals. They would do what they were paid to do. And she had other stops to make.

Land in a popular resort community is at a premium; the local lumberyard was off the island. Josie glanced down at her watch. It seemed, once again, to have stopped. Well, it was as good an excuse as any to be late. She turned her truck toward the old drawbridge at the south end of the island.

Her destination was only a few miles from the bridge. She figured the island police were busy guarding their hardened criminal, and pushed the gas pedal to the floor. The yard was called Timmons Lumber, but everyone on the island referred to it as *the twins' place*. It was owned, of course, by the Timmons twins. Betty had dated both of them (although not, she assured whoever would listen, at the same time), and had remained friends with both men throughout their subsequent marriages.

Tim Timmons was stacking wheelbarrows next to the front door as she parked in the lot. He stood up, pushed his hat back on his head, grinned, and waited for her to join him. "Good to see you, Josie. Come inside and have some coffee. I'll call Tom."

"Great. I wanted to talk with you both."

"I assume this is about Betty rather than problems with your order."

Josie felt herself moving into panic mode. "What problems with the order?"

"There aren't any that I know of. Your deliveries have been on time and everything is waiting in the back lot. So I hope you're here about Betty."

"Yeah, we're all ready to do anything we can to help." Tom had joined them.

The twins looked as different as they possibly could. Tom's blond hair hung to his shoulders and his beard started where that left off. He also wore tiny gold-rimmed glasses. Tim's hair was worn in a buzzcut and he had invested in contact lenses years ago. But both were tall and well built. That wasn't a surprise, Josie reflected. Most of the men Betty dated were tall and well built.

"Have either of you seen Betty recently?" Josie asked.

"We both went down to the police station as soon as we heard she'd been arrested, but she refused to see us."

"To see anybody is what I hear."

"When was the last time you saw her before the murder?"

"She delivered your order just a few days earlier," Tim answered.

"Did you talk with her then? You know, about anything significant?"

"Well, actually, we spent some time kidding about whether or not you and Sam were going to announce your engagement at Christmas . . ."

"Tom." Tim said his brother's name in a cautionary tone of voice.

"What?" Josie picked up on the mystery immediately. "What do you mean? Did Betty . . . ?"

"It has nothing to do with Betty," Tom said. "She saw Sam coming out of a jewelry store and jumped to what she thought was the logical conclusion."

Josie had conflicting emotions. She was here to discover any changes in Betty's recent life. But if Sam had been shopping in a jewelry store . . . She shook off the many questions that possibility raised and returned to the subject at hand. "How do you know Betty wants to get married?"

"She talks about it all the time," Tim answered.

"She does? Betty Patrick talks about wanting to get married? I heard that she had almost stopped dating. . . . She's not in love with someone who's already married, is she?" Josie suddenly realized there was a new possibility which she hadn't considered. One that might, after all, have some significance here. By the time the twins had answered her question, she was wondering if possibly Betty had met Caroline and Layne's ex-husband and if, perhaps, that might have had something to do with the murder. . . . But then Josie was actually considering Betty as a possible suspect! "Are you sure about this?"

"We know Sam . . ." Tom began.

"Sam's shopping habits are not what Josie is asking about," his brother interrupted. "And you've always been bad at keeping holiday secrets."

"Yeah, sorry. I didn't mean to be the one to spill the beans," Tom said. "But what we know about Betty wanting to get married sure isn't a secret. She told everyone around the table on Thanksgiving. You heard her," he added to his brother.

"Betty spent Thanksgiving with you two?" Josie asked. If Risa had known Betty was going to be free, she would certainly have invited her to join them at her home.

"And the rest of the family. There were thirty-one of us this year. My wife's family makes a big deal about inviting people who have nowhere else to go for the holiday. I haven't had a decent-sized plate of leftover turkey since we got married."

"But did Betty mention anyone in particular that she wanted to marry?"

"I got the impression that it's more a change of attitude than someone new in her life," Tom said.

"If there's a new man, she sure is keeping it quiet," his brother agreed. "So, Josie, how are you going to get Betty released?"

"Damned if I know."

"Well, the entire island is depending on you. Everyone has been talking about it."

Good. Nothing like a bit of pressure.

"And I hear Tyler is coming home today. And bringing Sam's mother along with him."

"Actually, she's bringing him."

"Well, tell him to stop over at the house sometime. We're setting up the train set for the holidays. He's always loved that."

"I'll be sure to let him know," she said, getting ready to leave.

"And tell him my wife has been baking gingerbread boys and spritz trees for days now. I know how he enjoys eating her cookies."

"Actually, I'm going to be doing a lot of baking myself this year," Josie said. She left the lumberyard ignoring the twin skeptical expressions on the brothers' faces. She assumed their looks had more to do with her cooking abilities than her investigative powers.

Not that she was getting anywhere. Everyone on the island seemed to know that Betty was anxious to get married—everyone except for Josie, that is. And she really had to get back to work. If only she could bake cookies and remodel houses at the same time.

She glanced at her watch (apparently a habit hard to break) and decided there was time to stop at the deli and pick up lunch. In fact, maybe she'd get an extra sandwich and bring it over to Betty. It wouldn't hurt for Betty to know that Josie was thinking about her, she decided, ordering two large hoagies with extra oregano to go and wandering around the small deli. Tables had been added by the cash register and they were filled with holiday goodies. Boxes of candy canes in all flavors and colors nudged bags of foil-covered chocolates. There were cellophane bags of Moravian ginger cookies and Josie wondered briefly whether or not she might pass them off as her own (without the bags, of course). She was tempted by a box of ribbon candy and, finally, decided it would be foolish to put off buying the chocolate orange which tradition demanded Tyler find in the bottom of his Christmas stocking. And with what, she wondered, driving to the police station, was she going to fill that stocking?

An anthropologist could track Tyler's life through the annual contents of that stocking, she thought. From the rattles and stuffed animals of his infancy, through the Matchbox cars and dinosaurs of his elementary years, to the batteries and tiny computer games which had recently been popular—what Tyler loved had been discovered in the fuzzy felt stocking. She had no idea what to put in it this year. Last year she'd had the same problem. Her solution had been a stocking full of school supplies. Tyler had been polite, sweet, but definitely unenthusiastic. Maybe this year she'd just fill the entire thing with chocolates—although he had been worried about his skin breaking out when she saw him in the fall.

She was at the police station before she had figured out a solution to this problem. The strange sight that greeted her in the lobby drove these worries from her mind.

John Jacobs, wearing an expensive Armani suit (possibly the only one on the island during the off-season), which he had crumpled and stained almost beyond recognition, was sitting on a long wooden bench surrounded by baskets, boxes, tins, and plastic storage containers of food.

TWENTY-THREE

"IF THE THREE kings lived on this island, Mary and Joseph sure wouldn't have had to spend a lot of time buying groceries." John Jacobs stood up and greeted Josie with a lopsided grin.

"I brought Betty some lunch." Josie held up the bag. "It's a hoagie from the deli."

"Let's see, she already has a pan of lasagna, a pot of baked beans with hot dogs, a good-sized bowl of tuna salad and a loaf of rye, cheese and crackers on a bread board, three jello molds—or molds of jello and fruit to be more exact—at least four thermoses of homemade soup, one of which is clam chowder, my very favorite and which I may sample sometime soon, and too many plates of homemade cookies to count. I feel like I've stumbled into the middle of a lavish church supper."

"Are any of the cookies Christmas cookies?"

"All of the cookies are Christmas cookies as far as I can tell. And the few I've snitched have been wonderful."

"I wonder if anyone would mind if I took some home with me," Josie said, thinking of her son and his friend and the bag of Oreos sitting in the truck. The kids would certainly prefer the best that the best bakers on the island had produced—and so would she.

"Don't see why not. They're just going to go to waste here."

"Has Betty eaten anything?"

"She was refusing all food this morning. And then, about an hour ago, this extraordinary-looking woman sort of swooped in the doorway, clothing and hair flying out in all

directions. She was carrying a casserole which smelled irre-
sistibly delicious and garlicky. Apparently Ms. Patrick had
the same impression because that casserole was accepted
immediately."

"Risa."

"Risotto? I was thinking pesto, for some reason, but it could
have been risotto, I guess."

"It may have been risotto, but I said Risa. She's my landlady
and the best cook on the island. I recognized her from your
description."

"Oh. Interesting woman. She acted as though she really
didn't care when Ms. Patrick refused to see her. She just
shrugged, gathered a scarf or two around her shoulders, and
flounced out. I'd heard of people flouncing out," he added, "but
I don't think I'd actually seen it done before."

"Has Betty seen you?"

"Nope. But I'll wait here until she does. She will, of course.
They usually do."

"She confessed."

"Yes, but that really doesn't mean much at this stage. She
refused to answer any questions, to explain how the poison got
in Caroline's food. It will be a piece of cake to talk it away
when we get to court."

Josie frowned. She sure hoped he knew what he was talking
about. "I guess there really isn't anything I can do here."

"Leave your name and another note, if you want. I'll be
happy to pass it on when I see her."

"Good idea. What should I say? I mean, I want to do anything I can to help."

"What would you normally say?"

"That I'm working to find out who really killed Caroline.
That she shouldn't worry."

"Good idea. And why don't you tell her that your son is on
his way home today? Sam told me," he added when Josie
looked puzzled.

"Yes, she would like to know that."

"Hmm. And maybe she'll see Tyler. He's a bright kid, Sam

says. He might even convince her to start talking to other people. Don't you think?"

What Josie thought, as she left the police station with two tins of cookies under her arms, was that Sam was right. John Jacobs was one smart man.

She ate Betty's hoagie as she drove back to the Professor's house. Then she ate the other while she joined her crew, which was working on the the new bathroom. The crew was unusually quiet while they worked—and remarkably productive. They had moved into the bedroom before quitting time.

"I'm planning on staying late," Pam reminded Josie as the other women were beginning to wind down around five.

"You know, the two of us could probably get the new doorway framed in another hour or so," Josie suggested.

"No problem. I just won't leave until we finish."

"I'm only here until Tyler and his friend arrive," Josie admitted. She had informed the crew earlier of her son's imminent appearance on the island.

"Then let's get going."

"You don't want us to stay around, do you?" Layne asked. "The police called early this morning and said that Caroline's body is going to be released tomorrow. I should call her family tonight and see what arrangements they've made for burial."

"Of course. Leave right now if you need to," Josie insisted. "Pam and I can manage this on our own."

"Are you sure? I . . . I sort of made plans," Sandy added. Since she was practically heading for the door as she spoke, Josie just waved her onward. She and Pam got to work immediately, ripping apart the wall to make a space for the new doorway. Once they were alone, Pam became talkative. That suited Josie just fine. Not only did it distract her from wondering—okay, worrying—about whether or not her son had managed to meet Sam's mother or was wandering the streets of New York City, but she was also interested in learning more about Caroline and Layne. Getting the door framed would be gravy after a long and productive workday.

Pam, she had come to realize, was something of a chatterbox, inclined to follow her own thoughts and assume that whoever was around would find them as interesting as she did.

"I just love this time of year, don't you? The decorations, the food, the carols. Just turning on the radio is fun. I was a bit worried about being here for Christmas. I mean, an almost deserted resort island on the Atlantic coast isn't exactly what one thinks of when one thinks of Christmas, is it? But I knew I was wrong about that when I drove across the bridge and saw that cute little village under the Christmas tree in the town square. I could just tell that I was going to feel right at home here. Did your family make a big deal out of Christmas when you were growing up?"

"Yeah. . . . Could you prop that up a bit higher?" Josie hoped Pam didn't ask any more questions.

"My family did. I have three sisters and we started preparing for Christmas on Thanksgiving night. While we cleaned up the kitchen, we would make out our Christmas wish lists. Then on Friday morning, we all went shopping for presents to send the relatives who lived out of town. And then later that weekend we all cut up candied fruit and nuts for the fruitcake my mother would make while we were at school. I loved it all."

"Sounds like fun," Josie admitted, remembering the holidays from her childhood despite herself. There had been nice times. She remembered decorating gingerbread men in a kitchen which smelled wonderfully spicy. And the excitement when packages arrived from her grandparents in Montana. Hanging the stockings on Christmas Eve . . .

" . . . and then there was the time one of the little boys in the choir set fire to the robe of the girl standing in front of him," Pam was saying when Josie wrenched her mind from the past. "That was the last time anyone held real candles in the candle-light service, I can tell you. The Methodist church was completely battery powered by the next Christmas."

"Good thinking. . . . You said you were there for the first winter Caroline and Layne's school was open. Did you spend Christmases there every year?"

"No, but there were other students who did. They didn't teach classes at that time—it was sort of between semesters, so to speak. But a lot of the women didn't have families or had left their families, and they really needed a place to live. It sounds like they had a lot of fun. Both Caroline and Layne did a lot of crafts. And I can remember Caroline collecting pinecones to string for garlands in the middle of summer. Those garlands may be the same ones hanging on the tree in the living room right now." Pam gulped, and Josie remembered that she had lost a friend recently.

"Were you close to Caroline?" she asked.

"Yes. For a while. I was really hurting when I started at the school. Everything that mattered in my life seemed to be gone. I had no idea what I was going to do when I got up each morning—to say nothing of the next day, week, month, year. Caroline rescued me."

"That's right. You said you were working as a waitress and she convinced you to come take classes at the school."

"Well, I didn't take much convincing. I was pretty sick of being a waitress and there weren't a whole lot of options in that little town."

"But most women traveled to get to the school, didn't they? I mean they were there to go to school."

"Oh, yes. There weren't a whole lot of people around otherwise."

"What about the women who lived in the area?"

"There weren't many women around. That part of Maine is fairly unpopulated. And the ones there were busy raising children or holding jobs."

Josie looked for the large level and spied it across the room. "What about the money that allowed the school to keep going? From the anonymous donor. Do you know where it came from? Who the donor was?"

"Well, I was just a student, but there was talk . . ."

Josie picked up the spirit level and walked back to the doorway.

Pam seemed reluctant to answer her question. "Tell me something," she asked. "How well did you know Caroline before she died? I mean, did you know her before she came to work for you?"

"Nope."

"Well, I remember someone at the school saying that Layne and Caroline were like a couple who had been married for a long time. They had divided running the school into two parts and they each did what they were good at, you know?"

"Layne said that Caroline took care of the finances."

"Exactly."

Josie wondered how she could get back to the topic of the money which had allowed the school to survive. Obviously Pam wanted to talk about other things.

"You're wondering about that money, aren't you?" Pam said, maybe reading Josie's mind.

"It . . . isn't it a little strange that Layne apparently doesn't know where it came from?"

"I thought about that when she was talking about it the other day," Pam admitted. "There was a rumor or two at the time."

"When it was given?"

"Yeah. I was at the school then. In fact, I later began to wonder if I was at the school just to fill a space. There certainly weren't women lined up at the door desperate to get in. There are now, of course. I understand that there is a waiting list for next summer's classes. Of course, the news of Caroline's death might change all that."

"You said there was talk about the donation that kept the school open," Josie reminded her.

"Yeah, I don't remember exactly how it came up. I mean, I remember when we got the donation. Everyone was thrilled. There was some sort of dinner celebration with champagne—not exactly the way we were usually fed. We worked hard—well, you know that—and there were a lot of women who thought we should have had more than the vegetarian diet which was provided. We sang songs and got giggly . . . It sounds stupid, but that night everyone was relieved. The school meant a lot to us."

"It doesn't sound stupid at all," Josie said. She remembered a few of Island Contracting's celebrations over the years which had resembled teenage slumber parties more than anything else.

"Well, everyone was really happy that night, but then the next morning, one of the women at breakfast said something about how lucky it was that the donation had come just in time, and someone else said that it probably wasn't an accident—that Caroline was always good at . . . at managing something like that."

"Meaning that she had waited until the times were desperate before announcing the donation," Josie guessed.

"That's what I would have thought too, but that wasn't what she meant. At least, that's not what I think she meant. I got the impression that she thought Caroline had something to do with the school getting the donation."

"You mean like applying for it in the first place?"

"Or being a bit more connected to the mysterious donor than anyone was admitting."

"What do you mean?"

"That the donation might have been money coming to her rather than to the school. Or that it came from a relative of Caroline's. There were even people who thought the money came from Ben."

"Caroline's ex-husband."

"Yes. But I can't believe that. He didn't seem to be a man with any extra money."

"He was still around when you were attending the school?"

"Not living in Maine. I think he'd moved to the Southwest. Someplace in Arizona. But he came back for a visit once. He struck me as one of those people who was spending his life regretting not being around for the sixties. Certainly not someone who had a lot of extra money."

"So there was some question of who the money came from."

"Yup."

Pam had given Josie a lot to think about. And she'd think about it when she had a bit more time. Right now she was finding it necessary to fling her arms around her son and hug him.

TWENTY-FOUR

"**S**HE ALWAYS DOES this when I come home. Don't worry. She'll detach soon."

Josie heard the embarrassment in Tyler's voice and removed her arms from his neck. "Sorry. I get carried away sometimes," she admitted to the tall young man standing beside her son.

"Don't worry about it. I think families should be close," he said, offering his hand. "I'm Hastings. Tyler and I are roommates."

Josie took Hastings's hands in both of hers and squeezed—before she realized that she was leaving filthy streaks on him. "Oh, I'm sorry. Occupational hazard."

"Please. Don't worry about it. It's good to finally meet you."

"Isn't anyone going to tell me how good it is to see me?" Carol Greenbaum was standing next to Sam, beaming at the scene before her as though she had arranged it all. Which in a way, Josie realized, she had.

"Carol!" She threw her arms around Sam's mother with slightly less enthusiasm than she had used to greet her son. "It is good to see you. And thank you for picking up these guys and bringing them here."

"I was glad for the company on the drive down."

"You should thank her for feeding us," Tyler said. "We've been eating ever since we left Grand Central Station."

Josie thought of the food in the truck. "I thought you might be starving when you arrived. I even have homemade Christmas cookies." Okay, so it wasn't her home they were made in, but they didn't need to know that!

"We're pretty full now, Mom. Maybe later. Carol baked this

incredible sour cream coffee cake and brought a thermos of hot chocolate. We gorged all the way here."

"And that marshmallow fudge! Just like one of my nannies used to make when I was a kid," Hastings added, almost smacking his lips.

"You're so sweet to enjoy it," Carol said. "I'll give you the rest of the box. I can make more if Sammy wants some."

"Thank you, Mother. I don't think I need the calories. I'm not a growing boy anymore."

"Well, we can use them." Tyler's red hair stood up when he was excited, just as his mother's did. "Hastings and I are going to do lots of surfing . . ."

"Tyler, it's winter!"

"Don't worry, Mom. Hastings has wet suits and we've been practicing in the school pool. We'll be fine."

"You brought wet suits with you?"

"They're being shipped, Ms. Pigeon. FedEx. They should be here sometime tomorrow."

Josie knew her son went to school with rich kids, so the fact that Hastings would have an extra wet suit and the means to pay a premium to ship them around the country didn't surprise her—much. "You'll take turns with Tyler's board?"

"My parents promised to ship my board before they left for India. It should be here any day now."

"Can't wait to try it. Mom, Hastings has a Custom-X."

"Wow." She had no idea what it was, just that she was supposed to be impressed.

"I'll straighten up here, if you want to get going," Pam spoke up.

"I'd really appreciate it, if you don't mind. Sam is taking us all to dinner and I'd better get these guys home, put away the groceries I bought this morning, and shower so we can leave on time."

"Oh, but Sammy, I brought dinner with me. Everything except the wine—and soda for the boys. I thought you probably carried soft drinks at your store. The salad just needs to be tossed and everything else popped in the oven. If you'll drop me off at your house, I can have a meal ready in less than an hour."

"Mother, I promised Josie . . ."

"That sounds wonderful, Sam," Josie interrupted. "We can go out with you tomorrow night—or later in the week." And every night until Christmas Eve, as far as she was concerned.

"If it's okay with you." Sam looked at her quizzically.

"Definitely. Really. Believe me," Josie insisted. "And I'm starving, so if we could just get going, I'd really appreciate it."

"Great. We can go in my mom's truck," Tyler told his friend. "Let's get our bags and dump them in the back—we can ride back there too, if you want."

"Cool. I've never ridden in the back of a real truck," Hastings said. "Land Rovers and HumVs, yes. But not a real working truck."

"My truck is a real working truck. And you might get your clothing dirty."

"No problem. I have more with me." Hastings and Tyler ran out of the house.

"And his parents can always have some flown to him from Brooks Brothers if he gets those dirty," Sam whispered to Josie.

"Sammy, Hastings seems like a very nice boy. He wouldn't be friends with Tyler if he wasn't. It's not his fault that his parents would rather buy him things than spend time with him," Carol said. "They were talking a whole lot on the way down while they ate, and I got the impression that Hastings was thrilled to be spending the holidays with people who value family—and teenage boys."

"We'll just have to make sure they both have a nice holiday," Josie said, determined to do just that. No one should feel neglected by their family this time of year.

"So let's get going and meet at my house ASAP," Sam suggested. "I'll stop at the store on the way and pick up some wine. What do you think those guys like to drink?"

"Coke, Sprite."

"Mountain Dew, 7UP."

Sam chuckled. "I'll mix up a few six-packs. Just one of the advantages of owning the store."

Josie and Carol followed Sam from the room. "Did you have any trouble finding them at the train station?"

"Not at all. They found me. How have you been, Josie? Sam told me about the murder and Betty's arrest. She is the young woman with the rather extraordinary body, isn't she?"

Well, that was one way to describe her. "Yes. She's a good friend."

"So this must be very upsetting for you. I brought down a chocolate cake from Balducci's for her. It's not homemade, but I'm sure it will be better than anything served in jail."

"That's very nice of you." Josie saw no reason to mention the veritable feast the islanders had provided for Betty—or the part of it she had "borrowed."

"And I brought something for you, too," Carol continued. "I know how you don't like to cook, and you must be extra busy with your work now that Betty is locked up. I must admit, I was very surprised to hear that you had been baking Christmas cookies."

"I . . ."

"Mother, we really have to get going." Sam stuck his head back in the door. "Josie's been working all day. I'm sure she's starving."

Never one to resist an opportunity to feed the starving masses, Carol hurried to the door. "See you in a few, dear," she called back to Josie.

"Great." Josie felt a bit guilty about letting everyone think she had been baking, but decided she had other things to worry about.

The boys were sprawled among their luggage in the flatbed of the truck.

"You guys are going to be cold back there," Josie called out.

"The cab seemed to be full of groceries and . . . and home-made Christmas cookies," Tyler called out in his mother's ear, hanging over the back of the truck.

"Well . . ." She should have known her son wouldn't believe that she had been baking day and night.

"We sampled them, Ms. Pigeon. The little almond crescents are wonderful!" Hastings peered in the other window.

Josie and her son exchanged grins. "I'm glad you like them. Just sit down. We'll be home in no time at all."

Tyler, as an intelligent only child of a single working mother, was very self-reliant and, once home, Josie left him to settle in his friend. She put away the groceries (sampling a few of the cookies as well) and hurried off to shower and change.

She was dressed in clean jeans and a new forest green velour tunic she had been saving for the holidays when she returned to her living room. The boys were sprawled on the couch, open tins of cookies in their laps, cans of Coke by their sides. Josie, who had given up being surprised by how many calories teenage boys could consume without putting on a pound, smiled and asked them if they were ready to go.

"Yes. We're looking forward to it," Hastings said politely.

"Yup, we're starving," Tyler added. Urchin lay contentedly in his arms, happier when Tyler was home than at any other time.

"Have you gone downstairs and said hello to Risa?" Josie asked, realizing she should have thought of it sooner.

"I knocked on her door, but no one answered."

"Really? Well, she's bound to be home soon." Now that she thought about it, it was unlike Risa to be out when Tyler arrived home. Usually, she was standing on the front porch with a plate of Tyler's favorite, spaghetti and meatballs, in her hands.

"There was a note though," Tyler continued. "She said she was bringing dinner to Betty at the police station and would be back soon."

"Why don't you run down and leave her a note telling her we're going to Sam's for dinner. She knows she'd be welcome if she wants to join us. And be sure to add that Sam's mother is cooking or, if I know Risa, she'll show up with a meal."

"Boy, if I'd known everyone on the island liked feeding people so much, I'd have come home with you before," Josie heard Hastings saying as the two boys clopped down the stairway.

The boys rode over to Sam's house in the cab of the truck,

discussing plans for their vacation as they went. Besides winter surfing, there was talk of running on the beach each day to build up their leg muscles, weight lifting in the garage of a friend of Tyler's on the island and, unlikely as it sounded, learning to make Carol's fudge.

"She said it would be easy to make on a hot plate or something in the dorm, Mom. Do you think maybe I could add a hot plate to my Christmas list?"

"Well, I . . ."

"And I've been thinking. If you did get me that computer, it would really help if you also got me a computer chess game. Chess is very good training in ah . . . logic. At least that's what my advisor says."

"That's Mr. Cutler. He knows what he's talking about, Ms. Pigeon. He went to Harvard and majored in . . . ah, philosophy or something really smart like that," Hastings supported his friend.

Josie just smiled. "We'll just have to see what's under the tree on Christmas morning," she said as she had been saying for the last fourteen of his fifteen years. Ah, holiday traditions, she thought fondly, as she parked the truck behind Carol's white Lincoln Town Car in Sam's driveway.

There was a wreath hanging on Sam's front door and a large balsam pine standing in a bucket of water nearby.

"Welcome. You're just in time." Carol opened the door and greeted them. "Look what Sammy bought this afternoon. We're going to have a tree-decorating party Friday night."

"Mother, that's your idea, not mine." Sam gave Josie a quick kiss and led his guests inside his by-the-beach ranch house. Built in the fifties, he had been remodeling it (with Josie's help) for the past two years. Most of the knotty pine had been replaced with wallboard, and the linoleum floors were now hardwood. But the pride and joy of Carol's life was the new kitchen which Island Contracting had installed during a lull in their workload in the fall. Bright white cabinets hung on the walls over granite countertops. New appliances were in place, and the Jenn-Air oven was emitting wonderfully enticing smells.

"The table is set. There's just time for a drink before dinner."

Sam and Tyler had made a coffee table from driftwood and a large sheet of glass. It was actually very attractive, especially when it was covered with goodies, as it was at present.

"Hmm. Crab dip."

"And guacamole," Tyler cried. "The food here is certainly better than at school, isn't it?"

"Wait. Hang on. Let's have some of this champagne— Sprite for the guys—and toast the beginning of the Christmas season!" Sam suggested.

Everyone grabbed a glass and was about to do as he suggested when there was a knock at the door. Sam ran to open it and Risa and John Jacobs entered the room.

TWENTY-FIVE

THEY BOTH LOOKED extremely unhappy. Until Risa spied Tyler.

"Tyler! *Caro!* How wonderful to see you! How you've grown, you sweet thing. You go to school a little boy and come home a grown-up man!" And Risa threw her arms about Tyler, causing him to drop the chunk of cheese he had been about to cram in his mouth.

"Risa, nice to see you." Tyler looked over Risa's shoulder at John Jacobs and frowned.

Josie, guessing what was causing his unhappiness, hurried to introduce John Jacobs, but, realizing suddenly that Tyler hadn't heard of either the murder or Betty's arrest, she didn't explain what another lawyer was doing on the island.

"Very nice to meet you, sir." Tyler shook hands with John. "This is Hastings Hudson, one of my suitemates from school. You might be interested in talking to him. He's thinking about becoming a lawyer."

Josie, who hadn't heard the boy's full name before, grinned and introduced Risa.

"Hastings knows all about Risa, Mom. She's my friend who sends the homemade biscotti," Tyler explained to Hastings.

Josie, to whom this was news, didn't say anything as Hastings was appropriately appreciative of Risa's generosity, raving about the pistachio biscotti as though they were his idea of heaven.

"Ah, *caro*, anything I can do for poor motherless boys . . ."

"Risa, both Tyler and Hastings have mothers . . ." Josie began.

"Why don't we all sit down and I can get John and Risa a drink. We're drinking champagne, but I also have a new Merlot you both might enjoy."

"And I think maybe we should tell Tyler more about what's been going on around here," Josie added.

"If you mean about the murder and Betty being arrested, I know," came her son's surprise statement.

"I'm afraid I let the cat slip out of the bag on the drive down," Carol admitted. "I thought you would have told him . . ."

"Yeah, but don't worry, Mom. Hastings and I have a plan."

"A plan?" John Jacobs accepted a glass of wine and sat down.

"To free Betty. She's not guilty, you know, sir."

"I'm inclined to agree with you," John said, taking their boyish enthusiasm seriously. "But she is doing a very good job of acting as though she were."

"She probably thinks she's protecting Island Contracting," Tyler said earnestly.

Josie took a sip of her champagne and looked at her son. "You know, that makes sense."

Sam frowned. "Now let's think for a minute. There have been two other murders connected with Island Contracting's work. Why is this one different?"

"Well, someone on the crew was murdered. That hasn't been true before," Josie suggested.

"But it isn't the first time a crew member was a suspect," Sam said.

"One of Mom's employees actually killed someone," Tyler explained to his friend.

"Yeah. I remember you told us that at school," Hastings said.

Josie wondered exactly what Tyler was telling people about her. "So that's what's different this time—I mean, the crew members are the only suspects here."

"Well, that does seem to be the case. Was it at all possible for anyone else besides the crew to have put poison in Caroline's food?" John was listening intently to the conversation, having put his glass down, untouched, on the coffee table.

"Not at the work site . . ."

"What about the people unloading the delivery? Or the Professor's aide? Or the Professor himself?" Sam asked.

All the eyes in the room were on Josie as she thought about an answer to that question. "I don't think the Professor is capable of doing that. He seems to have very limited use of his arms, but his hands don't work. And I can't imagine Nellie doing anything like that."

"Who's Nellie?" John asked.

"She's his aide. She was there that morning. In fact, she actually made wonderful Christmas cookies and gave them to us for our break that day. She's very sweet," Josie added, unwilling to think that a woman who baked so well could be a murderer. "And she had no reason to want Caroline dead."

"You don't really know that," John said.

"Where was the poison found? In Caroline's snack? Or were you all sharing?" Sam asked.

"I can answer that question. And then, since we're talking about this right now, I have some questions to ask. If this is an appropriate moment . . ." John was hesitant, glancing at the teens.

"The sooner Betty gets out of jail the better," Josie insisted. Everyone nodded in agreement.

"Well, like everything else in this case, the quality of the evidence is rather poor, but when the food was finally collected, identified, and tested, there was digitalis found in what was identified as a bowl of tofu meat substitute and brown rice soaked in tamari sauce and sprinkled with sesame seeds and powdered seaweed."

"Nothing else?"

"Nope. There were two containers of this particular dish, but only one contained the digitalis. But of course the question is why Caroline was the only person who ate out of this particular bowl—and who was intended to eat from it."

"Josie?"

"Well, we shared food, Sam. And Caroline and Layne frequently ate the same lunch." Josie shrugged. "I can't imagine exactly how anyone would put poison in the food ahead of time and then be absolutely sure only Caroline would eat it. I mean, suppose Layne put poison in the food at home and then just waited for Caroline to eat it."

"Okay, suppose it happened that way." John leaned forward to listen to her answer.

"Well, Caroline sits down to eat her snack and she opens her container and everyone says something like, 'what the hell is that shi . . .'" She glanced at her son before finishing. "'What is that stuff?'"

"My mother doesn't think I know words like *shit*," Tyler informed his friend.

"Actually, she was just hoping you wouldn't use them in front of her," Josie said. "Well, where was I?"

"You were explaining that if someone intended to poison Caroline by putting something in her food, they were just as likely to end up accidentally poisoning someone she shared her food with," Sam reminded her.

"Exactly."

"And everyone on the crew would know that? Everyone who had eaten with you? Everyone saw you tasting each other's meals—or snacks?"

"Sure."

"But not Nellie or the Professor?" John asked.

"Not the Professor," Josie answered slowly, thinking about what she was saying. "He's never been around when we're either taking a break or having lunch. He's not there all that much, after all, and we . . . well, we try to give the impression that we're working, working, working when he is. Which we are, of course. It's just that we do take two breaks a day, as well as stopping for about half an hour for lunch. Sometimes that looks like a lot to a homeowner who is anxious for us to get the job completed and get out of their house."

"Understandable. But Nellie knew about your breaks—in fact, she baked cookies and gave them to you."

"Yes. But why would she want to kill Caroline? Or anyone else, for that matter?"

"What about that nurse who killed hundreds of patients over the years?" Hastings spoke up for the first time. "It's true. I read about it in the newspaper."

"We're not allowed to watch television during the week at school," Tyler explained. "And on weekends we can only watch approved shows. Not things like *Hard Copy*."

"But why would Nellie want to kill Caroline?" Josie repeated the question she thought was significant.

"We don't know anything about her background, do we?" John asked.

"No," Sam answered.

"And we don't know anything about the Professor's background either. Not even how he ended up paralyzed . . ."

"No again," Sam said.

"I don't see how we can learn these things . . ." Josie started.

"Easy. We'll just hire someone," John answered, taking a small notebook from his pocket and writing something in it. "I've been thinking about that since I got involved in this case."

"Betty doesn't have much money . . ." Sam began.

"A detective? A private dick? Just like in the movies? Can we meet him?" Tyler and Hastings could barely control their enthusiasm.

"A private detective, yes. And I can't imagine any reason for her to come to the island, so no, you won't be meeting her. And if you did, you'd probably be disappointed. The woman I'm thinking of is more like your average accountant than any of the private detectives you meet in fiction or on TV," John answered. "And as for the cost, why don't you let me worry about it?" he added to Sam.

"Maybe this person—the detective—could look into Caroline's background too?" Josie suggested. "And Layne? And the school they run?"

"I must admit that Layne is the logical suspect for me too," Sam admitted. "She and Caroline had a lot in common and a long history together. And it's likely that Layne will benefit from Caroline's death—inheriting the school and the house."

"There is Caroline's fiancé, of course," Josie suggested.

"A fiancé? Caroline was going to be married?"

"That's what Layne said," Josie answered.

"When did you learn this?" Sam asked.

"When I went over to Layne's house the night after the murder. She said something about having to notify people that Caroline had died. And then she mentioned this fiancé—whoever he is."

"We'll find out. In fact, why don't I get working on this right away? What's the name of the town they lived in?"

"Ah . . . It's someplace in northern Maine. I know it's in the forms Caroline and Layne filled out—the job applications and all."

"The sooner I get them the sooner we'll have some answers."

"I could take you to the office . . ." Josie began.

"Does that mean they're lost somewhere in your unique filing system?" Sam asked.

Josie knew the term *unique* was generous. What he probably meant was either nonexistent, incompetent, or just plain messy. "Actually, they're sitting right in the middle of my desk. I could give you the key if you want to go over now. Or I could go over with you after we eat."

"After dinner will be soon enough. I'm going to make a few phone calls if no one minds. This woman I know can get started checking out the Professor and his aide. I don't suppose you know either the last name of the aide or the name of the college where the Professor teaches."

"I don't know her last name, but I can tell you where he works," Josie said, and did so.

John wrote down the information as she gave it and then headed for the kitchen and, presumably, the phone.

"I have a few things to finish up in the kitchen," Carol began.

"Why don't you let John make his calls, then we'll all help you get dinner on the table," her son suggested.

"Do you think Layne did it?" Josie asked.

"Well, she's always been the logical suspect."

"That's what she said the night after the murder," Josie said.

"I remember you telling me about that," Sam said. "That's one of the reasons I think she probably didn't do it."

"What do you mean?"

"Well, it's possible that she was trying to deflect suspicion by asking you that, but frankly, it seems a little calculating to me."

"You know, lots of serial killers are just like that, sir," Hastings said earnestly. "I read a book all about it."

"I don't think there's any evidence to lead anyone to believe that Layne is a serial killer," Sam said.

Josie realized he was taking the boy's ideas seriously. No wonder they liked him so much. "What about Pam, though?" she asked. "I mean, isn't it a rather large coincidence that she just happened to show up on the island two days after the murder of her teacher and mentor?"

"Who's Pam?" Carol asked.

Josie explained about their new crew member.

"You know, she really is worth a bit more investigation," Sam said. "John should pick up her employment papers as well as Layne's and Caroline's."

"Well, she didn't actually fill out the usual forms—yet," Josie admitted.

"Now that's interesting," Hastings said, excited by the news. "Maybe this Pam person is the murderer. Serial killers are very good at avoiding things like that. That guy in Chicago hadn't filed an income tax form for years, and the one in Florida had never signed a rental agreement, although he had been renting one place or another for over a decade."

"When it comes to paperwork, they all would have been right at home working for Island Contracting," was all Sam said.

TWENTY-SIX

"AS LONG AS we're considering possible suspects, what about Sandy?" Josie asked, choosing to ignore Sam's rather sarcastic comment about her paperwork.

"Are she and Caroline connected in some way?" Sam asked.

"Not that I know of. But she could have lied about it."

"Wouldn't that suggest that Caroline was lying too?" Sam asked.

"You mean Sandy and Caroline would both have had to lie if we weren't to find out about a connection. Yeah, I suppose that's true," Josie admitted. "And why would Caroline lie to protect the person who was going to murder her?"

"Well, I don't think . . ." Sam began to refute her argument.

"I don't know about the rest of you, but I think better on a full stomach," Carol insisted, apparently becoming bored with their conversation.

"And I'm off the phone, so the kitchen is free." John Jacobs reappeared, tucking his notebook back in his pocket.

"Then I'll just put the finishing touches on our dinner." Carol got up.

"Would you like me to help?" Josie offered halfheartedly.

"I will help Carol," Risa announced. "We will catch up with news."

Josie was fairly sure that the first order of business would be what she and Sam had been up to. She frowned. "Maybe you and Hastings could help with the table?" she suggested to her son.

"Sure, Mom." He grinned. "If I hear anything interesting, I'll let you know."

Hastings and Tyler bounded from the room.

"Have you ever noticed that they don't seem to be able to just walk slowly?" Sam asked no one in particular. "They're either running, or jogging, or dashing between places."

"Not true. You should see Tyler when there's a good-looking girl around his age present. He sort of saunters from place to place, lounging against walls or leaning on furniture. Apparently sitting isn't cool."

"The two of them do fill a room," Sam commented at the raucous laughter coming from the kitchen.

"This should be a very interesting case," John said, sitting down on the couch, picking up his full wine glass and draining it.

"Whoa, I never thought I'd see you chug a glass of French wine. I mean, I know you've had a hard day, but still," Sam said, refilling his glass.

"Betty Patrick is the most impossible person I've ever met. And in my line of work, that's saying a lot. I don't know what the hell is going on with her. First I think maybe she's just an innocent victim of a completely incompetent police department. Then I think she's just a spectacularly beautiful example of a woman determined to ruin her own life. Now I'm beginning to suspect that the incompetent police department might just be the victim here."

"What do you mean?" Josie asked.

"She stopped the entire investigation."

"Yes, you could say that, but . . ."

"That's a good point," Sam interrupted Josie to admire John's thinking. "And your guess is that it's intentional. That Betty's confession has a purpose."

"Yes."

"But what?" Josie asked.

"I think you should listen to your son. The best guess anyone has made so far is that she's doing it to protect you—or, since we know you didn't kill Caroline, your company," John answered.

"But what does Island Contracting have to do with Caroline's death?"

"That's something you'll have to ask yourself."

"Do you know something you're not saying?" Sam asked.

"No. And please don't read anything into any of this. I have no idea what is going on here. Betty seems like a sane young woman . . ."

"She is," Josie insisted.

"So we have to assume she has a good reason for confessing to a murder which she didn't commit."

"Unless she did kill Caro . . ."

"Sam! How can you even think such a thing? You know Betty isn't a killer. And what possible reason would she have to kill Caroline anyway?"

"Josie, I sure won't argue with you. So what John is asking is who might Betty be protecting. And what Tyler said makes sense. It almost certainly is Island Contracting."

Josie picked up her wineglass and drank the rest of the gleaming liquid. "From what? And how? Being involved in murders in the past hasn't destroyed the company."

"Okay. Fine. But that's not the question right now," said John. "The question is, why would Betty think this time is different?"

Sam nodded. "Good point. Think, Josie, is there any connection between Caroline and your company that you've overlooked?"

"Sam . . ."

"Wrong question, Sam," his friend corrected him. "Think again, Josie. What connection would Betty make between Caroline's murder and Island Contracting? It's entirely possible that she's wrong, that in reality there is no connection, but that doesn't make her idea any less significant."

Josie frowned. "I don't get it."

"Did the poisoned food come from your office?" John asked.

"No. None of the food came from my office."

"Could she have thought . . ."

"That it did," Josie finished for him. "Well, sure, I guess so, but I don't see why."

"Well, let's try looking at this from a different direction. Has

Island Contracting ever before hired anyone from the school Caroline and Layne ran?"

"Not that I know of."

"Do you think you'd know?"

"Probably. We talk while we work. Some people talk less than others, but we all know we're in the minority . . ."

"You mean being female carpenters?"

"Yes. So we usually tell each other how we ended up doing this. I've never heard of a school like this one until now. I'd remember," she added stubbornly.

John thought for a few minutes and then asked another question.

"Were you alone in the room where the food was stored?"

"It was all over the place. I mean, each of us carried our own snacks and lunches . . ."

"In what?"

Josie shrugged. "Whatever. In our toolboxes usually. Or any old canvas carryall. Betty carries a backpack for food and her wallet and other things she might need on the site. She can't trust the handle on her toolbox; it keeps breaking off."

"I assume none of you carries a purse on the job."

Josie grinned. "No, but it's an interesting image—carpenter with purse."

"I'm sorry. What I meant was, you all carry a variety of . . . of, well, carryalls."

"Yes. And we carry different things in them. And we dump them all over the place."

"You're saying it would be difficult to be sure who had access to Caroline's food that morning."

"Exactly. Unless Caroline kept it in her possession, I think almost anyone might have had access to it on the work site. And, of course, Layne might have put something in it before they left home."

"And then we're back to how did the poisoner know who would eat from that particular dish."

Josie sighed, discouraged—but still hungry. "I wonder when dinner's going to be ready."

"Right now. Carol and Risa want everyone sitting down at

the table immediately," Tyler said, appearing in the doorway to the kitchen. "You won't believe the food. Carol's made a huge pot of chicken and dumplings, and a pan of corn bread, and some sort of vegetable casserole that actually tastes good, and fruit salad . . . and there's dessert too."

The table looked like a photograph ripped from one of the magazines Josie had been studying for the past few weeks. Not only were there platters, bowls, and casseroles full of more food than Josie could imagine being ready at the same time, but Carol had apparently brought along holiday decorations. There was a large crystal bowl of greens, pinecones, and silver balls in the middle of the table. And green napkins which wished the person wiping their lips *Happy Holidays*.

Josie sat down between Sam and John Jacobs, filled her plate as the food was passed around the table, and started eating. Sam and John managed to do the same without interrupting their conversation.

"When will you get a report?" Sam asked, filling his plate.

"I told her to call with anything and everything she learned—as she learned it." John put most of a large dumpling in his mouth and kept talking as he chewed. "I want her out of there before someone has the sense to call in the state guys—I'd hate for this to get more serious."

"Any talk of that?" Sam asked.

"Nope. That young kid wants to run this thing so badly he can taste it. He's having a ball. I sure wish we could hire him off this island. My job would be a lot easier with an incompetent like him on the police department in New York City."

"You're really concerned," Sam said.

"I . . . sort of. I'd just hate to see a lovely young woman like Betty ruin her life because of some sort of mistaken heroic notion of 'doing the right thing' to protect someone."

Sam leaned farther around Josie and grinned. "Son of a gun. You've fallen for her. The serious, uninvolved John Jacobs, the man who's had half the women in New York City after him ever since the day he set up his practice, has fallen for a young carpenter on a barrier island."

"Okay, there's no need to gloat, you know."

"No need to gloat? After the shit you gave me when I told you about Josie . . ." Apparently realizing who was sitting right between them, listening to every word, Sam shut up.

Josie, however, had other things on her mind. "You know, I've been thinking about Sandy. She hasn't lived here long. She might have been connected with Caroline."

"At the school?"

"Probably not, since then she would have known Layne too, but Caroline spent years away from Maine, and she worked on construction crews when she couldn't get jobs in the art world. Maybe the two of them ran across each other at that time."

"I'll have complete employment records for both of them in less than twenty-four hours. If they were working legitimately— if they were officially on the books of a company—we'll know about it," John said.

"That soon?" Sam asked.

"This lady's good."

"But if either of them was moonlighting, working off the books, then you might not be able to find out?" Josie asked.

"Oh, that can be found out, from interviews with people who knew them at various times in their lives. But that type of research takes lots of time."

"Are you telling me my employment records are open for anyone to discover?" Josie asked, still wondering about the same thing.

"If an investigator has enough contacts, and can use the Internet to his advantage, there's not a lot of privacy anymore," John answered, apparently unconcerned about any distress this might be causing her.

"You know, I've been wondering about the Professor." Sam changed the subject.

"And whether the fact that the murder occurred on his property is significant." John nodded. "The thought crossed my mind too."

"How did he happen to choose Island Contracting rather than another company, Josie?"

"I'm not really sure."

"How many other contractors are there on the island?" John asked.

"Three companies, and more than a few people who do piecework—building additions and remodeling by themselves, or with one or two other workers, usually friends or relatives."

"And do homeowners hire companies that aren't . . . ah, in residence, so to speak?"

"Sure. Lots of the houses at this end of the island"—she resisted calling it the rich end—"were built by large builders from other places. Much as I don't like that, I can understand it. Big construction or remodeling jobs are expensive and time-consuming. A lot of people don't feel comfortable trusting someone they know very little about. And if they've worked with a builder in the past and been happy with him, they're surely going to want to hire that same person again."

"So how does the process work? An architect draws up the plans, then calls a bunch of contracting companies, shows them the plans, and accepts bids on the project?" John asked.

"Not necessarily, not for a remodeling project at least. Many homeowners—most, in fact—call contractors before architects. They know sort of what they want."

"Like an addition put on the back of the house?"

"Or a kitchen or bathroom remodeled, a deck added, even for something like a second floor added, many customers call the contractor first."

"And then you call an architect?"

"No, then we talk about what they really want. You know, some people know just what they want, others only know they want something different from what they have. Smart people talk to a few contractors and collect ideas—for free. Once you call in an architect, you're going to be paying for whatever they draw up. Then, after everyone has agreed on the plans— whether architect-drawn or not—we make bids and compete with everyone else."

"And so you beat out the other contractors on the island for the Professor's job."

"I don't know exactly. I mean, I'm not sure who else bid on

the job. I could find out easily though, if there were others on the island. Do you think it might be significant?"

"I haven't the foggiest. But I'd like to know."

"Then I'll make a few calls. . . . I could do it now. . . ."

"Great."

Josie headed off to the phone in the kitchen, taking her half-finished plate along with her.

TWENTY-SEVEN

J OSIE CALLED THE other contractors on the island while finishing her meal at the kitchen counter. It took a while to get the information she was after. Everyone insisted on asking about Betty before answering any questions. But by the time she was scraping her plate to pick up the last few bits of the best pie she'd ever eaten, she was sure no one else on the island had been approached by Professor Sylvester to remodel his home.

"Do you think it's significant?" she asked, back at the dinner table after explaining what she had discovered.

"It might be."

"You know, professors have a very high incidence of nervous breakdowns. Right before dentists, and right after journalists," Hastings announced. "I read about it in *People* magazine."

"Yeah, I read that too. What if this Professor went mad and killed Caroline himself? Then, because Betty was hopelessly in love with him, she confessed to a crime that she did not commit," Tyler began, obviously excited by his own deductions.

"Betty Patrick is in love with Professor Sylvester?" John was so concerned, he dropped his spoon right in the middle of the whipped cream covering the large slice of chocolate cream pie in front of him.

"I think Tyler is just making up possible scenarios," Josie suggested. "You don't have any reason to think that, do you?" she asked her son.

"No. I've never even met this Professor."

"But affairs between older men and younger women happen all the time," Hastings assured them all, his mouth full of creamy chocolate. "I read about it . . ." He stopped talking, swallowed, and looked from Josie to Sam and back again.

"You can read about that almost anywhere," Sam finished the sentence for him. "It's pretty common."

"Yes, sir, I guess you're right." And Hastings blushed.

"So did you find out anything else?"

"Nope." Josie yawned. "And, to tell you the truth, I'm completely whacked. If it wouldn't be rude, I think we'd better be heading home. Although I could leave the boys to do the dishes . . ."

"We have a lot of experience," Tyler explained earnestly. "At school, the houses take turns doing kitchen duty, and my suite always volunteers to do dishes."

"I have a dishwasher."

"We do at school too—a great big industrial one."

"Why do you volunteer for dishes?" Josie asked. She knew her son. He would have figured out all the angles.

"Kitchen cleanup is the last group to leave the kitchen."

"So you miss some of study hall?" Sam guessed.

"That, and also the paid staff likes to leave as soon as possible. So we're sometimes unsupervised. And that means extra eats!"

Josie looked at the two lean boys and wondered where they put all those calories. And then got her answer.

"If you don't mind, Mom, we were kind of thinking we could jog home tonight."

"Tyler! It's almost five miles."

"Shouldn't take much more than an hour."

"Nope, maybe less," Hastings agreed.

Josie glanced down at her watch—and then up at the clock on the wall. "It's almost nine. You promise you'll be home by ten-fifteen?"

"Yup. Don't worry. Hastings and I are always on time for curfew."

"Then I guess I'll be going," Josie stood up and offered Risa a ride, which she refused.

After much toing and froing (and some kissing and hugging from Sam), Josie was on her way home. She drove slowly down the mostly deserted island streets, admiring the cascades of lights which adorned some houses, the little electric candles twinkling in the windows of others. She would have to get cracking if she was going to have some decorations up before Christmas. On the other hand, Tyler and Hastings had free time. Maybe they could be bribed to hang lights from the roof outside her apartment.

Thinking of plans for the holidays, and happy that her son was safe at home, she didn't pay too much attention to the slight smell of decay hanging in the air as she unlocked the door of her home. Tomorrow she'd suggest to the boys that they select a nice fresh balsam pine from the lot the Boy Scouts ran. That should clear up the air, as well as adding to the holiday spirit.

Planning happily, Josie washed up, brushed her teeth, and headed for bed. She would get up early, leave a note for the boys, and start the new day nice and fresh.

She woke up with a start. Someone was screaming! She leapt out of bed and dashed into the living room, only to discover Tyler and Hastings making up for the fact that their television viewing was censored at school by watching middle-of-the-night reruns of a popular tabloid show. The screams were coming from two women who seemed to think an appearance on national TV was an appropriate moment to try to rip out each other's hair.

"Mom! Is everything okay?" Tyler looked up from the box of cookies he had been emptying into his mouth.

"Yes. Of course. Fine." Except for the fact that she was wearing a torn T-shirt advertising the Island Lifeguard Boat Fund beauty contest (which she surely wouldn't have entered, because she just as surely wouldn't have won). "I'm going back to bed." She hurried back to the privacy of her bedroom. "I'll leave a note for you guys if you're still asleep when I leave."

They didn't answer, and she fell into bed and into a deep sleep almost immediately.

* * *

The next morning, Josie was up at dawn, absolutely convinced that she had missed something significant in the discussion at Sam's house the night before. John's detective was going to investigate Layne, Caroline, Pam, Sandy, the school in Maine, and hopefully the source of the anonymous donation that had kept that place going. And then he was checking into the Professor and his aide. What else, she wondered, was there?

The answer struck her as she got in her truck. Betty. There still was no answer to the original question she and Sam had asked. Why all the changes in Betty's life recently? And if they didn't have anything to do with the murder (and certainly, Josie assured herself, they didn't), did they hold the key to her false confession? She suddenly realized she had forgotten to leave a note for Tyler. She'd call and leave a message on the answering machine for the boys. Tyler would check for messages when he woke up. She was reaching for the cell phone (tucked in the top of her toolbox) when she realized she had an ally she wasn't using—Betty's parents.

Instead of her home number, she dialed Miami information. Luckily, old people get up early, and the Patricks were alert and more than willing to help when she explained what she wanted.

After hanging up, she turned her truck around and headed for the police station. Things would be set up for her when she arrived. She was sure of it.

A hideous plastic wreath had been hung on the door, and directly inside, an anemic-looking artificial tree had been decorated with plastic ornaments and multicolored lights. Dozens of beautifully wrapped packages lay underneath.

The woman at the desk saw Josie looking at the display. "They're all for Betty. The islanders are really behind that young lady. I sure hope she appreciates it."

"I'm sure she does. We'll hear all about how she feels when this is all over," Josie assured her. "Have you seen Betty this morning?"

"Brought her some coffee and a slab of that marzipan coffee

cake that Madge at the bakery makes special this time of year. Don't know that she ate either, though. Getting hard to keep track. That hotshot lawyer from New York City has been snitching some of the things people bring to her. Two whole tins of Christmas cookies disappeared yesterday afternoon—as well as a thermos of the best homemade clam chowder on the island. I should know. Made it myself off of clams my husband dug yesterday morning."

Josie decided that this was not the time to confess to borrowing those tins of cookies. First things first, she assured herself. "Have any calls come in?"

"For Betty? This morning? Yup, her dad called. Thought Betty was going to refuse to talk to him, but he said the magic words—threatened to come up and see her in person unless she was willing to talk to him on the phone."

"So she talked to him?" First step accomplished.

"Yup. And to her mom too, sounded like."

"And then?" Josie held her breath, waiting for the answer.

"Then Betty hung up and told me that if you came, and if you wanted to talk to her, she'd listen. But she said for me to tell you something first."

"What?"

"She said to tell you you don't play fair."

"Sometimes," Josie said, heading for the door that led to the holding cells, "it's better to win."

John Jacobs was sitting in a chair beside Betty's cell, a wide grin on his face. "Well, Ms. Pigeon. Good to see you so bright and early this morning. I was just telling Betty about the wonderful evening we had at Sam's house last night. Well, I have a few phone calls to make, so I'll leave you two alone. See you later, Ms. Patrick."

"He's a nice guy," Josie commented as the door swung closed behind him and they were alone together.

"I'm not talking to you. I told my father I would see you. But I didn't say I would talk to you." Betty got up from the chair she was sitting on, turned its back to Josie, and sat down again. Facing the wall.

"Oh well, then I'll talk to you. Nice cell you have," Josie said sincerely. "Well decorated."

And it was. There was a small Christmas tree in one corner, decorated to death. Cookies, foil-covered chocolates, shimmering ornaments, tiny Santa Clauses and good luck angels, candy canes, chains made from popped corn and cranberries, and little notes of encouragement covered its boughs. More wrapped packages were tucked underneath. The cell, probably not more than eight feet square, was hung with Christmas cards. (At least, Josie realized, when you were living in a space defined by metal bars and cinder blocks, you didn't have to worry about tape damage.) Her own living room was bleak by comparison.

"I suppose a lot of people contributed to this," Josie continued, when Betty didn't answer her.

"Josie, you conned me. I wouldn't even be talking with you if my father hadn't said he would get on the first plane up here if I didn't." Betty spoke quietly. "And I don't want my parents to suffer because of this."

"Betty, you're under arrest. You've confessed to a murder. How the hell do you expect to prevent your parents from suffering?"

Betty sighed. "I . . . I'm doing what I think is right. I'm trying to live a better life. An intentional life. I'm trying to do the right thing instead of going through the days, having fun, doing nothing for anyone."

"But Betty, I don't understand. What does trying to be good have to do with confessing to a murder you didn't do?"

"You know I didn't do it?"

"Of course I know. You'd never murder anyone! Anyone who knows you knows that! Why do you think you're getting so much support from the town, for heaven's sake?"

Betty repeated her first statement. "You know I didn't do it?"

"Yes, of course. That's what I just said." Josie looked intently at her friend and then turned around to look over her shoulder. John Jacobs had firmly closed the door behind him. They were alone, and anything that was said would be confidential.

"You're trying to tell me something, and I'm just not getting it."

Betty looked down at the floor. "I don't know how to say it."

"What do you mean?"

"I don't want to hurt . . . or insult you."

"Betty, I'm going nuts. I know you didn't kill Caroline. And I don't have any idea why you confessed to a murder you didn't commit."

"You don't?"

"Of course I don't. I've been asking around town and I understand that you've been talking about becoming more serious. That you want to get married and all. There are even people who think you might be involved . . . involved with the wrong man." She had a hard time finishing her statement. It suddenly struck her that maybe the problem was Sam. Maybe Betty had fallen in love with Sam. Josie was so shocked by the thought that she didn't hear what Betty was saying.

" . . . as you should know."

"I should know what?" Josie asked, returning to reality.

"Josie, I'm trying to tell you. . . ." She took a deep breath.

"Trying to tell me what? Why don't you stop trying? Just tell me what it is. I'll understand. Even if you're in love with Sam, I promise I'll understand. . . ."

"In love with Sam? Your Sam? Sam Richardson? Josie, what the hell are you talking about?"

"I'm trying to figure out why you've done this. Why you confessed to a murder you didn't do . . ."

"Because I saw you."

"What?"

"I saw you in the living room. I saw you with the toolboxes. I saw you opening and closing toolboxes that morning. Right before Caroline died."

TWENTY-EIGHT

"**Y**OU THINK I did it." Josie stood up. Sat down. And stood up again. She ran her hands through her hair a few times and then took a seat. She had no idea what to do. "I never thought you killed her. And you . . . You think I did it! How could you have so little faith in me? And . . ."

"Josie, I'm sitting here because I care about you." Betty spoke quietly, but firmly.

"I . . . Of course. I'm being an idiot. But Betty, I didn't have anything to do with Caroline's death. I was checking out your toolbox because I—well, this is going to ruin your Christmas surprise, but I suppose that doesn't matter now—because I've ordered a new one for you for Christmas and I wanted to make sure it had the same interior as your old one. I know how people get attached to their stuff, and just that morning you had mentioned that you really liked the style of your box and I just went there to check it all out, to make sure you would like what I bought for you. . . ." Josie stopped speaking and grimaced. "It's all so stupid. Sort of like that O. Henry short story," she added. "By trying to make Christmas nice for you, I ended up putting you in jail, right?"

"Yeah. But I was the one that screwed everything up by lying to everyone, didn't I?"

Josie looked around her cell before answering. "You got a lot of cookies and some wonderful decorations. So I guess things could be worse."

"I need a shower. And I can't tell you how much I'd like to go for a run. Besides, you must be getting behind with work on the Professor's house while I'm just hanging around here."

"We actually hired an extra person—not that we don't need you," Josie added quickly. "Listen, we can chat later. Let's call your lawyer and get you out of here."

"Good idea."

Josie noticed that Betty had grabbed her comb and was running it through her hair as she left the room.

John Jacobs was sitting on a desk in the reception area, chatting with the woman sitting there and eating a slice of what looked like fruitcake.

"She wants to leave," Josie announced.

"Of course she does. It must be terrible to be locked up over the holidays," the woman said.

John's response was cooler, and more cautious. "What do you mean?"

"She didn't do it. She wants to take back her confession. She wants to go home."

"I'll call Mike, and get the key." The woman behind the desk reached for the phone.

"Ladies, it's not quite that simple."

"Because she was arrested before she confessed," Josie said, realizing suddenly that she had been ignoring that.

"That and the fact that she can't just take back a confession. There's a process here."

"Oh. She's going to be very disappointed. She really wants out of there."

"Why don't I go talk with her?"

"Shall I hang around? There is a reason Betty confessed, you know. She thought I was the murderer."

"She thought . . ." John Jacobs turned and stared at Josie. "Why would she ever think such a thing?"

"Because . . ."

"Wait. Why don't you tell me when we have a bit more privacy?" He glanced over at their companion.

"You don't have to worry about me. I know how to keep a secret. There are a lot of people in town whose dirty laundry would be hung out in public if I didn't. I work as a dispatcher in the summer. The name of every drunk on the road passes through my hands—as well as people committing even more serious crimes."

"I still think . . ." John began.

"We should get back to Betty. I hate to think of her packing up her stuff and then having to stay in jail," Josie urged.

"Of course."

"Do you want me to call the chief? Or the chief's kid, I suppose I should say."

"Why don't you just wait a bit? I'd like some time with my client."

"Sure. Take all the time you want. I brought my Christmas cards along today. Going to spend the afternoon addressing them. This may be the first year they've been mailed out on time in a long while."

Josie decided she would think about Christmas cards when she had some free time—possibly around Saint Patrick's Day. She followed John through the door.

Betty was sitting on the edge of her bed, looking happy and excited. "When can I leave?" she asked. "I can come back for this stuff tomorrow, if that's okay with everyone here."

"You can't leave. You're still under arrest."

Josie would have broken the news a bit more gently, and she flinched as the pain crossed over Betty's face.

"I only confessed because I thought Josie did it," Betty responded.

"Josie already told me that. Now why don't you explain exactly what happened that day?"

Betty did just that, going into a bit more detail regarding where she had been standing while Josie was surreptitiously going through her toolbox. Then Josie explained why she'd been doing what she'd been doing. Then it was John's turn.

"What Mike is going to say—if he has half a brain in his head—is that the two of you got together and cooked up this story. And it still doesn't explain away the original reason he saw Betty as the murderer. Caroline's final words included her name."

"That doesn't prove anything."

"Of course it doesn't. Any defense attorney worth his salt

could—and would—argue that Caroline might have meant any number of innocent things. But I think the only way you're going to get out of jail is to find the person who did this."

"That's what I've been thinking all along," Josie confessed. "But I don't think we're a whole lot closer now than the day Caroline died."

"Is it possible that someone else saw Josie messing around with your toolbox?" John asked Betty.

"I suppose so. But I wasn't conscious of anyone else being right there watching, if that's what you mean."

"And you just looked in Betty's toolbox," he continued his questioning, looking at Josie. "Nothing else? You didn't put anything in or take anything out?"

"There was no reason in the world for me to look in anyone else's box. It was only Betty's box that worried me."

"And you didn't touch any other boxes?"

"I may have . . ."

"You did," Betty interrupted. "Layne's box was on top of mine. You must have moved it to get to mine."

"You're sure?" John asked.

"Yup. Because I had put it there. I was looking inside for a wrench I needed. Mine was lost, and she suggested I borrow hers."

"You're thinking that someone else might believe I put poison into Caroline's food," Josie said, thinking she understood.

"Nope. But look. You didn't put poison in Caroline's snack. Betty didn't put poison in Caroline's snack. I think we can assume Caroline didn't put poison in her snack—there's no hint that this was a suicide. And it's a bit public for that type of thing anyway. So the remaining suspects are Layne and Sandy. And if there's no connection between Sandy and Caroline, then Layne is the obvious suspect. . . ."

"You're not considering Pam or Nellie, I gather," Josie broke into his reasoning.

"Who's Pam?" Betty asked.

"She's the carpenter I hired to help us get this job done on time."

"My replacement." Betty sounded sad.

"No one could replace you," Josie assured her, and quickly explained Pam's background.

"Why would you include her in the list of suspects?" Betty asked, apparently surprised by the idea.

"Well, if you include Sandy, you must include Nellie. Because she was there that morning too. And there could be a connection between them. And Pam—well, doesn't it strike anyone as strange that Pam just happened to show up when she did? Isn't it possible that she was on the island the day of the murder? That she is the murderer?"

"We'll have to wait for the detective's reports," John suggested. "If we're lucky, there will be an obvious connection between some of these people. Something we missed—or just didn't know about."

"Detective? What detective?" Betty was mystified.

"Oh, you don't know. John hired a detective to look into some of the questions we have about this," Josie explained.

"John did? You did?" Betty looked up at her lawyer. "Who is going to pay for all this?"

"I don't think you should worry about that right now."

"You don't? Did this detective tell you that I'm about to become a rich woman? Someone who can pay for expensive New York lawyers to defend me and private detectives to . . . to do research? If they did, they're not very good. Because I'm a carpenter, John Jacobs. And that's all I'm ever going to be. There's no way I can afford you—or him—or all these things. And if I can't get out of jail unless I have them, then I'm going to end up in jail for the rest of my life." And Betty bit her bottom lip and stared down at the floor.

"Go tell the woman at the desk to come in here and open up the door to this cell. She shouldn't be alone right now," John stated flatly.

Josie ran.

When she left the police station fifteen minutes later, she was sad and perplexed. And more than a little curious about the relationship developing between John and Betty. Apparently

Sam's teasing of his friend at dinner last night had been right on the mark. The way the two of them had been clutching each other certainly seemed to indicate something other than a merely professional relationship. John, looking over Betty's head as he held her in his arms, had promised to call Josie as soon as he knew anything more. She assumed that meant his detective was going to be making a report. She sure hoped so. Betty in jail because she was trying to protect a friend was sure different than Betty in jail because an idiot police department wouldn't believe in her innocence.

The Professor was waiting to talk with Josie.

"Good morning. Any problems?" She asked the question as brightly as she could, forcing a smile on her face.

"Not with my house. But I've been thinking about your problem."

"My problem?"

"You don't consider one of your crew members being arrested for the murder of another to be a problem?"

Why did he make her so angry? "Yes, of course I do."

"Well, I think I might be able to help you. To clear up some things relating to the murder."

"Really? If I could just check on the work . . ." Josie said, glancing toward the sound of hammers, which was coming from the back of the house.

"Sure. Take your time. I'll just sit here and read my book."

Josie left the room, noticing that the Professor was turning pages of the book in his lap by using a peg attached to his wrist.

Everyone on the crew was working hard—as they always did when the owner was present. The radio was playing "Grandma Got Run Over by a Reindeer" and hammers banged in time with the tune. Josie explained what was going on before returning to Hugh Sylvester.

"I got a few phone calls this morning. One from my office at the university and one from a colleague. Someone has been asking questions about me and, I would assume, about my staff."

"Well." There was, she decided, nothing to be gained by lying. "Yes. Betty's legal team has hired a detective to look into the backgrounds of people involved in this murder. Not that we think you are involved, but because you . . . you own this house and about Nellie—because she was here the morning that Caroline died."

"She had left by the time of the poisoning. At least, that's what I understood."

"Yes. But the poison could have been placed in the food earlier in the day. Before our break."

"Must have been earlier, in fact. I can't imagine anyone reaching over and sprinkling digitalis on the food while everyone else was present."

Josie started to grin and then realized what he had just said. There was that stuff Layne and Caroline used to sprinkle over their food. . . . She made a mental note to check to see if any of the poison had been in that container. She didn't see exactly what difference it would make, but still . . .

"Have I said something you don't understand?"

"No, just something that that made me think."

The Professor chuckled. "If only you were one of my students. I have a very difficult time inspiring them to the same task."

Josie was astounded. Was that a compliment? "The detective who was checking out Nellie and you was only looking for a connection to Caroline. Not trying to"—what would he call it?—". . . to invade your privacy."

"I'm not upset. In fact, I've been more than surprised that the local police department hasn't been asking more questions. I don't mean to worry you, but they do seem convinced of your buxom carpenter's guilt."

"Yes, but they're wrong."

"I'm willing to accept that as our working thesis. And apparently, you believe Nellie and I are suspects."

"No! I mean, it's possible, and . . ." She took a deep breath and continued. "And we don't have any choice but to consider everyone."

"Good enough. I know about myself, and I would bet anything on Nellie. She might kill someone, but never with poison. She has too much invested in her reputation as an exceptional cook. Which leaves us with the other two women on your crew."

"Thanks for leaving me off the list," Josie said.

"It's not that I don't consider you a suspect. I just don't think I'd get anywhere considering your story with you."

"If I were going to kill someone, I sure wouldn't kill them on my own work site," Josie argued.

"Before you get huffy, you might remember that you're having me investigated."

"Oh, yeah, well . . ."

"But you do have a point. Why was this woman killed here?"

Josie had some experience with this type of thing. Maybe she'd impress him a second time this morning. "So that there would be a lot of suspects."

"Three? Four?"

"I guess that doesn't make a lot of sense."

"No."

"So it must be something else."

"Excellent thinking."

The last was said sarcastically, and Josie realized she was rapidly losing his respect. "Perhaps the murderer didn't have any choice. Perhaps it wasn't that Caroline had to die here as much as that she had to die right away. The killer didn't have time to wait for a more private place. Or something." She ended less confidently than she had begun.

"Or something," the Professor said grimly. "But you could be right, and it's an excellent idea to look at a problem from as many angles as possible."

Josie smiled.

"As long as we don't merely confuse the central issue."

TWENTY-NINE

SAM AND JOSIE were meeting for lunch at his liquor store. Tyler and Hastings had been planning to join them, but Tyler had called Sam and explained that, after getting up late, the boys were on their way to pick out a Christmas tree.

"He said they were going to get the best tree on the island," explained Sam, who had taken the message on the phone at home.

"I hope he remembers to buy a balsam—that scent really puts me in the mood for Christmas."

"I'm sure they'll do a good job," Sam said, opening the refrigerator which held chilled wines and beers. Lunch was stored within. "You said on the phone that you talked with Professor Sylvester about the murder."

"Yes, and he was really helpful. . . . I mean, I got the impression he was trying to be helpful."

"That's interesting."

"Do you think it's significant? Maybe he is involved in this?"

"I think that's highly unlikely, but the detective should be able to tell us if there's any connection between him and Caroline. If he's not upset about his past being looked into, he's probably uninvolved. It's more likely that he's trying to be helpful. He's gotten to know you through the work you do, and he's impressed. Or maybe he just likes puzzles. But I have good news for you," Sam added. "The detective has checked in. John is on the phone with her back in my office right now."

"Sam, that's wonderful. Why didn't you tell me right away?"

"You walked in the door talking and complaining of starvation. I thought you wanted your lunch." He was laying out three matching orange Tupperware dishes, a loaf of bread, napkins, utensils, and plates as he spoke. There was also a bottle of beer for him and a diet Coke for Josie.

"Your mother made all this? After that amazing dinner last night?" It was a wonderful spread. Shrimp cocktail with sauce, crab salad, and a tomato, mozzarella, and basil salad.

"Yes. She also made plans for dinner tonight—we're all going over to Risa's. Apparently Risa felt that Tyler couldn't live a day longer without one of her special meals."

"Sounds good to me." Josie was sticking her fork into the various containers and tasting while speaking. "Where did your mother get fresh tomatoes and basil at this time of year?"

"Balducci's. She brought them out from the city."

"Of course." She wondered if they had a takeout service for Christmas Day. "I . . . You're done!" She interrupted herself as John appeared. "What did she learn?"

"Lora—that's her name, Lora Smith. Tall, blond, thin, with a graduate degree in Japanese Lit from Princeton. She's one smart cookie."

"Any particular reason why you're talking like a character in a Raymond Chandler novel?" Sam asked.

"Sorry. There's something about hiring a private detective that makes me feel rather louche."

Josie wasn't at all interested in this exchange. "So what did this Lora Smith learn?"

"Lots. But not much that would lead to the murderer. In fact, I think her information may have confused the issue even more."

"Have some lunch and explain," Sam suggested. "Do you want a beer?"

"Thanks. I took some notes," John said, flipping open a pad of paper. "Let's take the Professor and his aide first."

"No connection?"

"None that I can see, but here are the facts. Professor Sylvester is exactly what he claims to be, a professor of psychology who specializes in what is now called intelligence theory—the many ways people learn. He has his doctorate from Yale and has been working at the best universities in the country ever since getting his degree—except for the year after his accident."

"It was an auto accident that put him in the wheelchair?"

"Yes. He was driving and was hit from behind by a truck which was out of control on an icy highway. The Professor was alone in the car, and his spine was severed. He was paralyzed instantly. The trucker died. This happened in Kansas, where he was giving a speech at a university symposium. He was stabilized at a local hospital and then went on to do rehabilitation at Craig in Colorado. He was back to teaching full-time a little over a year later."

"Impressive," Sam said.

"Yes."

"But he's not working now, is he?" Josie asked.

"He's on sabbatical, and will be until the middle of January.

"Lora couldn't find any connection between the Professor and Caroline. He didn't teach at the college she attended, didn't live in the same city. If he's ever been to Maine, it was to vacation, not to go to a school for female carpenters. There's also no unaccounted for cash in his life. He didn't sue for damages after his accident, and has lived pretty much on his salary for years. The house Island Contracting is remodeling belonged to his parents—they left it to him when they died, and he's been renting it out summers ever since then. He's single, and lives very frugally, but there's no way he could be the donor whose cash kept the school going. He just doesn't have that type of money."

"And Nellie?"

"Nellie is what she claims to be—his aide. She is paid by his insurance company. And she's been working for him since six months after he came out of rehab."

"Is that timing significant?" Sam asked.

"Nope. Apparently he had a number of aides before Nellie—he claimed were incompetent, and they left. The insurance company has voluminous notes on the subject."

Josie noticed that neither Sam nor John seemed surprised

that a private investigator had access to insurance company files. She'd remember this when Sam nagged her about her sloppy record-keeping—what wasn't written down couldn't, after all, be read. "He is very good at expressing himself when he's unhappy," was all she said.

"Well, he's happy with Nellie and, I assume, she with him. Except for vacations, she's been with him since then. And there's absolutely no way to connect her with Caroline—or her school."

"It was a long shot," Sam said, spearing a shrimp, dipping it in sauce, and popping it in his mouth.

"Yes." John paused to do the same.

"So that leaves Sandy, Layne, and Pam," Josie said, busy with a pile of crab salad.

"And Caroline herself," John added. "But I'll tell you about her last of all."

"Sandy first, since we've been assuming that she wasn't in any way connected with Caroline," Sam suggested.

"Not true. But the connection is very thin. Sandy worked for three years for a company up in Rhode Island. Two other women hired by that company were trained at Build Your Freedom."

"What?"

"What?"

Sam and Josie spoke as one.

"Build Your Freedom. That was the name of the school."

Sam glanced at Josie. "I don't think either of us knew that."

"I sure didn't. It's a weird name."

"I think the idea is that a woman who acquires the ability to build a home acquires a certain amount of personal freedom at the same time."

"Interesting," Sam said.

"Nuts," was Josie's assessment.

"It may be rather idealistic. But that doesn't matter now. The point is that Sandy unquestionably knew about the school. The women Lora spoke with could hardly stop raving about it—those are her words. So she assumed Sandy would have heard about it more than once if they worked together all those years."

"But?" Sam evidently heard something in his friend's voice that Josie didn't.

"Well, did she say anything about it when she met Caroline and Layne?" John asked Josie.

"Not that I know of, but maybe she didn't connect them to the school. I mean, even if they chatted about their school in Maine, it might have been a different school they were talking about."

"And possibly Sandy didn't ask," Sam added.

"You must not have spent a lot of time with Sandy. If she thinks it, she says it," Josie explained.

"So she would have asked."

"Yeah, probably."

"Then I suppose we have to count that as a connection," John said, writing in his notebook.

"But if they—the women Sandy worked with—were happy with the school and what it taught them and all, well then, I don't understand," Josie said, as confused as her statement. "What I mean is, just because there is a connection, doesn't mean there's a reason for Caroline's murder."

"Absolutely. We're just doing pure research here."

"So tell us what you learned about Pam next. Josie should find that interesting." Sam had been looking over John's shoulder and reading ahead in the notes.

"Of course. It's always interesting when someone lies."

"I suppose you two will get around to telling me what you're talking about eventually." Josie reached out for some bread.

"About a fair amount actually," John said. "To begin with, Sam tells me that the story Pam told about her background was . . . well, was somewhat similar to your own."

"Sort of," Josie admitted, a little surprised that Sam had talked about her background to John. Had the two of them discussed the possibility that she was the murderer?

"Not true. Pam is a carpenter just like her father and her two brothers. She was raised to be a part of the family business.

And probably would be right now if she could get along with her brothers' wives."

"What do they have to do with it?"

"The family company was divided equally between the three kids when the parents retired."

"Both of her parents were carpenters?" Josie asked, finding this almost as interesting as the fact that Pam had lied to her.

"No. The mother worked in the office. Bookkeeping, payroll, and the like. I guess there's a fair amount of that type of thing in your business."

"More than you can imagine," Josie said. "I sure wish I had a wife to do it for me."

"I . . ."

"Thanks, Sam, but every time I even let you peek into a file drawer, I worry that you'll have a heart attack."

John was grinning. "So the tradition of the wife in the office was passed from generation to generation. And the brothers' wives share that task. I would expect some conflict with each other, but apparently that isn't the problem. The problem is that Pam can't stand either of them. After some sort of big argument, she left and moved to a competing company. Which made no one happy—not even Pam apparently, as she didn't stay at that job long either. And she's been drifting from company to company ever since then."

"When was this?"

"A year or two ago. I'm sorry if I made it sound as though she'd spent years on the road. She worked for three different companies around New York City in that time. And then she went to Maine and ended up going to the school."

"That's odd, but not . . . um . . ." Josie looked at Sam. "What am I trying to say?"

"Ominous? Significant?" he suggested.

"I think it must be significant. After all, why would she end up in Maine pretending to be completely ignorant of carpentry skills and in need of school?"

"Excellent question," Sam said.

Josie agreed.

"That's what Lora was wondering. She's going to have

some connections in Maine check it out. They've been in contact already, of course."

"Getting information about Caroline, Layne, and the school," Josie guessed.

"Yes."

"I don't mean to sound crass, but who is paying for all this?" she asked. "Betty's worried about it."

"Their services are billed to my office."

"And you pass along those costs, right?"

"I don't think we have to worry about that this time."

"You lose money on your cases?" Josie asked, incredulous.

"I do a fair amount of pro bono work, yes."

"John and I have spoken about this, Josie. Everything's going to be taken care of."

"Well, okay." What could she do? She couldn't afford to pay for it herself, that was for sure. "So tell me what your detective—and her assistants—learned in Maine."

THIRTY

"**I**'LL TELL YOU everything I know. A lot of it won't be new, of course. But there are one or two things that will come as a big surprise, I think."

"Just tell," Sam insisted.

"Okay. Well, let's start with Layne. She's a multitalented woman. And if her carpentry skills are comparable to her writing skills, any crew she works on is lucky to have her."

"So she is a serious writer. I wondered," Josie admitted.

"She's a well-respected poet. Published in excellent journals and magazines. She's won two major awards."

"Is she still writing?" Sam asked. "I mean, is any of this current?"

"Yes." John flipped through his notes. "She had a series of poems published in the fall that received substantial acclaim in certain quarters."

"I assume she can't make a living as a poet?"

"No, but other people in her position have managed to carve out respectable careers teaching—and there's fellowship money available as well. As far as anyone could discover, Layne hasn't tried to live that particular lifestyle. It's strange. Although, of course, she might just prefer to work as a carpenter and teach building skills."

Josie got the impression that John didn't quite believe this was an option—for a sane person, at least.

"That's interesting."

Josie glanced over at Sam. Were he and John thinking the same thing? "Just because Layne made an unconventional career choice . . ."

"We're not implying anything here, Josie," Sam insisted.

"Actually, there is more to this, Sam. But I'd rather go into it when I tell you about the school."

"Oh. Fine. So go on."

"Well, Layne is the product of an upper-middle-class family. Both of her parents are physicians, and she went to exceptional private schools and a prestigious university. She was an excellent student in college, but like many other excellent students"—he glanced over at Josie before continuing—"both male and female, she made an unfortunate choice when it came to romance. She fell for another writer—a scholarship student from the wrong side of the tracks—her senior year of college. All plans for graduate school vanished fairly quickly, and she and this young man—also a poet although not, I'd guess, as talented—ended up living in a small town in Maine."

"The town where Caroline was living," Sam guessed.

"Yes. They were next-door neighbors, in fact. If you can call two houses on a dirt road about seven miles from the nearest town a neighborhood."

"Layne told me that she and Caroline didn't get along at first," Josie said.

"That may be true. Their backgrounds were different, of course. It wasn't as though Caroline was poor, but her family certainly couldn't provide for her the things that, in Layne's life, were automatic. Caroline was one of nine children. Her father was a mechanic in a garage and her mother a housewife. She only made it to college because of a generous scholarship—and she had to work her way through as well."

"How did she end up in Maine?" Josie asked.

"Well, for a scholarship student, she wasn't too practical. She majored in art, thinking that, somehow, a job in a gallery in a large city would just fall into her lap. It was foolish, of course. That type of job goes to young people with connections or—rarely—to interns from a few select art schools with enough money behind them to work for free and survive in the city. Caroline was neither and, after a few months spent knocking on doors that didn't open and filling out applications that were tossed in the wastebasket unread, she met another young man in a similar situation. Like Caroline, Ben was angry at the lack of recognition of what he thought of as his obvious artistic talent, and he also didn't have very much money. Maine looked like a pretty good solution to their particular problem. Land was cheap inland. There are a number of craftspeople who manage to create a life for themselves up there. Unfortunately, both Ben and Caroline had invested a lot of themselves in the concept of being serious artists and not selling out and becoming commercial. They were almost bound to starve from day one. And they would have if Caroline hadn't turned out to be more practical than even she, I imagine, suspected."

"You mean the school."

"Well, the house first. I don't know many people who, if they found themselves living in a dump with no money, would learn to fix it themselves," John said.

"I think you might be wrong there," said Sam. "What other choice did she have? Apparently job offers weren't just flooding in. She didn't have family to fall back on. And probably no friends who could afford to lend her enough money to get started somewhere else. Remember your years after law school? How many people had those sorts of resources?"

"And she probably didn't want to admit that she'd made a mistake anyway," Josie suggested.

Both men looked at her, then at each other. "You know, you're probably right," John said slowly.

"Probably," Sam agreed.

"So she started rebuilding her house and, after a while, became friendly with Layne. But apparently Ben and she didn't have much of a relationship, and she up and left him to return to the big city and try the art world again. Which she did—for a few years. But the second time wasn't a charm. She did, however, have a salable skill this time, and she hired herself out as an unlicensed carpenter. She even helped in the remodeling of a new art gallery down in Chelsea and then one on the waterfront in Boston before returning to Maine."

"Where she and Layne founded their school."

"Yes. She even brought a few students up to Maine with her from her last job in Boston."

"The story I was told is that the students she brought with her kept the school in business for a while and then, when they were really in desperate straits and almost forced to close, this mysterious donor appeared with money to keep them going."

"Which sounds more than a little fishy," Sam added to Josie's story.

"It is. In fact, it's a flat-out lie. The money isn't legitimate."

"What do you mean, *legitimate*?" Josie leaned forward.

"Is it unaccounted for? Or is it illegal?" Sam's question was more specific.

"We don't know yet. Lora's got people looking into it. She'll let me know when someone discovers something more. All we know for sure is that it was completely off the books. The school is a nonprofit organization and the records are pretty clear. Layne and Caroline were joint directors of it—as well as the founders and teachers. Caroline may have done all the bookkeeping, but she had an accountant who did their taxes. Apparently everything was completely legit. Until this mysterious donation.

"No record of where it came from. No one would actually even know it was there—nothing coming in. But there was evidence of it going out. A large amount of cash went out, in fact—long-overdue bills were paid, supplies ordered, there were very expensive ads placed in prominent media, and a public relations firm was hired for a few months to try to create some much-needed publicity for the school."

"And the money came in one chunk."

"We think so. I'm not sure of the . . . uh . . . nature of the source of this information. Lora . . . well . . ."

"She gave you the impression that you'd rather not know," Sam suggested.

"Exactly."

Josie looked at them. "I don't understand."

"When it comes to the law, ignorance is no excuse," Sam said.

"On the other hand, what you don't know, you can't lie about."

"But you are pretty sure this wasn't a legitimate donation from a foundation of some sort."

"Definitely not. There were no records kept. And up until this time, the financial records of the school are fine—complete and accurate—rather ordinary, in fact."

"Any foundation would require accurate record-keeping," Sam mused.

"Sure would. They have to pay their taxes just like everyone else. But to continue, the school got on its feet and has kept both Caroline and Layne gainfully employed. And, not incidentally, has quite a good reputation both in Maine and around New England."

"And Caroline and Layne are both content to be divorced from this Ben?" Sam asked.

"Apparently he's an excellent ex-husband. Layne dates, but no one in particular. And Caroline too."

"No, she's engaged. Layne told me."

"She told you Caroline was engaged?"

"Yes."

"When?"

"When did she tell me? It was the morning after Caroline died. Layne was going through the list of people she needed to call to let them know what had happened, and she mentioned Caroline's fiancé."

"Has he been here?" Sam asked.

"On the island? I don't think so."

"Who claimed the body?"

Josie stood up. "You know, I have no idea. Who would normally? I mean, if I dropped over dead, what would happen?"

"Your closest blood relations would be notified and expected to take care of things—burial and such."

"Not Tyler!"

"No, I don't think anyone would expect a teenager to carry that sort of burden," Sam reassured her.

"Probably your parents," John suggested.

Josie wondered what her parents would do if they got a call telling them that the daughter they hadn't seen in sixteen years had died, leaving them the trouble of disposing of her body.

Sam seemed to know what she was thinking. "I don't think you have to worry about that now," he insisted. "Besides, if you get married, it will be your husband who takes care of all those details."

If he outlives me, Josie thought. But she didn't say anything. Tyler and Hastings were crashing through the door, followed by gusts of freezing air, scented with the sharp smell of balsam.

"We brought you a wreath, Sam!"

"A big one!" Hastings added, although they were quite capable of seeing that for themselves.

"It's the biggest one on the lot this year. And we got it for half price."

Their prize was in danger of knocking down a display of imported champagne, and Sam jumped up to accept his gift and rescue his stock.

"Hey, food!"

"Help yourself."

"Where's the tree?" Josie asked.

"At home. We need a new tree stand, Mom. Remember we threw out the old one last year? It leaked. Remember?"

"Yes. I do." There was still a large stain on the floor under the window, which she had discovered when she took down the tree last January. She had spent much of the holiday wondering how the tree had managed to dry out and consume so much water simultaneously. "If you buy one at the hardware store, you can just charge it."

"Great. We'll do that on the way home, right after we finish our surprise."

"What surprise?" Josie knew she sounded less than enthusiastic, but she had been on the receiving end of her son's surprises in the past.

"It wouldn't be a surprise if you knew about it," Hastings explained seriously, as though that might be a new concept to her.

"You'll like it, Mom. It's a great surprise."

"That's what you said the time you decided to paint the refrigerator with leftover model airplane paint," she reminded him.

"I was just trying to make you happy. You were always

saying you hated the avocado green. Besides, I was just a kid then," Tyler protested.

"Ah yes, I remember." It was less than two years ago, in fact. It was easy to date—the replacement refrigerator was almost two years old.

"And this is really cool—it's a Christmas surprise!"

"Well, this is a good time of year for surprises," Sam agreed, examining the pink bow which decorated the surprise the boys had given him.

"Yeah. You'll like it, Mom. Risa thought it was a great idea. . . ."

"Although she didn't want us to do it to her house, remember?" Hastings said.

"But she was right. It looks more impressive . . ." Tyler glanced at his mother and stopped talking. "We'll stop at the hardware store on the way home and pick up the stand, okay?" he asked, changing the subject.

"Good."

"I'll stop over before dinner and we can get the tree up then, if you'd like," Sam suggested.

"Great!" The boys had finished every single bit of food during this short discussion, and Sam noticed Tyler's longing looks at the bags of chips hanging near the cases of beer.

"If you guys would like some Fritos or potato chips," he began to offer.

"Yeah. We're working hard. We're also thirsty."

"Then take some soda too." Sam recognized a hint when he heard one.

"I've got to get back to the job." Josie stood up.

"You're going to the house you're working on, right?" Tyler asked.

"Right." Josie suddenly realized that her surprise must be located at Island Contracting's office.

"Maybe you should spend a little time this afternoon finding out more about Caroline's phantom fiancé," Sam suggested.

"And I'll call when I hear from Lora again. . . . Unless that's her calling on the phone right now," John said, getting up to answer it.

THIRTY-ONE

JOSIE ARRANGED THE afternoon's work so that she and Layne were alone together. And then she popped the question.

"Did you ever get in touch with Caroline's fiancé?"

As Layne was holding a two-by-four for Josie to hammer in place, she wasn't in any position to leave, even if she did find it difficult to talk about her old friend.

"No, and I've been worrying about it . . . him. As far as I know, he has no idea she's dead."

"You didn't call him?"

"I have no idea who he is. And you know, the strangest thing is, Caroline's parents didn't even know she was engaged."

"Are you sure?"

"Yes. I asked the second time I called them. . . ."

"You called twice?"

"Three times. The first time just to let them know she had died. And then I called back later that day. I thought they might have some questions. Which they did, of course, although I didn't have too many answers. And I wanted to help out, you know, to ask if they needed me to do anything, to call anyone."

"And did they?"

"Yes. In fact, they asked if I would make sure all Caroline's friends in Maine knew about her death. So I . . . well, I didn't think there was anything odd about it. . . . I asked if they would like me to call her fiancé."

"And?"

"And they were shocked. It's just like I said. They had no idea she was engaged. I felt terrible. They were already so upset about her death. And then discovering that it was murder. And then to find out that she had become engaged and not told them about it. Well, I sure wished I had just kept my mouth shut."

"So you didn't know who to call."

"No. And I called our friends. You know, people we both knew in Maine. And no one had any idea who he is."

"She told you she was engaged and she didn't tell you who she was engaged to?"

"Yes. But, now that I think about it, I realize that she probably didn't even want to tell me about it."

"What do you mean?"

"Well, I've been trying to remember. It all started the day before Thanksgiving, I think. At least, that's when I noticed the first phone call. . . . It just wasn't like Caroline . . ." She stopped talking and thought for a moment.

"I guess I'd better explain. You see, Caroline and I ran the school out of an office that we shared in the house. Well, it's not really an office. It's the balcony studio in our house. It was originally planned as an artist's studio—Caroline's when she was living with Ben. And then, when she moved out and I moved in, I used it as a study."

"A place to write."

"Yes, but that didn't work, because it's open to the floor below, and frankly, I prefer to write in a place where I'm alone, and if people want to reach me, there's a door for them to knock on and let me know. I finally took over the second bedroom to write in. But then Ben and I got a divorce. And when Caroline came back, she needed to use that room. She thought I should move back to the studio, but if that room hadn't been private when Ben was there, you should have seen it when we started the school. We pretty much ran everything out of the house—we even fed all the students their meals there. There was no way I could write there. I moved my typewriter into a corner of my bedroom and that's where I wrote—and still write when I have the time."

"And the studio became your office?"

"Yes, and it's a great office space for the same reasons it was a rotten place for me to write. You can sit up there and order supplies or do paperwork or whatever and keep an eye on what's going on in the house, or peek out the window to where the students are practicing framing in or whatever."

"You were starting to tell me about a phone call," Josie reminded her. "The day before Thanksgiving."

"It may have started earlier than that, and I just didn't recognize it. But it was the Wednesday before Thanksgiving. We had closed the school for the winter a week earlier, and we were going to leave Maine in a week or two. But we had invited all our friends and neighbors in for a huge Thanksgiving dinner, and we'd been getting ready—shopping and cooking and cleaning—for almost a week. You know how long it takes to create a big dinner party like that."

"Yes. Of course," Josie lied.

"Well, I love to cook, and I was downstairs in the kitchen making pies that day and I noticed that Caroline was on the phone and she was upset. Very upset."

"You could hear her?"

"Not really, but I could see her, and she was agitated and angry—furious actually. Really, it was unusual. I didn't want to interrupt, and she could have easily called down to me if there was anything I could have done, so I just decided to wait until she hung up and talk to her then. The fact that I had to get six pies in and out of the oven in an hour if I was going to stay on schedule probably had something to do with that decision.

"Well, she finally hung up and came downstairs. I don't remember now exactly what I said to her. Probably something about how upset she seemed and was there anything I could do. And she blew up at me. I was shocked. Caroline had a temper, but when she got mad, there was always a reason. And not something minor either."

"What did she say?"

"Well, first she accused me of spying on her, listening in on her private conversations. And then she started talking about how I didn't appreciate her and everything she did. That I was always cooking and doing the fun stuff while she did the real work, and without her there wouldn't even be a school. I was shocked."

"Because of what she said?"

"Yes. And because it was completely untrue. Completely. And we both knew it. We were always talking about what a good team we made. What I was good at, Caroline wasn't, and what she did well, I didn't. That sort of thing."

"Did she explain the phone call—that was what had upset her, right?" Josie asked, wondering what this had to do with Caroline's fiancé.

"No. She didn't explain anything. She just said she was going to go for a walk, and stamped out of the house and off toward the path through the woods and down to our pond. When she came back, it was almost evening. She apologized for yelling at me, didn't explain a damn thing, and got to work getting ready for our company."

"What does this have to do with her engagement?" Josie finally asked.

"It's just the beginning of the story. You see, the day after Thanksgiving, I walked in on another phone conversation that she was having—this time in her bedroom—and she was upset again. I backed out immediately, but I was curious, wondering what was going on. And this time, when she came out she said she was having man trouble. Well, we'd both been through a lot of that over the years, and I just made sure I gave her a lot of space so she and this guy could work out whatever their problem was."

"But you still didn't know who he was."

"Nope. And I didn't ask. I knew she would tell me in her own time. But things got worse. I realized Caroline was running to answer the phone when it rang, and then, when she hung up, she'd be upset. I might not even have noticed all this if we hadn't been getting ready to leave Maine. We were spending more time together than we usually do."

"And then?"

"Well, she was so upset. One night, when a call had interrupted dinner for the second night in a row and she was too upset to eat, I just asked her why she was bothering with this guy—what was so special about him that she would keep letting him upset her like this."

"Good question."

"And the answer was the one it always is—she said she was in love with this man—engaged to be married to him."

"Weren't you surprised?"

"Yes, but not shocked, if you know what I mean. Caroline and I lived together, but we're adults. We didn't intertwine our lives too much, and we gave each other a lot of space. It might have been unusual that she had met a man, fallen in love, and gotten engaged without me knowing, but not impossible." Layne stopped talking and looked down at the work she was doing.

"It hurt your feelings," Josie guessed. But enough to be a motive for Layne to kill Caroline?

"Yes. Yes, it did. But maybe I should have expected it. Caroline and I were growing apart."

"Really?" Josie hammered away. They were setting in the new doors, and she just hoped Layne would keep talking.

"Yes. You know, it was such fun in the beginning. Starting the school was Caroline's idea, and we felt like we were breaking through barriers, opening new frontiers for women. Does that sound stupid?"

"Nope. And you probably were." Josie resisted the urge to get on her hobbyhorse and talk about women in construction.

"Well, we thought so. We were so excited every single step of the way. When the original bunkhouses were built, we could hardly contain our joy. Really. And even the struggles of those early years were okay. More of a challenge than anything else. Know what I mean?"

"Yes." And this time she did.

"There were some really tough times. We really believed that we were going to have to close down the school at one point. No students and not enough money either to pay our bills or to advertise and let prospective students even know that we existed.

"And then we got that anonymous donation, and I thought we were set for life."

"And you weren't?"

"We were. . . . At least, I guess we were. But it changed everything. Suddenly it wasn't Caroline and I against the world as much as Caroline doing the paperwork and me teaching the classes and . . . Oh, I don't know how to explain it. It doesn't make any sense."

Josie thought that perhaps it did. It was the same thing that made couples who had raised children and paid off mortgages and slaved to have some sort of security and peace of mind get divorced after they had achieved success. Once the school was a success, once they weren't fighting shoulder to shoulder against life, they weren't together. And apparently Caroline was becoming serious about someone else. . . . Josie suddenly realized that Layne might have been facing the possibility of a future alone. That Caroline might have gone off to get married and left Layne to run the school alone—or sell it—or whatever. She would have to ask John what the possible options were. She glanced under her eyelashes at Layne. The other woman was obviously upset.

"It sounds like the last few years haven't been easy." But had they been difficult enough to drive Layne to murder?

"I don't mean to make them sound all bad—it's more that things changed. And I'm not sure I realized just how much until Caroline was killed and I started thinking. You know, I understood exactly how her parents felt when they heard Caroline was engaged. I felt badly too."

"Did you ask about this man? What he did? Where she had met him?"

"Yes. She . . . she didn't want to tell me."

"Did she give you any reason for that?"

"No. But she said I would understand soon. That she wasn't telling me because she had a surprise for me."

"Like a Christmas present?"

"She didn't say it like that at all. She said it like the surprise wouldn't be very pleasant."

THIRTY-TWO

PAM HAD COME in then, offering to help with their work, and Josie couldn't ask any more questions. Not that she was sure exactly what to ask, as she was explaining to Sam on the phone a few minutes later.

"I have to get back to work," she insisted, after giving him a brief synopsis of the conversation.

"Just a few questions," Sam insisted.

"Okay . . ."

"First, do you really think Layne is telling the truth? Is it possible that she killed Caroline and then made up this story about a fiancé to complicate things?"

"You may be right, Sam." Josie spoke slowly, but she was thinking furiously. "And maybe she not only made up the fiancé, but also the conflict. Perhaps she did kill Caroline, and now she's trying to set this fictional person up as the primary suspect in the murder. If, I mean, *when* Betty gets out of jail and they have to find a suspect, here's this unknown man that Caroline was always fighting with the last few weeks of her life. He sounds like the perfect suspect to me. You know, there could even end up being this nationwide search for the killer. He might even end up on *America's Most Wanted*—and not even exist!"

"Do you think maybe, just maybe, you've spent a bit too much time watching the type of television shows that are banned at Tyler's school?"

"Sam! I'm trying to figure this thing out. I'm . . . I'm thinking out loud. Brainstorming. And it might be true! You know you keep saying Layne is the most logical suspect."

"I'm willing to admit that I don't have a better solution to the mystery," he said. "Do you have a minute? There are a few more things bothering me."

"Shoot."

"Is it possible that either Pam or Sandy was listening in on your conversation with Layne?"

"It's possible, but I doubt it. They were working together in the bathroom, putting down the mud floor, and it's unlikely that either of them would stop until they were finished. That mud is pretty fast-drying. But I could check to make sure. Do you still consider them suspects?"

"I haven't eliminated anybody. Do you think you could find out a little more about Pam? But be careful. We know she lied to you—as well as to Caroline and Layne—about her background, and she just might think that keeping her past a secret is worth killing over."

Josie nodded. "You're right. She could be the killer. Well, I'll ask more questions and see you tonight at home. What time is Risa expecting us?" Josie, always hungry, felt her stomach grow larger at the thought of one of her landlady's delicious meals.

"She said early. So I suppose that means around six-thirty—do you want me to pick you up? I told Tyler that I'd be at your place around five to help him put up the Christmas tree, but I could do that and then come back for you."

"Nope. I'll drive home. I have a few errands to do tonight on the way. I'll be fine."

"Oh, and Josie, you might want to drive by your office on the way home."

"I fed the cat this morning . . ." she began.

"No need to go inside. Just drive by. See you later."

Was it her imagination, or had Sam been chuckling when he hung up?

She looked up to find Sandy leaning against the brand-new doorjamb, cleaning her fingernails with a Swiss Army knife. "Were you waiting to talk to me?"

"Yeah." She flipped the knife closed and slipped it into her pocket. "Sorry to be so disgusting. That damn mud is impossible to wash away once it dries up."

"So you're finished in the bathroom?"

"Yeah. The tilers can come on in. Then I'll set the bowl and get the sink hooked up."

"Betty and I usually do the tile work," Josie said. "I hadn't even considered hiring the work out." She sighed. "Shit."

"I can do plumbing and electrical, but tile is beyond me. And this isn't an ordinary tile job either. Wall-to-wall and floor-to-ceiling. One mistake and the Professor will get vertigo every time he uses that room."

"Shit." It was repetitive, but appropriate. She knew of one other good tiler on the island. And he was taking his grandchildren to Disney World for Christmas.

"You might ask Layne if she's ever done any tiling. Who knows? They might have taught tile-laying at that school. I don't think Pam can do it though. She would have mentioned it to me. She's mentioned everything else. I'll bet a hundred bucks she was called chatty Pammy in grade school."

Josie, who had a strict policy against gossiping with employees about employees, couldn't resist grinning. "And she didn't mention doing tile work?"

"I don't think so. After a while, it's easy to stop listening. I always do when I'm bored. Which reminds me . . ." Sandy did something entirely uncharacteristic—she hesitated.

"Yes?"

"I've been thinking that I should tell you something. About that school in Maine."

"Yes?"

"I told you I'd never heard of it before. But I think I had. It's sort of like with Pam. I stop paying attention when people talk too much. You see, I used to work with some women who had gone to that school Layne and Caroline ran. They were real flakes. Feminists. The kind that make me wish I were a man. You know the type."

"No. I don't."

"Always talking about equality. And the female agenda. And abortion rights. And goddesses, for god's sake! I thought I

would throw up one day when they were talking about the need
to get in touch with your own body, and some woman claimed
you weren't liberated until you'd tasted your own menstrual
blood."

"Is that why you didn't say anything when Caroline and
Layne explained about the school?"

"God, yes. I was afraid they were like that too. But Layne, at
least, seems like a sensible person."

"You didn't think Caroline was?"

"Sort of. But nervous, you know?"

"No, I didn't get that impression of her at all," Josie said.

"Well, maybe it's just a case of selective memory. You know
how, when terrible things happen, you go back over all the
details and suddenly things seem significant that didn't at the
time?"

"Yeah. Like what? Did something strike you as odd about
that morning?"

Sandy thought for a moment. "It's pretty well known on the
island that you investigate murders. I'd heard about it even
before Caroline's murder."

"Really?" Josie couldn't help but be flattered.

"Yeah. Frankly, I thought it was just a crock when I first
heard about it, but apparently you've actually accomplished
something in the past."

So much for being flattered. "Yes."

"And you probably don't think Betty killed Caroline."

"Of course not."

"Which means you must be thinking it's Layne."

"Layne?"

"They were friends—or maybe enemies. But certainly the
person who killed Caroline knew her."

"Pam knew her," Josie said.

"Yeah, I thought about that. You think she was in town
before she claims to have been?"

"I have no idea. You were telling me about the day of the
murder. Something you remembered."

"Yeah. Well, I don't think you want to hear this."

"Why not?"

"Because I was with Layne all morning. Because she'd had some sort of fight with Caroline before they came to work. At least that's the impression I got. . . ."

"That's what Layne told you?"

"No. That's what Caroline told me."

"I don't get it. What did Caroline say?"

"I've been trying to remember exactly."

"Yeah, that's good."

"Caroline and Layne had just gotten to work. They drove to work together, right?"

"Probably."

"Well, they came in together and dumped their stuff on the floor and started to argue."

"About what?"

"I have no idea. And when I walked into the room, they shut up immediately."

"You didn't hear anything?"

"Just enough to know that they were both unhappy about something."

"Unhappy or angry?"

"Both, I guess. Look, I don't have anything against Layne or Caroline. And to tell you the truth, I don't want to get involved."

"But Betty shouldn't be in jail. She didn't kill anybody."

"I heard she had confessed." Sandy looked suspicious.

"She just did that because she thought I was the murderer," Josie explained without thinking.

"Why?"

"She thought she saw me putting poison in Caroline's food—I didn't, of course, but that's what she thought."

"And I'm thinking that Layne and Caroline were arguing the morning of Caroline's death. Arguing about that damn school."

"What about the school?"

"I don't know. Something about some policy. At least that's what Caroline said. Probably whether or not they were going to accept women who weren't liberated or something."

"A school policy? That's all you remember?"

"That's all I heard. Caroline was talking when they walked

in the room, and when she saw me, she shut up. And Layne said something to the Professor's aide—Nellie—and everyone ended up exchanging recipes for Christmas cookies, for heaven's sake."

Josie was amused by Sandy's dislike of both the liberated and the domestic, but she had no time to consider it now. "Is there anything else about that morning that you think might be significant for some reason? You said you were with Layne the entire time?"

"Yeah. I know you don't want to hear this. But we all hung around listening to Layne and Nellie discussing the differences between molasses with sulfur and molasses without or something else completely insignificant, and then Caroline said something about getting to work. And then she and Betty went off to start ripping out the walls in the bedroom and Layne and I started on the bathroom."

"Excuse me? You and Layne and Caroline and Betty?"

"Yup. I think maybe you were busy talking to the Professor . . ."

"Not an unusual occurrence," Josie muttered.

"Well, Caroline suggested to Betty that the two of them work together, so that left Layne and me."

"Strange though, wasn't it? I mean, usually Layne and Caroline would work as a team."

"I thought about that later. At the time, it didn't seem all that unusual. I mean, I knew they had been arguing. And if I thought about it at all, I would have assumed that it was temporary. You and Betty usually work together and I probably would have expected things to change when you came in."

"And they didn't?"

"No, I think you joined Betty and Caroline for a while and then Layne and me for a bit. And then there was that delivery . . ."

"And you were with Layne the entire morning?"

"Yeah. So if she put poison in Caroline's food, she must have done it before they left home. That's what you're thinking, isn't it?"

It was. And she didn't see any reason to deny it.

THIRTY-THREE

"I CAN'T BELIEVE IT."

There was no one around to hear her, but she said it again regardless.

"I cannot believe it." Then Josie grinned. "Those kids. I can't believe it." And she put her truck in gear and headed off in the direction of the Fish Wish bait shop. She had finally decided to get Sam a heavy-duty surf fishing pole for Christmas, and she wanted to make sure they were holding the one she had picked out. While she was there, she'd buy a few crab traps for Hastings. Apparently his parents owned a house on the bay out at Montauk, but he'd never done any crabbing. It wasn't the type of luxurious gift he was accustomed to getting, but he still might enjoy using them next summer.

And she supposed she might as well stop at the hardware store and pick up Betty's toolbox. Although she wished now that she had selected something else to give her. If she hadn't decided on a toolbox, if Betty hadn't mentioned liking the interior of the one she already owned, if she hadn't decided to check it out the morning Caroline was killed, if Betty hadn't seen her doing that very thing . . . then Betty wouldn't be in jail, arrested for murder.

Josie hopped down from the cab of her truck and stopped dead. That wasn't right! She wasn't right! Betty had been arrested because Mike had thought Caroline accused her of the murder, because Caroline had said her name just before she died.

Why?

She was asking Sam the same question a few minutes later.

229

"Because Mike Rodney is an idiot. I thought we both agreed about that," he answered.

"So let me ask you another question." Josie pulled her jacket closer around her neck. "Why the hell are we standing out here in the cold?"

"Because Tyler and Hastings have a surprise for you."

"Another one?" She had a thought—a dreadful one. "Sam, they didn't wrap lights around the house like they did down at my office, did they? I mean, the office is sort of cute all lit up in the night, but I really don't think Risa would appreciate . . ."

"Why do you think your office is decorated? When Tyler told Risa about his plan to trim the house with lights, she suggested that it would be better down at Island Contracting's office."

"Smart woman. So what's going on here?"

"Just one more minute. They were almost ready when I left . . . There!"

And her second-floor living room window was illuminated with the glow of her very own Christmas tree.

"Oh, Sam, it's beautiful. You all decorated the tree."

"The boys did it with very little help from me. I just made sure it was firmly in the stand and insisted they make sure the lights were safe. Those two did all the rest. They're waiting upstairs for lots of compliments."

"And they're going to get them," she called back over her shoulder as she ran toward the house.

Tyler and Hastings were, as Sam had promised, waiting for her. One on either side of the tree, they were both grinning. Hastings looked slightly embarrassed as well.

"It's wonderful! It is absolutely, perfectly, truly, fabulously wonderful! Thank you so much!" And she hugged her son and then his embarrassed guest. And then her son again.

"We hung up those shell ornaments that were sitting on top of the microwave," Tyler pointed out.

"They look nice, don't they? I saw one at the Professor's house and thought I could make them myself. So I collected the shells, spray-painted them, and then glued on the ribbons so they could be tied on the tree." Josie didn't admit it, but she had felt more than a little like Martha Stewart while doing it—a new feeling for her.

"And we hung up those origami birds that Tyler made when he was little. They were a little squashed, but he insisted," Hastings pointed out, punching his friend on the shoulder.

"I knew you'd be upset if we didn't use them," Tyler explained earnestly to his mother.

"I would have been," Josie assured him. She took a step back and examined the tree more carefully. "It smells just like Christmas, and it really looks wonderful. And different . . . Tyler, you bought new ornaments! Wherever did you find this little hammer? And the little saw! And . . . Oh, I've never seen anything so cute!" A tiny red pickup truck, decorated with an even tinier wreath, was hanging from an upper limb.

"Sam bought them, Ma. He brought them over when he came this afternoon."

"And don't forget all those little red hearts. They're an early Christmas present from my mother. Bloomingdale's," Sam added. Josie understood it was a reference to one of his mother's favorite haunts. Sam, arms crossed, smile on his face, was leaning against the open doorway.

"Oh, Sam . . ." He had remembered what she'd said about her Christmas tree. In the midst of everything—Caroline's murder, Betty's arrest, John Jacobs coming to town, his mother and Tyler's early arrival—in spite of all these things, he'd remembered what she'd said and done something about it. What could she say? She was so happy.

"Sammy!"

It was Carol.

"Sammy, dinner's ready!"

She was yelling up the stairs from Risa's apartment. Josie grinned at her son. "Guess I'm not the only mother who embarrasses her son to death."

"Guess not," Sam agreed. "Turn off those lights, guys, and let's all head downstairs."

"I need to wash up. Tell Risa I'll be down in a few minutes." Josie hurried to her bedroom. As usual, her clothing was tossed all over the place. Additionally, there were piles of cookbooks everywhere. And lists. But Josie, taking off her filthy work clothes and, mindful of her son's visit, throwing them in the hamper, felt something begin to nudge the edges of her mind. There was something . . .

The phone rang before she could figure it out.

"Josie? John Jacobs here. I have some more information. About the school. And I think it's a motive for murder."

Josie listened for ten minutes and then hung up, after assuring him that she would pass on the information to Sam. John was at the jail and would let Betty know that things were moving forward.

"Who was that?"

Josie, still trying to assimilate what she'd just learned on the phone, almost jumped into the air, the voice frightened her so. "Sam! How long have you been here?"

"Just long enough to hear you telling John that you'd let me know what he said. That was John, wasn't it?"

"Yes." She reached out for the jade earrings Sam had given her for her birthday.

"And are you going to tell me what he said?"

"Dinner . . ."

"Risa is busy stuffing your son and his friend with bruschetta slathered with cheeses and olives and some sort of paste that Tyler seems to love. They won't even notice if we're a few minutes late."

"So . . ."

"So talk."

"Well, Lora Smith's contacts in Maine checked in, and it turns out that the school is about to be involved in a scandal." She knelt down on the floor as she spoke.

"The endowment?"

"Exactly . . ."

"Josie, what are you doing?"

"Looking for my other shoe. Ah . . . there it is!" She pulled a green suede loafer out from under her bed and waved it in the air. "Think your mother will approve?"

"They're devastatingly chic," he said, completely disinterested. "So talk!"

"There was no anonymous donor . . ."

"I was wondering about that. The whole thing sounded just a bit too convenient. You need money. You get money. The world just doesn't work that way, not in my experience. Not legally."

"Well, you're right this time. According to this detective, the money wasn't a legal donation. In fact, if Caroline had lived, she could have been arrested for fraud."

"Where did it come from?"

"Layne's family. . . ."

"And Layne never said anything about it . . ."

"Sam, if you want to hear this story, you're going to have to let me tell it. Layne didn't tell us about the money coming from her family for the simple reason that she didn't know. Apparently Caroline contacted Layne's family without letting her know about it—for the excellent reason that she pretended to be Layne when she contacted them."

"You're kidding!"

"Nope. Amazing, isn't it? Caroline was desperate for cash to keep the school going, and she knew that Layne's family had money. She also knew that Layne wouldn't ask for money." Josie paused for a second. "I understand that. I never went to my family. If they didn't approve of my lifestyle, I certainly couldn't ask them to support it. Besides, it's important to do things by yourself."

Sam just nodded.

"Well, Caroline wrote a letter to Layne's father, explained the situation, and asked for the cash. And then signed the letter as though it was from Layne. They had known each other for years and years. They'd probably exchanged stories about their families many, many times. And they were living in the same house. It wouldn't have been difficult. As long as Caroline made sure she picked up the mail, and as long as she made sure they didn't call the house . . ."

"How did she manage that?"

"Simple. She just wrote, as Layne, explaining that it was very important that Caroline not get wind of where the money was coming from, and asked that any communications about this be in writing, and to her. And her father apparently honored this. There is absolutely no evidence that Layne has any idea about any of this. When her plan began to fall apart, she created a fictional fiancé to explain the phone calls to the house."

"How much money was it?"

"Seventy thousand dollars."

"And was it a check?"

"I don't know. John didn't say. Would it make any difference?"

"Only if she forged Layne's signature to cash it."

"She must have forged her signature on the letter to ask for the money, right?"

"Probably."

"So if she did it once, it was just easier the second time."

"And there's no evidence that Layne suspected any of this?"

"None. But that was going to change apparently."

"Why?"

"Layne's father has cancer. This will probably be his last Christmas. Both Layne and Caroline knew that. Remember, you told me that Layne was going to visit her family early next year. And when he dies, there's no way Layne is not going to know that she received part—even if it's only a small part—of her inheritance ahead of time."

"Interesting. Very interesting." Sam walked over to the window and looked out onto the deserted street below. Snow was beginning to fall. "Maybe Tyler and Hastings should think about sledding rather than surfing if the weather doesn't clear up."

"Hmm." She knew he was thinking things through. She wondered if he was coming to the same conclusions as she was. "It is puzzling though," he started, turning back to her. "John said that the school was jointly owned, right?"

"Yup."

"And if something happened to one of them, the other would own it in its entirety."

"Right."

"So the school now belongs to Layne."

"Yes."

"But it doesn't make any sense. The story you just told means that there's a reason for Caroline to kill Layne. Right?"

Josie just sat on the edge of her bed, staring at the green suede shoes on her feet.

"Josie? Am I making sense? Do you think I'm right?"

Her answer came slowly, in a voice almost too soft for him to hear. "I think I know what happened, Sam. I think Betty was right. I think maybe I did kill Caroline."

THIRTY-FOUR

"**J**OSIE, I DON'T know where you're on your way to, but I'm going with you."

She didn't want to take the time to argue. "Fine, but we should stop by Risa's and explain that we'll be late for dinner."

"I don't think I want any dinner, Sam." She was so worried, she didn't even notice the look he gave her.

"Look, I'll tell Risa that we're busy and you go ahead and get into the car."

She grabbed her coat and ran down the stairs without another word.

"Where . . . ?"

"Layne's house," she answered the question she hadn't allowed him to ask, and added the address.

They arrived in minutes. "Do you think she's home?" Sam asked, flinching as Josie slammed the car door into the curb.

"Maybe. And Pam is staying with Layne. But they don't matter. It's Caroline who matters." She hurried up the sidewalk, Sam following close behind.

Layne and Pam, caught in the middle of a pepperoni pizza, were surprised by Josie's request to look at Caroline's room, but willing to accommodate.

"I suppose I should have thought about packing everything up and sending it on to her family, but frankly, I just haven't had the heart to do it," Layne said sadly, opening the door to the messy room.

"Yes. And we thought about cleaning up, of course, but it didn't seem respectful somehow," Pam added, following them down the hallway. "Do you want my help with whatever you're looking for? I'm pretty good at finding things."

"I think," Sam said slowly, "we're fine. We'll call if we need anything."

"Good, because . . ." The door closed in Pam's face, muffling the end of her sentence.

"So what are we looking for?" Sam asked Josie. She was standing completely still, staring at the bed as though mesmerized by the hideous coverlet lying bunched up on the lumpy mattress.

"Poison. But I assume that she would have hidden it, don't you?"

"Poison? Josie, what are you talking about? Are you saying you think Caroline killed herself? Committed suicide because she didn't want to be caught and charged with stealing money from Layne's family . . . from Layne . . . with fraud . . . for heaven's sake, there must be dozens of things she could be charged with. But still . . ."

"Yes. I think she killed herself, but I don't think she meant to. Sam, let's just see if we can find the poison. It wouldn't take too much, would it? I mean, we're probably looking for something pretty small. And I suppose she might not even have had a whole lot extra—just a second dose in case the first didn't work."

"I . . ."

"Don't ask me any more questions, Sam. If I don't find anything, I'm completely off track, and I'd rather just not talk about it."

Sam leaned against the doorway. "I was just going to say that I'll stay right here so you're not interrupted while you work."

But forty-five minutes later even Josie had to admit that if there was poison in this room, she sure couldn't find it.

"What about the kitchen?" Sam asked. "Isn't it possible that if Caroline wanted to hide the poison it would be in some of that food only she liked?"

"No, I don't think so. In the first place, Layne might have gone into anything in the kitchen. And in the second place, something like that would lead anyone investigating right to Caroline. If it's not here, I would think it's in some neutral place. Someplace like . . ." Josie stopped talking and opened her eyes wide. "Sam, I know where it is. It's hanging on the Christmas tree in the living room!"

"I'm not going to ask. Just lead the way," Sam said, opening the door for her.

Layne and Pam were sitting at opposite ends of the couch. Pam was reading aloud from the newspaper. Layne didn't appear to be paying much attention. They both looked up when Josie and Sam reappeared.

"Your tree," Josie began, walking straight up to it. The lights weren't on, and apparently no one was watering it. Needles were beginning to fall on the floor and some of the boughs were drooping. "Your decorations. You told me Caroline was making some of them right before she died."

Layne smiled gently. "Yes. We always tried to make something new each year. This year Caroline was working on those little yellow felt stars—the embroidered ones. She saw the design in a magazine and copied it. There are three, I think. She started making them right after Thanksgiving, but the pattern is rather complicated and each one took quite a while. . . . Why are you taking them?"

"I think they have something to do with her death," Josie said. "If I'm right, they're evidence. And if I'm not, I'll bring them back as soon as possible. Okay?"

"Okay." Layne looked confused. "I don't understand, but if it will help answer some questions . . ."

"I think it will help answer all our questions," Josie said gently. "And I don't think you have to worry. What happened . . . it was horrible . . . but it's over. I don't think anyone else is going to have to suffer."

Layne just nodded. And for once Pam kept quiet too.

"Come on, Sam," Josie said, and they left without saying good-bye.

"We need to cut into these things to see if they have poison in them," Josie said, getting into his car, the ornaments still in her hands.

"Josie, if there's digitalis in those things, I don't want it anywhere near my home, and you don't want it in yours either. Let's go over to the police station. John's probably there, and you might as well explain what you think happened as few times as possible."

"Fine." She didn't say any more until they were in the police station, standing around a table set up outside Betty's cell, shreds of embroidery thread, felt, and cotton batting on one side of the table, a tiny vial of powder on the other.

"Is that digitalis?" Josie asked.

"It will have to be analyzed, but probably. I can't imagine why Caroline would be hiding anything else in a Christmas tree ornament, can you?" Sam asked.

"Frankly, I can't quite imagine why you think Caroline is the person who hid this," John stated flatly. "If she wanted to kill herself, she sure picked a pretty dramatic way to do it. Unless you're both thinking she did it in such a way that Layne would be accused of murder intentionally. Only, of course, she didn't have any idea how incompetent the local police would turn out to be."

"That's not what happened, is it?" Betty spoke up for the first time, her face paler than Josie had ever seen it. "It . . . it had to do with my . . . with my Christmas present. Didn't it?"

"Exactly. It's my fault Caroline is dead," Josie said, reaching through the bars and grasping her friend's hands.

"Josie, you said that before. I think it's time to explain everything," Sam insisted, putting an arm around her shoulder.

"It's simple," she answered. "You see, Caroline didn't want to get caught, and the only way she could prevent that from happening was to kill Layne. That way, she would inherit the school and no one would ever know that the money hadn't come to Layne when the school was in crisis."

"So she poisoned her own food and ate it? What sort of incompetent murderer was she?"

"She poisoned food that she thought Layne would eat—there were two different containers. One was poisoned and one not, right?"

"Yes."

"And they each had their container in their own toolbox. But then I moved them. I moved Layne's and Caroline's toolboxes to get to Betty's. And Caroline ended up eating the poison that she had intended for Layne. Simple. If I hadn't moved the boxes that morning, Caroline would still be alive . . ."

"But Layne would be dead," Betty reminded her. "You saved Layne's life."

"And the person who died was the murderer. There's a natural justice to that," John reminded her.

"I know," Josie said, trying not to cry. "I know, but somehow that doesn't make it a whole lot easier."

Before anyone else could reassure her, the door to the room slammed open, and Mike Rodney Senior entered, his face scarlet with rage.

"What the hell is this? A goddamn Christmas party in a jail cell? Where's my idiot son? And what the hell is the prettiest girl on the island doing in a cell and that pain in the butt Josie Pigeon doing outside of one?"

THIRTY-FIVE

"**J**OSIE, I'VE GOT to admit it. I never thought you'd manage to cook a meal like this one."

"Betty's right, Mom! This is great. We sure don't get meat like this at school!"

"Bella, cara. Bella!" Risa called from the middle of the table.

Or actually, from the middle of the three card tables which were lined up and, along with the Christmas tree, filling Josie's living room. The china, cutlery, and crystal didn't match. In fact, most of the crystal was cheap glass. The napkins were paper, the crust on the mushroom pie was scorched, and the large wooden salad bowl was cracked.

But Josie thought everything looked wonderful. She smiled at Sam, seated at the opposite end of the table. His mother intercepted the look.

"It would be a perfect Christmas if only we had an engagement to celebrate," she hinted broadly.

"Oh, but we do," Josie insisted.

"We . . ."

"What? . . ."

"Cara . . ."

Tyler, Risa, and Carol rose as one.

"We should be congratulating Betty and John," Sam quickly added.

"We . . . we got engaged last night after the parade," Betty admitted, a shy smile appearing on her pretty face.

"I had to ask her," John said. "She gave me a bag of candy."

241

"Since she threw candy to everyone on the island, I don't think you had much reason to feel singled out." Sam grinned.

Betty had replaced the Santa who usually rode the fire truck through the streets tossing candy to the island's children. The cheers which greeted her had been even more enthusiastic than those usually reserved for jolly old Saint Nick. And she had been looking her prettiest, flushed with excitement and relief, when John met her back at the firehouse. He had proposed immediately. And had been accepted. So today they were cele-brating more than Christmas with the champagne Sam had brought from his store.

"Things are going to be different down at Island Contracting once Betty leaves the island," Risa said.

Josie glanced under the tree at the Swatch Betty had given her. Then at the Timex which Layne, Sandy, and Pam had all chipped in to buy her. Then at the wall clock shaped like a house which had come from the Professor. And at the elegant little gold watch Risa had given her. As well as at the chic man's-style watch from Barneys that had accompanied Carol to the island. And up at the large grandfather clock that Tyler had spent the last few months making in his school's shop classes. (And which had been sitting in Sam's neighbor's house for the last few weeks, mailed to her office early by a suitemate's parents from their home in Massachusetts.) And, finally, down at her wrist to the Rolex Sam had ordered at the local jewelry shop. "Sure things will be different, I won't have any excuses to be late anymore."

Everyone chuckled.

"It was nice of the Professor to give you a Christmas pres-ent," Betty said. "After all, it certainly wasn't your standard remodeling job."

"True. But he really didn't expect it to be an easy job. We had a long talk the night before last, when we did the final walk-though on the job, and he gave me the last payment on our contract. He's really wonderful. Do you know, he hired Island Contracting after researching all the various options on the island? Someone told him about our policy of helping out women who need a second chance. He said the time he spent in rehab taught him just how many people wake up one day and discover that a second chance is just what they need. And he's also discovered just how rarely those second chances come along in life." She stuck her fork in her salad and smiled. "He's really a nice man. I hope you have professors like him when you go to college, Tyler."

"Actually, Ms. Pigeon, Tyler and I are thinking of skipping college," Hastings explained earnestly. "We think world travel is probably a more educational alternative, don't you?"

It was Christmas. Most of her son's harebrained schemes never got past the thinking stage. Why worry? Josie just smiled. "Well, I'm sure glad the Professor liked his house. We did a good job."

"Thanks to Pam and Layne and Sandy," Betty said. "I was amazed how much you'd all accomplished when I got out of jail. And Layne, at least, must have been awfully upset. First Caroline dies and then she discovers that Caroline had been trying to poison her."

"Yes. She was heading to her parents' home the last time I saw her. Her father's condition has gotten worse." And Josie frowned. "On the other hand, Pam was feeling pretty lousy too."

"She deserved to," Sam said. "Lying all that time. First to everyone at the school about her background and then about how she just happened to be on the island right after Caroline died, instead of admitting that she had come here at Caroline's invitation."

"Why did Caroline invite her anyway?" Betty asked.

"I suppose so she could tell us what a wonderful person Caroline was. Pam seemed to have a slight case of hero worship there. And, of course, anything she said she would have said over and over and over."

"Yeah, there's a kid like that at school," Tyler said, not particularly interested.

"Yeah. I read how repeating yourself is a sign of insecurity," Hastings supported his friend. "This person you're talking about probably didn't have enough self-esteem. Self-esteem is very important. Tyler and I saw it on TV the other night."

"Have you boys tried out the computer program I gave you?" Carol asked innocently.

"Yeah, it's really cool. Thank you," Tyler said.

"But we haven't even opened some of the boxes my parents sent," Hastings reminded him.

"I think we're supposed to wait around for the plum pudding," Tyler said, not giving the impression that the possibility interested him.

"You've sat still long enough. Why don't you grab some of the cookies that Risa brought up . . ."

"And some of my egg nog," Carol added. "Take it from the green pitcher. I left the rum out of that batch."

"Good idea. Be sure to have some egg nog. You can take everything to your room and eat and work on the computer."

The boys burst out of their seats and, with appreciative comments about the meal, grabbed cookies and egg nog, and vanished.

"I'll clear the table while you get the pièce de résistance ready," Sam offered, standing up and, squeezing through the small space between the Christmas tree and the table, following Josie to the kitchen. "Josie, everything's wonderful, really wonderful. And I love my present. I'll invite you over to eat the first flounder I catch."

"And I love my watch too, Sam," she interrupted, waving her arm in the air.

"Well." He chuckled. "I guess it's one of those occasions that proves that great minds really do run in the same direction. But . . ."

Josie didn't have any trouble sensing his reluctance to continue. "What's wrong?" She pulled the tin mold from the deep pot it had been steaming in for the last few hours. "Smell this, please," she added before he could answer her question. "Does this smell like seafood? I scrubbed and scrubbed, but this is the pan I use to boil crabs and I think it still has just a slight odor." She sniffed.

"That's sort of what I wanted to talk to you about," Sam answered. "Oh, not the pan. It smells like cloves to me, not crab. But at my end of the table there is this . . . this smell in the air . . ."

"Oh, Sam!" Josie started to giggle. "The boys and I must have missed one of the ornaments."

"Ornaments? Believe me, Josie, this is not a Christmassy smell."

"Little do you know," she said, running a knife around the edge of the mold to loosen the pudding. "I saw these really pretty ornaments. They were shells, gilded with gold paint and tied on a Christmas tree. Well, I thought, we have shells; I do a lot of painting. I'll just make some of them myself. And I did, and they were really pretty. But I guess . . . Well, I guess I didn't clean them out enough. The apartment started to smell. And then the boys got the tree, and it smelled like Christmas. But in a few days, it smelled like rot again. Last night we were sitting down to open the one present we allow ourselves to open on Christmas Eve and Tyler was sitting right next to this little spiral conch shell . . ."

"And he realized it smelled," Sam finished for her, chuckling.

"It reeked. We tossed them all out. At least I thought we did. Apparently we missed one or two."

Sam reached over and hugged her. "So you had rotting shell-fish hanging on your Christmas tree. Well, it's original. Josie, that's one of the things I love about you. You're never really sure what's going to happen when you're around."

"I . . ." She smacked the bottom of the mold and nothing happened. "Well, I . . ." She smacked it again. "Damn it. I . . ." The third smack worked. Miraculously, the plum pudding fell exactly on the middle of the plate. "Wow! Look at that! Where's the brandy you brought?" she asked, distracted.

"Right here." Sam had the bottle in his hand.

"Okay." She plucked a sprig of holly from the glass near her sink where it had been waiting, and perched it on top. "You pour the brandy over the pudding and I'll light the match, and . . . Oh!"

The pudding flamed up and her guests simultaneously murmured their appreciation of the sight.

"So Merry Christmas everyone, as Tiny Tim said," Sam said, following Josie to the table.

"Josie, it's wonderful. A wonderful ending to a wonderful day."

"Hey, Mom, great!"

"Yeah, great!"

The boys had left their computer and were standing in the doorway.

Josie looked around at the smiling faces of her family and her guests and giggled. "Merry Christmas, one and all." She took a deep breath and blew on the pudding with all her might. The flames wavered and straightened up. She blew again and the same thing happened.

"Sam . . ."

"Josie . . ."

"Mom . . ."

"Tyler, open the window!"

"The curtains!" Risa cried. "Be careful of the curtains."

Josie dashed to the window and, plate and all, tossed the pudding to the ground below.

There was a moment of silence.

"I guess we were lucky to have snow," Risa said, staring out the window. "To have a white Christmas to put out the fire."

Sam put one arm around Josie's shoulder and one around Tyler's. "I think we're lucky for a whole lot of things. Very lucky. But next year, if none of you mind, I'll bring the dessert."

A Conversation with Valerie Wolzien

Q: Valerie, let's talk about one of your recurrent themes: holidays and murder. What inspired you to start writing holiday mysteries?

A: Do you ever wonder about the people who buy the Christmas magazines that sit next to the cash register at the grocery store in the middle of August? The sunbathers who read Christmas mysteries while sprawled on the beach? Well, I'm one of them. I love Christmas. Gingerbread men are my comfort food. Balsam is my Chanel No. 5. I plan for the holiday all year long. I also spend between seven months and a year writing each mystery novel. It occurred to me that by writing about Christmas, I could think about cookies, presents, and decorations as I wrote. And have some of the fun without all the work—or all the calories. That's how my first Christmas mystery, *We Wish You a Merry Murder*, was born.

Q: What holidays other than Christmas are featured in your books?

A: *All Hallows' Evil* takes place during Halloween. *A Star Spangled Murder* takes place on an island in Maine during July Fourth celebrations.

Q: Do your family holiday rituals figure into your mysteries? How so?

A: No one in my family has actually killed anyone over the holidays—yet. In *We Wish You a Merry*

Murder, all the cookies mentioned are baked by members of my family—mainly my grandmothers. I come from a line of dedicated bakers, and food is very important to us all at Christmas. That said, I should admit that the meals in *'Tis the Season to Be Murdered* are amazingly elaborate. No one in my family is a professional chef. But Kathleen Gordon comes from an Italian background, and she creates a wonderful traditional Italian seafood feast on Christmas Eve. My brother's wife is Italian, and I'm always sitting at her father's dining-room table on the twenty-fourth!

Q: Are the murders in your mysteries committed with holiday-related items?
A: It's amazing how many common holiday plants are poisonous—mistletoe, poinsettias, English ivy. Even the bottle of preservatives that can be poured into the water the Christmas tree sits in will make anyone who ingests it pretty ill. But that, it turns out, is the problem. Most of these poisons will only make a person ill. I played around with poisons for my first Christmas murder and then decided that a gun was an efficient weapon—no matter what the season. In *'Tis the Season to Be Murdered*, the victim is strangled. Once again, I did consider poison. Since Z Holly is part owner of a catering company, it seemed like a logical way for him to die. But strangling was easier. Besides, food poisoning is part of the plot, and one scene with people throwing up is enough.

Q: Why did you write more than one Christmas mystery?
A: Both *We Wish You a Merry Murder* and *'Tis the Season to Be Murdered* are set at Christmastime, but they cover different aspects of the season—the

week before Christmas and the week after. In *We Wish You a Merry Murder*, Susan and her friends shop for presents. In *'Tis the Season to Be Murdered*, they go back to the malls only to run into people returning the gifts they gave them just a few days ago. The original title of *'Tis the Season to Be Murdered* was *And a Lethal New Year*. It isn't a New Year's book—the action starts on Christmas Day and continues during the week until New Year's Eve—but I thought it would be cute to have two titles that were sequential. But, since both are Christmas books, it was thought that the second title might be confusing.

Q: Is it difficult to put an established series character like Susan Henshaw in several holiday murders? Does she begin to dread holidays?

A: Well, Susan Henshaw did hire a caterer in the second book, so maybe the cooking is getting to her. (Although, knowing Susan as I do, I suspect it's the cleaning up that's making her nuts.) But Susan's views on holidays are mine: Celebrations are one of the things that make life fun, that bring us together, that create and define a family or a community.

Q: Do you feel different about the holidays now that you have written murder mysteries about them?

A: This year I definitely am going to try baking that Swiss pear bread in *'Tis the Season to Be Murdered*! Sometimes I do think about keeping up with the Henshaws—which could be a little difficult. Susan is fictional, and she has unlimited money and time. I sit at my computer during the day and bake in the evening. But this time of year, the days seem a little longer, I get a little more done—and then I have time to read holiday mysteries other people write.

Q: Tell us a little about your other series character, Josie Pigeon—who now has her own holiday mystery in **Deck the Halls with Murder.**

A: Josie was introduced in a Susan Henshaw book, *Remodeled to Death.* She is a carpenter in her early thirties who, in *Shore to Die*, inherits Island Contracting, a company made up entirely of female workers. The business is located on a barrier island within commuting distance of New York City. Josie is a single mother who hates to cook, wouldn't think of baking something that doesn't come out of a box, and is not interested in being domestic. That makes her a nice contrast with Susan Henshaw.

This interview originally appeared in a slightly different form in **Murder on the Internet.**